POLLY AND THE ONE AND ONLY WORLD

DON BREDES

GREEN WRITERS PRESS *Brattleboro, Vermont*

Printed in the United States

10 9 8 7 6 5 4 3 2 1

Green Writers Press is a Vermont-based publisher whose mission is to spread a message of hope and renewal through the words and images we publish. Throughout we will adhere to our commitment to preserving and protecting the natural resources of the earth. To that end, a percentage of our proceeds will be donated to the environmental activist group, 350.org. Green Writers Press gratefully acknowledges support from individual donors, friends, and readers to help support the environment and our publishing initiative.

green writers press

Giving Voice to Writers Who Will Make the World a Better Place
Green Writers Press |Brattleboro, Vermont
www.greenwriterspress.com

Library of Congress Cataloging-in-Publication Data is available upon request.

ISBN: 978-0989983891

PRINTED ON PAPER WITH PULP THAT COMES FROM FSC-CERTIFIED FORESTS, MANAGED FORESTS THAT GUARANTEE RESPONSIBLE ENVIRONMENTAL, SOCIAL, AND ECONOMIC PRACTICES BY LIGHTNING SOURCE ALL WOOD PRODUCT COMPONENTS USED IN BLACK & WHITE, STANDARD COLOR, OR SELECT COLOR PAPERBACK BOOKS, UTILIZING EITHER CREAM OR WHITE BOOKBLOCK PAPER, THAT ARE MANUFACTURED IN THE LAVERGNE, TENNESSEE PRODUCTION CENTER ARE SUSTAINABLE FORESTRY INITIATIVE® (SFI®) CERTIFIED SOURCING

While the sun and moon endure
Luck's a chance but trouble's sure.

— A.E. Housman

All religion, my friend, is simply evolved out of fraud, fear, greed, imagination, and poetry.

— Edgar Allan Poe

For Nora and Jack's three boys,

Nathan, Toby, and Gabe

ONE

1

WENDELL WAS AWAY for the weekend. She could tell as soon as she hopped off the trolley—the carport was empty, and he never fired up his sports car unless he had to drive to the transport hub. Uncle Wendell worked as an agent for Sunshine Properties half a mile down Mariposa, but he had clients all over New Florida, so he traveled a lot.

He also hated her. Ever since Polly arrived in Orlando five months ago, he'd been threatening to turn her in to the Faith and Truth Board. So far he hadn't, and that was no small thing, she knew. As an officer in the reserves, Wendell had a Class-A fuel card, free housing, and health benefits for him and Aunt Leslie. They'd lose all that if they were caught harboring a heretic.

Back in December when her father sent her away, he told her that Orlando would be as safe a place as any in the Protectorates. "You can pass there," he said, "as long as you're clever about it." An old friend of his from college, Byron Morgan, ran a girls' tennis academy over on the west side. Byron agreed to admit Polly, but only as a day student. She'd have to find her own lodging. Fortunately, Aran's half-sister Leslie happened to live in Orlando, too, and even though they hadn't spoken in 30 years, once he'd reached her on the phone, Leslie didn't hesitate. *Send her down.* She didn't mention Wendell, not that it would have mattered. There was no place else for Polly to go, and time was short. Ten thousand Home Guard troops were already massed along the shore of the lake from Ticonderoga to Plattsburg, poised to commence the sweep.

Last fall when the Faith and Redemption Amendment became law, all the "heretics, apostates, and followers of false creeds" anywhere in the Protectorates had 90 days to register for assignment to a ReBirthing facility. Either that or apply for bondservant status. Anyone who failed to comply with the FRA, citizen or outlier, would face arrest and exile, or consignment to a work camp, or death.

By the end of October almost everyone Polly knew had fled the Regions for the wilds of Newfoundland or the barren west. Some were planning to travel east over the mountains to the seacoast, where, if you had the money, you could book passage a freighter bound for one of the refugee colonies in ice-bound Europe. A few were determined to stay put—defiant farmers and woodsmen, the TwiceBorn, anyone too old or sick to travel, and those witches and warlocks committed to the resistance, like her father.

And Polly. At the Great Gathering a year ago, she had sworn to stand and fight alongside Aran and the last stubborn remnant of the Old League. But days before the invasion, Aran sat her down at the kitchen table to say he'd changed his mind. The dangers ahead were too great for any child to face, not if she had a safer option. His decision did not surprise her. It was a relief, in fact. What did surprise her was what he said next. "Your safety is the main thing, Polly, of course. But there's another reason I want to send you away." He took her hand in his. "I have a mission for you."

5

☾

"Polly? For heaven's sake, what *happened* to you? It's almost seven!"Aunt Leslie was calling from the computer room upstairs."You find something to eat?"

"Not yet."

"OK, but before you do that, we have an appointment."

"What appointment?"

"At seven. Up here."

"On the screen, you mean?"

"Yes, Hon." Leslie appeared at the top of the stairs. She was in her pink bathrobe. Her hair looked wet. "It's a little intervention we want to try."

"Who?"

"Me and Wendell and I think Pastor Baxter. And *you*." Meredith Baxter was the new minister at the Church of the Resurrection over on First Avenue.

"I thought you had class tonight."

"Sweetie, I know you must be hungry and all, but after what happened last Sunday? Pastor Baxter is very concerned about the spiritual health of our household."

Each Sunday Polly prepared a brunch for Leslie, Wendell, Wendell's demented mother, Doris, and Pastor Baxter. She didn't mind the chore because when they had company Wendell made an effort to show her some kindness. But last Sunday Pastor Baxter and Doris were late, and while Polly was setting the table Wendell spotted her triquetra. She'd been wearing it ever since the day her mother presented it to her in parting, a year ago.

"There. What is *that*?" He was pointing.

She pressed her hand to her chest. "Just a necklace."

"It's more *witch* crap! I don't believe it."

"Maybe you shouldn't be peeking down my shirt."

"Don't get smart with me! Take that thing off and put it on the placemat. Now."

"I can't." The triquetra was a looping, three-lobed symbol etched into a thick disk of clear amber, framed in scalloped gold, on a fine gold chain. Lil had charged it for her health and alertness to harm. She was never to be without it.

Her first night here, even before he'd showed her into the guest room, Wendell had gone through her footlocker. He confiscated her ivory wand, her silk altar cloth, her pentacle, her silver bell, her crystals and shells, her pearl-handled athame, and her alabaster chalice. He missed the red sewing box containing her herbs, candles, salves, and oils, the grimoire she had hidden at the bottom of her backpack, and the triquetra at her breast.

"First night you set foot in this house, I *told* you, we will tolerate none of your blasphemy! Take it off!"

"Can't you two get *along*?" Leslie called from their bedroom. "It's Sunday!"

"Please," Polly said. "It was a gift from my mother. It has nothing to do with you."

"From what I hear about your mother—"

"*That's enough!*" Leslie shouted.

Wendell reached out and grabbed her by the arm. Grimacing, he pulled her against the edge of the table. The pepper mill fell over. "Take it off," he said through his teeth.

Leslie's sandals clattered on the stairs. Wendell let her go with a shove.

Polly looked down at the table top, rubbing her arm and blinking back tears. Leslie's pewter napkin rings were each inscribed with a fish formed by two arcs that crossed at one end to make the fish's tail. She picked one up and held it out to him.

"You know what this is, don't you, Uncle Wendell?"

"Yes, it's Ichthus. It stands for Jesus, the Son of God."

"For you it does. But before the time of Jesus, your *Ichthus* was the Great Mother, and this shape—" she turned the fish to the vertical—"was the entrance to the womb."

"*Polly!*" Leslie said.

Wendell's face turned red. "See how she mocks us?"

"I'm not mocking you, Uncle Wendell." A symbol was just a shape, that was all she wanted him to see. The only meaning it had was the meaning you gave it. "I'm just saying my triquetra means *nothing* to you."

"Bullcrap! I *know* what it means. It means you're *possessed!*"

"I am not! That's *crazy.*"

"Take it off and leave it on the table. Now. You have no choice."

"Maybe you should, Pol," her aunt said.

The doorbell chimed.

Leslie gave her a pleading look.

Polly's cheeks burned. She reached under her collar, undid the double clasp, and placed the triquetra on the table, its chain pooling, her eyes brimming again.

"Thank you, Jesus," Wendell breathed.

Leslie gave her a grateful smile.

But as her uncle turned to answer the door, she snatched it back.

Wendell spun around. She slipped past him into the vestibule. He lunged for her, sideswiping the brass coat tree. It fell sideways into his mother's French antique mirror, a family heirloom, which cracked with a hiss.

Wendell dropped to his knees, hands out, as if he could make the big glass oval whole again. "Noooo!"

Polly yanked the door open. On the other side of the

grille Pastor Baxter and Doris Houghton stood staring at her. She couldn't leave.

"Aw, you *guys!*" Leslie said behind her. "What a *shame!*"

Polly righted the coat tree. Doris looked on, patting her hair in confusion. Wendell was kneeling on the floor with his back to them.

"I'm very sorry this had to happen, Uncle Wendell," she said to his face in the mirror. The crack was like a silver ribbon pressed into his forehead.

"That's just it! It *didn't* have to happen." He shook his fist at Leslie. Mimicking her voice, he said, "'Why can't you just let her *be,* Wendell?' See? *See? This* is why." He rose and turned to Polly. "Give me that damned thing, or by the Lord Jesus Christ you have spent your last night in this house!"

"Polly," Pastor Baxter said, "you will obey your uncle in the Lord."

So, heartsick and fuming, she did, even as she knew it would not be enough.

☾

The screen was a watery blue.

Leslie patted the seat beside her. "You OK, Pol? You look stressed."

"My shoulder's sore." She'd strained it somehow in practice. "Will I have to say anything?"

"When they ask questions, sure. Just answer the best you can."

"Wendell's reported me. Hasn't he?"

"Oh, no, Polly, I don't think so. But this is serious, I know that."

The speaker pinged twice. The wall screen resolved into a chapel, maybe at a hotel. Wendell was sitting in a club chair in a white sweater with the sleeves pushed up.

He had a thick book in his lap. A frowning reverend stood at a tabletop lectern, holding a staff with a cross on top. His skin was black. Beside them a gold-fringed CPA flag hung slack on its pole.

"Good evening, ladies," Wendell said. "The gentleman with me here is the Reverend Dr. T. Bob Haselton, Executive Pastor of the Blood of the Lamb Evangelical Church in Pensacola. Reverend Haselton is the Dominion representative to the Faith Guidance Council up in Dallas. The power of the Holy Spirit is great within him. Reverend?"

Haselton made a smile. "I am surely blessed and pleased to meet you, Polly. And you, Mrs. Houghton. Let me offer a short prayer before we begin."

Polly raised her hand. "Excuse me, Reverend. Sorry, but first would you please tell me what this is about?" She touched the zoom to pull him closer.

The reverend turned to Wendell and nodded. Wendell opened his book to the page he'd been holding. "What we're going to do, Polly, is we're going to beseech 'the Creator of all things seen and unseen to rescue you from demonic torment and deliver you from the infernal invaders now commanding your soul.' He looked out at her. "We want to open your heart to the love of our Savior. That you may be redeemed for all eternity."

"That's what I was afraid of. Listen, I don't mind all this, Uncle Wendell, but before we start, I just want to assure you, both of you, that I'm *not* tormented or possessed or anything like that. I'm *fine*. I really am."

Wendell was about to reply, but the reverend raised his hand. "My child, do you not know that your body is a temple of the Holy Spirit, whom you have received from God? Who now writhes under the black boot of Satan?"

She thought it better not to answer.

"It's the Lord's truth, child! You are not your own!" He closed his eyes. "We shall begin."

"Be good, Polly," Leslie whispered. "Don't play games now."

Haselton raised the cross. "God of heaven, God of earth, God who has power to give life after death, because there is no other god than thee and there can be no other, for thou art the Creator of all things, of whose reign there shall be no end, we beseech thee to deliver this pure girl from the tyranny of Satan's infernal demons, their snares, their lies, their furious wickedness. O Lord, free her and grant her thy protection and keep her safe and pure. We beseech thee through Jesus Christ our Lord. Let us now join hands." He reached for Wendell's.

Leslie pressed Polly's fingers between her soft palms.

The reverend tipped his head back. "Be *gone,* Satan, inventor and master of all deceit, enemy of our salvation. The Sign of the Cross commands you! Give place to Christ! Stoop beneath the all-powerful Hand of God! *Tremble* and *flee* at the holy and terrible name of *Jesus*! We drive you from this pure girl, unclean spirits, satanic powers, diabolical legions! By the authority of *Jesus Christ*, I lay down my command. Depart this girl's life and *never* return!" He pounded the floor with his staff three times.

"Hear us, evil one, and *depart!*" Wendell said.

"Be *gone,* Satan!" Leslie cried.

"Rise, Polly! Rise up and resist! Cast him out!" shouted Haselton.

Polly stood, pushing her chair back. She threw her arms in the air. "I think it's working!"

Aunt Leslie shushed her.

Haselton rammed the butt of his staff into the floor once more. He was scowling. "The Dark One *defies* us!"

Wendell shouted, *"Be gone, Satan!"*

Haselton stared at Polly.

"Oops!" Leslie said. "Hang on, guys. Hold it a second. You're kind of flickering—" She leaned over her console and tapped POWER.

The two men dissolved into glittery shades. The panel went back to blue.

Polly turned to her. "Why did you do that?"

Leslie was flushed. "*Because you were jerking them around!*"

"I was only trying to help them out. There is no point—"

"You don't get it!" she shouted. "The *point* is you go along! You *let it happen! That* is the point!" Leslie covered her face with her hands. She was weeping. "Oh, dear God in heaven. We are in so much trouble now."

2

SHE TOASTED AN ONION BAGEL and took it out to the patio. Run away. That was all she could do. Only there was no place to run to except the maintenance shed behind the courts at St. Michael's, where Mr. Sanchez kept the brooms and the roller, and then what? The transport hubs and the highways were monitored by Security. And she had no ID. She'd have to walk. But even if she could avoid the main roads, any runaway traveling on foot through the countryside was bound to be reported and picked up by Wayward Youth. And yet she could not stay here.

Another starless, humid night. The moon was a dingy lump in the haze. It was May. At home the pasture brook was brimming with snow melt. She could see it running silver and loud under the alders. And the lilac buds were as big as grapes. And the sugar maples were all in flower along the lane.

"Hello."

She shook her head. *Balthazar?*

"Aye."

It was. The old tautness in her chest. *Where?* She scanned the rooftops.

Here.

There, perched on one of the loungers on the other

side of the patio, his yellow eye aglint in the shadows. The brook, the lilacs, the maples, those had been his, she realized—his way of announcing himself.

"B! It's so *wonderful* to see you! Great Mother, that must've been some trip! How long did it take?"

The topic didn't interest him. His ordeal was over. He was listening to a siren whooping somewhere, a helicopter, a woman shouting in Spanish. He fluffed his neck feathers.

Polly's parents had given Balthazar to her on her fifth birthday, at the start of her training. He was just two. She had not expected a raven, but he was perfect for her, she knew right away. Balthazar was less sure. The tether of the connection unnerved him. At first he chafed under its obligation, but after a week they were trading simple thoughts, then words, and before the end of the summer the husky raven had learned to take pride in his role as a guide and guardian. Leaving him in December had been wrenching for both of them, but no witch could keep a familiar in the Dominions without giving herself away. Now here he was. With a message for her, she was certain. She only hoped the news was not too terrible.

"You're hungry," she said. She could feel it.

Very.

From the fridge she took a block of cheddar in foil, a wedge of smoked Gouda, some julienned sun-dried tomatoes in a jar, and some green grapes. A feast.

Balthazar hopped from the lounger to the table but then held back, waiting for her to move to the other side of the glass slab before he would touch the food.

He ate fast.

"Don't make yourself sick."

He wagged his head.

"Did my father send you?"

"Aye."

"Is he all right?" She held her breath.

"Aye."

"What about the others?"

Ilsa is dead.

Aran's familiar had been a friend to Balthazar all his life. But Ilsa had been old for a marten, almost 20. "I'm sorry to hear that. What about Ophine and Tess and everybody?"

They need you.

"It's not over, is it?" she asked.

Maybe.

For the past month or two, whenever the Nightly Bulletin featured the purge, there was no mention of the resistance. Back in January the early reports were that "terrorist incidents" had slowed the sweep, and the Guard had suffered casualties, but that was all. For weeks now the resettlement of the Regions had apparently been proceeding without much trouble.

"OK. When do you want to leave?"

Now.

Of course. Now.

Balthazar raised his head. "Suit?"

Her flying leathers, he meant—what she used to call her "raven suit." But that and her helmet were on the top shelf of her closet at the farm. She had promised her father she would work no transformative magick while she was away on her own.

"I'll see what I can find."

Balthazar extended his wings and refolded them. "Book?" The grimoire, he meant.

"It's safe, don't worry." The book was hidden under her bed in an opening she'd made in the box spring. She'd coned it, because if Wendell ever tried to take it from her it would strike him dead. "But my uncle took my triquetra."

He made a knocking noise. *It is close.*

"How close?"

He hopped from the table and rose with three flaps to the rain gutter above Leslie and Wendell's bedroom window. He rocked his head side to side.

So much for blasphemy. Wendell had stashed it in their bedroom, the hypocrite.

She ran up the stairs, ducked into her room, and slipped out of her shorts. Her cotton-lined nylon warm-ups would have to do. She took her green fleece cap with the ear pieces, some wool socks, and a pair of old Speedo swim goggles from her footlocker.

What else? Her metal sewing box, the bird glasses, her pocketknife, a towel and soap, her spare tennis shoes, underwear, and extra socks and pants.

She dissolved the cone and worked the book out of its nest in the box spring. Of all the grimoires left in the world, *The Craeft* was possibly the rarest. An ordinary grimoire would contain the 24 standard spells and releases along with recipes for the rudimentary balms and powders, but *The Craeft* also included over a hundred recondite hexes, incantations, enchantments, countering spells, and reverses, along with a catalog of image magick that no witch had worked for centuries. Six hundred and twelve pages of faint brown calligraphy in Middle English and Latin. Authors unknown. Polly had read it all, with Lil and Ophine's help, but as a maiden in training she'd been limited to eight basic, versatile spells and their releases and nothing more.

She slipped into Leslie and Wendell's dim bedroom. The bed hadn't been made. Rumpled sheets, an empty champagne bottle, and men's pajamas on the floor. A gilt-framed portrait of the Virgin hung above the padded headboard.

She turned to the quarters of the room. It was here. She

addressed the quarters again but slowly . . . and *bink*, she spied it on Wendell's bureau in a wooden bowl with his golf tees, spare keys, coins, and seashells.

In the kitchen she took what was left of the cheddar and Gouda, two bottles of water, two bananas, and another bagel, then helped herself to a flashlight, extra batteries, and a box of wooden matches from the utility drawer.

Out on the patio, she called for Balthazar. "B? I'm ready."

"Polly?" Leslie had come up behind her in the patio doorway. "Are you talking to somebody?"

"Just myself."

"Thank God! I thought they were here already. Listen, Pol—" The microwave beeped. "Face it, first thing Monday morning that Reverend Haselton's gonna have you up before the FTB. That's happening, OK? So, when they ask you— Yikes." She let the screen door slide shut in its track. "What are you *wearing*?"

The fleece hat and the swim goggles. She pulled them off and shook out her hair. "We're doing that skit, remember? For history?"

"OK, but listen to what I'm telling you now. Because I'm very, very serious. You have got to accept the Lord Jesus Christ as your Savior. Cast out those demons! If they send you to a facility . . . well, let's just hope that'll be enough. I mean, for the FTB. Because you *could* get the death penalty, Polly! Do you realize that?"

"Yes, I do. What I don't get is why they're so *afraid* of me."

"They're *not* afraid! They want to *save* you!"

"By killing me?"

"Of *course* not! But the thing is, if you're *not* saved, you'll burn in hell for all eternity, so it's like what difference does it make?"

She had no reply.

"This is about your *eternal salvation,* Polly! You get *that,* right? You have to open your heart to Jesus. And you can *do* it, I *know* you can!" Leslie stood there for a moment, then pleaded, "*Tell* me you'll try. Will you?"

"I'll try, Aunt Leslie."

She shook her head and left the kitchen.

Polly untied the grimoire's oiled-goatskin wrapper. The book's heavy hasp and corner pieces glimmered. Five turns of the clasp wheel, *Mithras, Crescent, Quincunx, Pillar, Cube.* The tongue piece fell free and clacked on the glass. She had Dispersal down cold, but she hadn't worked any magick in so long that she wanted to be absolutely sure.

Balthazar landed on the table. He folded his wings and opened them. *Men come.*

"For me? Is that what you mean?"

"Aye."

She grabbed the poolside broom and swept a circle on the tiles. "Render the place herein a place apart, the locus of my lifting energy and dispersal. Let nothing untoward intrude."

She held out her hands. "Great Mother, heed my will and favor my purpose." She turned to the quarters and requested the aid of the elements.

Be quick!

"I'm trying!"

Even the most skilled witches rarely took to the sky unless they had to, and hardly anyone flew for the fun of it. The effort was too taxing. When she was little, Polly used to imagine that flying would be like swimming underwater. Insulating and beautiful. And holding the charge would be like holding your breath. It was nothing like that. It was grueling, noisy, and more strenuous than swimming. More exhilarating, too—although that could be a danger in itself.

She cleared her throat. "Where are we going?"

Balthazar hopped up to the chair back. *The sea.*

"You sure that's a good idea?"

"No," he said.

"Do you have a route in mind?" An open-water crossings was nothing to take lightly—if your focus went off, you'd have no place to land.

He shifted foot to foot. *Follow the shore.*

That made sense. Outside the harbor towns, the storm-ravaged coast was mostly empty all the way up to the Exclusion Zone. And this time of year there would be food to forage.

A gas-powered vehicle rumbled up Palm. She heard the *eeeeek* of its brakes in front of the bungalow.

B flapped to the peak of the Binghams' tile roof. *Hurry!*

Polly tied her chin cord and pulled her ponytail through the split strap of her goggles.

She spoke the spell's eleven phrases, the seven and the four. She took a dab of flying ointment from its tin. Inside her warm-ups, with her finger she painted a line of ointment from between her legs up her belly to her collarbone. A fiery streak rose from her womb to her throat.

"*Polly!*" Leslie shouted from the living room. "It's the Guard! Oh, my dear God, they're *here!*"

Her form twitched and loosened, thinning in its interstices. She pushed the book and the sewing box down into the backpack, cinched it closed, threw it on, and snugged the straps tight.

Her feet left the slate. She rose, slow. Then faster. Faster.

Harsh voices echoed up from the street. A radio crackled. A patrol wagon's lights flashed blue in the bougainvillea and against the windows of the bungalows below. The Ionatti twins had come out into their yard to see what was going on. *Goodbye, girls.*

The curving rows of rooftops and the lamplit streets of The Ponds spread out beneath her. A hatch of flies pattered against her cheeks and goggles. Glade Avenue, Mariposa, the Orange County East Mall. Traffic.

Off in the distance she could see the inner fence--a long line of sharp, white lights. Scattered vehicles sliding along Highway 4. The luminous expanse of DisneyWorld. The transport hub's approach lights like blue beads on velvet. All the blackness of the bogs.

She followed Balthazar's silhouette. He kept the walled communities to their left, trending northeast toward the empty flood plain and the dark, punishing ocean beyond it. Not high, just high enough to avoid any manmade obstacles.

She felt her familiar's satisfaction. The gassy numbness in her arms and legs reassured her, too. When your toes and fingers began tingling, that meant you were regaining your density and it was time to come to ground, but for now the charge held steady and strong. Her focus was a vivid filament at her center.

How long could she keep this up? No idea. In training, two hours had been her limit. The Adepts, like Lil, could hold the charge all night if they had to. Polly could only hope she had inherited her mother's stamina. If not, then she would just have to hop along. Land and rest a few hours. Land and rest. Land and rest. Only landing safely in settled territory was no easy thing, especially in the dark. There were trees and wires to beware of. Also fences, waterways, vehicles, and people. But she probably wasn't more than an hour from the fence. Out in the

Wastes there would be fewer people, and on the seashore tomorrow she'd have a whole day to herself. Plenty of time to take stock and make plans.

Later, as they crossed the inner fence and the mottled plain of lights shrank away behind them, her altitude became harder to judge. She climbed, for safety.

How wonderful. She was *free* again. Free and on her own. And home was just a few days' journey up the coast.

She flew on. The cross-currents grew stronger in the salty air.

3

BALTHAZAR JOLTED HER ALERT. *Watch, watch, watch!*

The spell was fraying. Her feet crackled as if they were shedding sparks.

Follow.

She couldn't. All she could do was breast the air and glide. At her shoulder, the raven drifted toward the sea, urging her *slow, slow, slow,* and bending her course little by little as they descended. *Follow.*

It was nearly dawn. Polly could see the paling horizon and the frilly hem of the sea, nothing more.

Feet to the fore.

Her numb heels hit the ground. She skidded, lost her balance, and came down hard on her tailbone and backpack.

It took her a few seconds to be sure she wasn't hurt. Her bottom felt bruised. She'd wrenched her neck and torn the seat of her warmups. But fortunately, that was it.

She was sitting in the middle of a gritty lot that opened onto a shoreline boulevard that cut through the coastal ruins. To her left was a roofless building, to her right a flood baffle—packed rubble two stories high.

She massaged her thighs. She could hear gulls, mosquitoes, and the muffled thump of the surf. Woodsmoke mingled with the tang of the ocean and the smell of decay. Glass glinted on the asphalt.

The day brightened. Across the sand-ribbed boulevard, a high berm of bulldozed debris blocked the ocean from sight. In between, pools of standing water reflected the sky. The grassy sand was stitched with tracks.

She was too sore and tired to think. She knew this was no time to decide, but at the moment she didn't see how she could push on like this night after night after night. How many nights would it take? Ten? Fifteen? She couldn't do it.

B was nearby, perched on an overturned Dumpster. She could feel his nervousness.

What's wrong?

There are others.

"Where?"

Here. Wait.

Are they bad?

Maybe. Take care.

She couldn't hear anything over the wind and the surf. Her triquetra was inert. After a time she said, "I'm going to go pee."

Balthazar glided off. Gulls brayed as the black bird passed underneath them.

Polly stepped into the roofless building's vestibule through a twisted metal doorframe. A restaurant of some kind. Seaweed, tufts of beach grass, and pieces of glass covered the floor. She loosened her waist cord.

Behind her someone let out a deliberate cough.

She rose, tugging up her pants. "Who's that?"

The back wall of the space, she saw now, was a partition someone had built of salvaged sheet metal. Above it, the restaurant's shifted roof formed a sort of lean-to on the other side.

"Who are you?" a man demanded.

"My name is Polly Lightfoot, and I'm a traveler passing through." She stooped to pick up a strip of aluminum molding, then backed away toward the vestibule.

"Hold on now. Hold on a second."

A small brown man with a grizzled beard stepped out from behind the partition. He was wearing round eyeglasses, knee-length canvas pants, and tire-tread sandals, and he was carrying a cudgel—a stick with a knob of wire at the end.

"I'm sorry, sir," Polly said. "I didn't know there was anybody here. I was just looking for a little privacy."

He glanced behind him. "Just another goddamn runaway. How'd y'all get here?"

"I'm a traveler, I told you. I'm making my way up the coast."

"From where?"

"Orlando."

He stepped closer. "Like hell. Coast is infested for a hundred miles. Pretty little CivSide girl like you wouldn't last a day out in the open."

"I've gotten this far." She touched her triquetra through her shirt.

"Not up the beach you didn't."

"What makes you so sure?"

"There's wild hogs out there. Gators. Scavs rollin' by two, three times a day. Plus robbers and bounty hunters and every other goddamn thing."

"Thanks for the warning. If you don't mind, I'll be on my way."

"I wouldn't if I was you."

"Why?"

He paused. "Got anything to trade?"

She glanced out toward her pack out in the sandy lot. "For what?"

"Directions. Ain't nothin' free, girl, even in the Wastes."

"You know who you remind me of?"

"Who?"

"The troll."

"*Who?*"

"In the fairy tales—the guy that jumps out and says, 'You may not cross this bridge until you have answered three questions.'"

"Girl, you want to head up that beach, I ain't gonna stop you."

"I'm glad to hear it."

She dropped her strip of metal and backed out through the door frame into the vestibule. The bones of some small animal were sticking out of the sand. All she wanted to do was to curl up in the sun somewhere and sleep. She looked around for Balthazar.

Sparrows, sandpipers, terns, gulls. The sun was a wafer in the haze. *Where are you?*

He grawked. There, across the boulevard—a speck on the dike. She lifted her pack and put it on.

"Keep to the baffles," the brown man said behind her. "And steer clear of them shipbreakers up toward Augie. Worse than scavs, some of 'em."

"Thank you. I'll be fine, I'm sure."

"Lascomb!" A woman's high voice. "That's enough now. Bring the girl to me."

"Who is that?" Polly asked.

"That's Mrs. Hacker."

"No need to run off, Polly," the woman said. "Join us for breakfast, won't you? We have Chinese tea and ripe tomatoes. And we have sardines. And an abundance of oranges."

She searched again for Balthazar. He wasn't offering anything—maybe he was too far away. He would not have led her here, she decided, if he didn't think she'd be safe with these people, whoever they were. She said that some tea would be very nice.

"Lovely. Show the young lady to me, Lascomb."

The man nodded for her to go on ahead. He followed, walking backward so he could sweep away their footprints with a palm frond.

On the other side of a sailcloth curtain the shelter seemed bright and spacious. The roof sloped down to a set of shelves just off the ground that held an orderly array of plastic jugs, crates, and odds and ends.

Bars of sunlight slanted through openings in the wall overhead. At the far end of the space, an older woman, heavy, with thick gray hair, reclined on a platform piled with cushions. She had a shawl over her shoulders. On the wood table beside her were a ceremonial altar with brass pentacle, a crystal goblet, an iron cauldron with taloned feet, and a few candles. A radio, some books, and a marble mortar and pestle stood on the floor.

A solitary in exile, that's what she was. That's why Balthazar led her to this place—he'd felt the hum of the Braid. He wouldn't know that nowadays lesser witches could not be trusted. They tended to be fearful and desperate. Only this Mrs. Hacker didn't seem fearful. Or desperate. She was lonely, no doubt, living way out here.

"You're a witch, I gather."

She waved her hand. "I putter."

"Both of my parents are mages," Polly said. "In the Old League."

"Aha. Gracious. And you've found your way here to me, Eleanor Hacker? How did you manage that?"

"My familiar guided me. He's a raven."

"Fascinating. Lascomb, old friend, we have an occasion. Open a tin of sardines, won't you? You like sardines, I hope?"

Polly didn't care much for sardines. "Do you have any Dijon mustard?"

Mrs. Hacker sat up with a laugh. "An epicure! My dear girl, we don't have a jar of grape jelly."

"Oh. Well, I have a wedge of cheese."

"Do you? Come closer, Polly, so I can see you better with these weak eyes." She nodded encouragingly. "You're safe here—safe as we are, anyway. We know this neighborhood, Lascomb and I."

"What neighborhood?"

"Palm Gardens!" Mrs. Hacker spread her fleshy arms. "*Very* upscale when I was your age and in bloom. Lascomb and I lived about a mile from here. The Sea Spray Inn, 880 Ocean Front. What a splendid inn it was! Designed and built back in 1912 for Willie K. Vanderbilt, the automobilist. We were famous hereabouts for our flowers, weren't we, Lascomb?"

"You lived in a hotel?"

"We *owned* it. Or I should say my parents did."

"Hibiscus and camellias," Lascomb said. "We surely was."

"Lascomb was our driver."

"Mercedes 600," he said.

"So you just stayed out here—after the Cataclysms? You didn't leave?"

"Oh, no, dear, we left. Of course we left. Only the seagulls stayed behind. We went to my brother's up in Dunwoody. Chad was *very* generous to take us in, considering the chaos of the times, and the sickness, and the panic." She laughed. "Damn city's just as inhospitable today, but for different reasons." Atlanta was the seat of government in the Second Dominion. The privileged and the well-connected lived there—clergy, government, military, and their servants.

"Got our asses evicted," Lascomb said. "Th'owed out in the hot heat of August."

"That's not *quite* true," Mrs. Hacker said. "We departed the metropolis on our own terms. However, as you can see, we've had to adjust to a reduction in circumstances."

Lascomb peeled the lid from the sardine tin. He forked the glistening fish out onto a scrap of formica, then took a saucepan of hot water from a camp stove and poured it into a china teapot with a broken spout.

"Come here, Polly, won't you? I'm terribly curious about your cheese."

Lascomb gave her two sardines head-to-tail on a slice of tomato, served on a page he'd torn from an old magazine. Polly cut three pieces of the Gouda with her Swiss Army knife. Mrs. Hacker served the tea in three pale blue cups.

"Lovely," the woman said, rubbing her hands together.

Lascomb sank to the floor beside Polly. She flinched at his smell.

Mrs. Hacker closed her eyes. Her fingers were crooked and swollen. "Oh, Great Mother, we thank you for the food and drink that you bestow, and for your protection from all the world's dangers. Do not slacken in your vigilance, we beg you, even as we may curse you in our despair."

Polly gave her a hard look. No witch she knew would ever curse the Great Mother.

Mrs. Hacker bit into her sandwich. "Now, my girl, tell us how you got here. You didn't walk. We know that."

She knew it was unwise for a witch to discuss her skills in the craft in the company of strangers, but just the same, when their eyes met, she said, "Actually, I flew. From Orlando." She decided it was better for Mrs. Hacker to understand what sort of witch she was dealing with than to take her lightly.

"Aha. You flew. Alone?"

She nodded.

"My. So you have mastered a flying spell. Which you can maintain all by yourself. As a *maiden*, no less."

"Well, I'm not very good at it."

"If I may be so bold, what is a maiden witch of your stature doing down in the Second Dominion?"

Polly told her.

Mrs. Hacker propped her chin in her palm. "And now you say you're headed *back*? All the way to the northeastern Regions?"

"That's right."

"And your familiar, has he been with you all this time?"

"Oh, no. He came for me just last night."

"I see." She beckoned for Polly to move closer.

A little reluctantly, Polly knelt on the platform and let the old woman draw her head into her deep, soft chest, her musky hair. Mrs. Hacker's knobby fingers found Polly's sore shoulder. She massaged the tendons. "Not just *any* witch, Lascomb. A *flying* witch."

"I don't believe that," he said. "Flying people goes against the laws of Nature."

"The laws of Nature are much more forgiving than most people realize, Lascomb."

"Oh, yeah? You seen what Nature done to *this* place. Don't seem too forgiving to me."

"There are limits to her tolerance. As we know too well."

"And too late," Lascomb said.

A cat yowled somewhere far off. A rising wind rustled the sailcloth overhead.

"Are there very many witches hiding out in the Wastes?" Polly asked.

"Oh, no, dear. A handful. All solitaries, I'm afraid. It's too risky to gather, even here." Mrs. Hacker took her hand. "You need to rest, my dear. You're spent."

Mrs. Hacker directed her to a heap of mildewed cushions in a corner of the ruin.

When she awoke again, at first she thought only a few minutes had passed, but the angle of the sun said it was almost evening. She'd slept all day.

She sat up, muzzy-headed. And *thirsty*.

Mrs. Hacker and Lascomb were standing together with their backs to her, peering out toward the boulevard through a crack in the cinderblock wall.

She cleared her throat. "May I have—"

The older woman whirled around. "*Hush*, now. Be silent."

"Why? What is it?"

"Scavs," she breathed. "The wind's off the sea. If they don't smell us, they'll pass by."

"Are they dangerous?"

"Of course. This bunch isn't foraging, at least. Ocean corridor's been picked clean."

Polly remembered when bands of wanderers used to pass through the northern Regions, migrants her parents called vagabonds. They were rough and dirty, but never threatening. Their harvest wagons were relics from the last days of large-scale agriculture out on the Great Plains—the high-sided fiberglass type with patched sails and no running lights. The vagabonds would do whatever needed doing—threshing, scything, cutting firewood, weeding gardens, pruning trees, harvesting beans, apples, wheat, potatoes—in exchange for food, medicine, and cider. Polly remembered she had not been allowed to play with their wild, dirty children. But no migrants had passed through the Regions for more than ten years now, all of them driven north into the Canadian marshes or rounded up and shipped to the camps in the west.

Lascomb still had his face pressed to the wall. Over the thud and shush of the surf, Polly could hear axles creaking, a dog barking, men singing in Spanish. Someone screamed and laughed. The wagons jingled. She could smell gasoline, tobacco, and dung. Dust drifted up past the gaps at the top of the shelter's sloping roof.

They waited. After a few minutes, the only sounds were the surf and the gulls. The sun was going down.

"Headed for Augie," Lascomb said.

"Nearest good water's in Augie," Mrs. Hacker told her. "And Monday's the bazaar."

"What's the bazaar?"

"It's a big fair—food, games, amusements. Bunch of merchants set it up once a year out where the airport used to be."

"Would they have robbed us if they'd found us?"

"Or worse."

"Savages," Lascomb said. "Rip off your arms to get that backpack of yours."

Mrs. Hacker frowned. "No need to worry, Polly. We'll protect you."

"Like hell!" Lascomb said. "We couldn't protect Mary Ellen Brainard's boy. How the hell we gonna protect this little thing?"

"By our wits, Lascomb."

"Our wits ain't worth a cup of sand. The Brainard boy was strong. He was armed, too, for all the good it did him."

"That boy was a dolt. Don't you understand? This is a *high witch* we have here. She has been delivered into our hands for a *reason*!"

"Well, if she flew in here like she says, then I say let her fly the hell out."

"Las. Just look at her. She needs our help. She wouldn't *be* here if she didn't. We're going to guide her to Jacksonville, you and I."

"Say what?"

"We've been called. I knew it when I heard her voice."

She turned to Polly. "Las and I can get you as far as Jax. Up there you'll be able to provision yourself without Security looking over your shoulder. After that, your best bet may be the sea ferry. It's dicey, but it's safer than flying. At least those ferry hands won't be checking for ID."

"That's kind of you, Mrs. Hacker, but I'm sure I'll be all right on my own. Really."

"My dear girl. The Wastes are *swarming* with scavs, thieves, slavers, and bounty hunters from here to Savannah. And you have *nothing*! A bottle of water, a box of herbs, a few candles, a folding knife, and a flashlight. Now, think. Do you honestly believe that's going to see you all the way home?"

Polly felt her scalp tingle. The woman had gone through her backpack. Still, there was truth in what she said. Polly was not equipped for weeks of scrounging in the wild and sheltering in the open. She needed supplies. She wouldn't be taking her chances on a ferry voyage, though, she knew that much. Yet it seemed Mrs. Hacker really did feel called upon to help her."How long would it take to get to Jacksonville?"

"Six hours to the fence and three more to South Bridge after that, if we can flag a coach."

"*Nine hours?*"

"Depending on the weather. And other hazards."

"Like what? Scavs?"

"Well, scavs aren't much of a bother after dark—not unless you blunder into their camp somehow. At night you have boars, snakes, coyotes, and gators. Also little things like chiggers, ticks, wasps, and brown spiders. Then, of course, you have your human predators—bounty hunters, vigilantes, and gangs of CivSide boys out for a little jolly mayhem. But we know the best route, Las and I, and we're in no hurry. With a bit of luck we can give trouble the dodge. We've done it before, eh, Las?"

☾

It didn't take long for the two of them to button up their shelter. Mrs. Hacker had velvet drawstring pouches for her altar pieces and a padded case to put them in, also bedrolls, ponchos, and framepacks. Whatever belongings they couldn't take with them they wrapped in canvas and plastic and hid inside a car mostly buried in sand under the back of the building, its glass intact.

They left the shelter just as the moon showed a cheek in the east. Lascomb listened for a minute, then headed out along the open boulevard for a short stretch before veering off onto a narrow path Polly would never have noticed on her own. The two of them each carried a machete in hand, its thong around the wrist. Polly's tennis shoes crunched on stone and shell. Mosquitoes whined. The soft breeze carried sharp smells—the acid ocean, decaying fish, and salt.

A rising wind chased the haze, and the stars multiplied. Lascomb led them to the northwest, following a trodden path between two baffle berms among grassy hummocks of broken concrete, sand, and weeds. Twice they stopped out of the wind to peel oranges and drink from their water bottles. Coyotes yipped out on the flats.

A series of switchbacks took them to a ridge top where Lascomb stopped to survey the terrain. Gusts of wind buffeted his pack, rattling his zippercords. Far to the west a winking stream of headlights and taillights marked Route One, well beyond the raised flood barrier. The band of brighter lights in between marked the security fence that separated the coastal wastes from the inland communities—CivSide. Lascomb pointed to the northeast. The dull glow from some settlement hung in the ocean mist.

South of that, the black, skeletal hulks of a dozen or more freighters lay in a row up the coast, the shipbreakers' fires like orange sparks among them. The flood plain looked bleak and barren.

Mrs. Hacker joined them. "Hoo!" she breathed. Her gray hair was wild.

"That's Jax?" Polly asked. "Across the flats?"

"That's Jax," the woman said. "Shame what a pestilent hole it's turned into."

"And over there, that's the security fence."

She nodded. "You can't see the utility gate from here, but that's where we're headed. Nearest Customs portal's way up at South Bridge."

"Why not just hike straight across the plain?" It looked easy compared to what they'd just been through.

"Farther than it seems. Besides, the flats are full of scavs, and there's no place to hide."

Polly's tennis shoes had taken a beating over the last four hours. She needed boots. Heavier pants. Her own machete. Rain gear.

"Gets harder on ahead," Lascomb said. He was crouching with his back to the wind, sipping water.

"We'll be picking our way along the baffle berm," Mrs. Hacker told her. "The footing is bad in places, so stay within arm's length of Lascomb and follow his step exactly. Lean into the slope. If it shifts, wait. If you slide, don't panic. Keep your arms and legs spread. You won't go very far."

Lascomb capped his bottle and set off, moonlight glinting on his pack frame.

Polly felt sore and twitchy. She was light-headed with hunger. Her two companions were tougher than they looked. She recalled the week she went hiking and camping high in the wind-swept White Mountains with her parents and a few others from the coven. She was so young back then, five or six, and she had had no experience with—

Her foot sank underneath her, her knees buckled, and she fell, *whump.* Headfirst, she slid down over the loose scree, everything giving way under her grasping hands.

4

LASCOMB SCRAMBLED AFTER HER down the slope. "Y'all OK?"

"I think so."

He knelt beside her. "No, you ain't. You got a cut on your neck."

She could feel it. A long slash, but not too deep.

"Let it bleed," Mrs. Hacker told her. "It's cleansing. Here, drink a little water." With her feet Mrs. Hacker leveled a clearing in the rubble where the three of them could sit side-by-side.

Lascomb held a flashlight while Mrs. Hacker sprinkled something from a vial into Polly's laceration. She pressed a wad of gauze over it.

"Is that cayenne?"

"How sharp of you," Mrs. Hacker said. "Yes, it is."

Humming, she fashioned a poultice of kelp and yarrow. "Now you hold this right there, just like that."

Polly sat listening to the song of the wind for a time as the edges of her cut drew together under the soothing pressure of the poultice. She would have crafted her own healing spell, but Mrs. Hacker's ministrations seemed sufficient. They rested, huddled together for warmth, Lascomb's spine and rump pressing against her on one side and Mrs. Hacker's meaty back on the other. They both snored. Polly watched the brittle stars, her eyes hot with tears, until sleep overtook her.

☾

From the top of the berm, with her bird glasses, Polly surveyed a sunny vale of speargrass and melaleuca through drifting smoke and dust. The opening in the security fence was marked by a pair of light posts, one on either side of a wire-mesh gate. Polly had seen the fence before, but only on television. Its implacable length seemed unsettling—a woven steel barrier reaching all the way to the horizon in both directions.

Lascomb pointed. "See the garbage trucks?"

On the other side of the gate a number of gray-green solarcrawlers stood idling in a line that stretched back toward Route One, where the occasional vehicle flickered by. Plumes of smoke hung in the west. To the north, a defunct wind farm undulated in the heat. Many of the towers still had their turbines and rotor blades attached.

"Come noontime, as long as we don't run into any trouble, we'll be waltzing right through that gate."

"How do we do that? Buy off Customs?"

"In a word, yes."

"It's that easy?"

"No, it's not easy at all. And we've still got to negotiate that jungle in between."

The vegetation belt, a two-mile swath of trees and speargrass criss-crossed by ditches dug to channel the storm surge, looked shady and calm from up here, but no doubt it harbored cottonmouths, gators, and worse.

"So what have we got to bribe the guards with? Sardines?"

Mrs. Hacker gave her a look. She drew a spotting scope with a collapsible monopod out of her pack and watched the gate for a while.

A glass-sided guard booth stood on stilts to the right of the gate. There were no people. Nothing moved but the gulls. Polly looked around for Balthazar. She could feel him. He wasn't far off, but she couldn't pick him out.

"What are we waiting for?"

"The juice," Lascomb said.

"Electricity's down," Mrs. Hacker said, yawning. "The gates won't open until the panhandle grid powers up."

A Guardian drone, a gray cross with a spiky yellow nose, came buzzing low out of the south, following the fence. They watched it until it disappeared in the sea haze. Finally, the cab door of the lead crawler slid back, and someone in desert fatigues jumped to the ground.

"Here we go, Las," said Mrs. Hacker. "Give her a sign."

Lascomb held his machete overhead, turning the blade to catch the sun.

The guard walked to the gatehouse entry and paused at a hooded panel to press in a code. She went up a short ladder and entered the gatehouse.

Mrs. Hacker clucked her tongue. "I'll be damned. She never looked."

"You sure that's her?" Lascomb knelt again.

"It's her. She better spot us before the crawlers get back, or we'll have to hike. We can't sit here all day."

"Why can't we just walk to the gate?" Polly asked.

"We have to catch her eye first, so she'll switch off her cams. We don't want your blond head popping up on Security screens all up and down the border, now, do we?"

"My familiar might be able to get her attention."

"Now that's a thought. Where is he?"

"He's around." *B?*

There. He came beating up the slope, just a few feet off the ground. He looped once around Polly and settled on a girder protruding from the berm.

"That is the biggest damn fish crow I ever seen," Lascomb said.

"These are my friends, Balthazar," Polly said, for their benefit, not his. "Mrs. Hacker is a solitary in exile and Lascomb is her partner."

Balthazar didn't respond.

"It's good to see you. Are you hungry?"

He looked away. *Aye.*

"I think we have some sardines."

"Hell if we do!" said Lascomb. "Birds get their own damn food."

B turned his yellow-green eye on Polly and twisted his purple head. *Leave now. Fly.*

You know I can't do that. Not in the light of day.

"Hah! See there?" Mrs. Hacker chirped.

The solarcrawlers had begun rolling through the gateway one by one and down the incline into the Wastes, dust churning in their wheelwells—eight long rigs towing trashwagons and, to the rear, a monstrous *Merriman-Drake Bros. Recovery* flatbed with its own crane. A gang of pickers, 40 or 50 of them, straggled along behind, pushing handcarts. A few had pack mules.

The gates slid closed.

"So, do you think we might send Balthazar down there with a note, say?" Mrs. Hacker asked.

"He'll do what I ask him to do, but he won't get very close. People shoot strange birds."

"I understand." Mrs. Hacker patted her pockets for something to write with. "Don't worry, Balthazar. Sophia's one of us. She won't mistake you for some germy fish crow."

Balthazar hopped into the air and glided off.

"Did I say the wrong thing?"

"It's better if I speak with him," Polly said. It seemed

odd that Mrs. Hacker did not know it was rude to freely address another witch's familiar.

"Tell him he has nothing to worry about. Sophia is a sister in the craft."

"She is? And she's a border guard?"

"Not in her heart of hearts. She's a *sympathizer*."

"How does a lapsed witch get a job with the federal government?"

"These days a poor witch must do whatever she can to survive."

"I'm sorry. But everyone knows you can't trust a turncoat."

"Oh, no. We can trust Sophia. I promise you."

"How do you know?"

"I'll tell you. After the Uprising, Sophia, her older sister, and their dear mother, witches all, turned themselves in to Security so that their lives might be spared. At some ReBirthing facility out in the Fifth Dominion, they were forced to repent of their sins and dedicate the rest of their miserable lives to the worship of the Lord Jesus Christ in anticipation of his glorious return and so on and so forth. Whereupon, after a few years, they were baptized and released. On probation. Some years after that, lovely Sophia met a military officer who forgave her her dark past and persuaded her to marry him. They moved to Georgia, where Sophia found herself recruited by Customs, and, to make a long story short, here she is, assigned to a utility gate guard booth all day long. She makes a very nice dollar, I might add. And yet, to this very day, by blood and temperament, lovely Sophia remains a *witch*. And a witch she will *always* be. As you should know, Polly."

"So she's a *spy*?"

"No. She's a *sympathizer*. As I said."

"So what's to keep her from turning me in for a bounty?"

"Her sympathy, my dear, of course."

Polly was not convinced. "What will the note say?"

"That we have gold."

"We have *gold*?"

Mrs. Hacker reached behind her and patted her framepack.

Balthazar?

He glided in out of the haze and settled on the protruding girder.

Polly nodded toward the fence. *The guard at the gate is a lapsed witch. If we can bribe her, she'll let us through.*

She is bad.

I don't doubt it. But my friends are trying to help me. Will you carry a message for us?

If you ask.

Mrs. Hacker folded the note over twice and handed it to Polly.

Polly gave it to Balthazar. "As soon as you catch the witch's eye, drop the paper."

She watched him through the binoculars.

Balthazar set the message in the middle of the rutted lane, then veered away, skimming the dusty ground.

The guardhouse door slid open. The woman in the military jumpsuit climbed down, jogged over, and retrieved the note.

"Hallelujah. Here we go. Strike a pose, Lascomb!"

Lascomb extended his machete overhead. Sweat streaked his brown arms.

The guard waved the note in the air.

Mrs. Hacker clapped her hands. "Praise the goddess."

They zigzagged down the berm of packed sand and debris toward the vegetation belt. Polly's cracked lips stung, and her shoulders ached under the bruising pack straps. She forced herself to concentrate on the backs of Lascomb's knotty calves, watching where he set his sandaled feet.

No one said anything. Behind her, Mrs. Hacker wheezed and coughed. In the distance she could hear the rumble of the refuse wagons.

The slope leveled off as the grass, bamboo, and melaleuca thickened. They proceeded more briskly on the less cluttered terrain. Until Lascomb stopped short and whirled around.

Polly turned, too. Back on the crest of the berm above the trail, a figure stood in crisp silhouette against the white sky. He dropped out of sight.

"*Bastards!*" Lascomb wiped his eyeglasses on the front of his shirt. "They got the trail *posted*."

"Who?"

"Shit and damn. *That's* why she never looked for us."

"*Who?*"

"Scavs," Mrs. Hacker said. "They'll be closing in soon."

Polly stopped her breath.

"Shit and *damn*." Lascomb slashed the air with his machete. "See what you done, you and your greedy little plan?"

"Shut up, Las," Mrs. Hacker growled.

"What's happening?" Polly said.

"Gonna come take everything we got," the small man said bitterly. "If you can fly, girl, now's the time."

"He's *right*, Polly!" the woman said, taking her by the shoulders. "You can make it. Just fly! Fly to Jacksonville—*fly*!"

"I *can't* just fly!" Mrs. Hacker knew nothing about transformative magick. "I need time to *prepare*!"

"Then *run*. Run and hide in the jungle till they quit looking for you. *Then* you can fly."

"Let's *all* run!" Polly said. "Let's run to the gate! Come on!"

"I'm too slow, Polly. Here, take my pack. It's lost if you don't." She unbuckled her hip belt and shrugged off her packframe.

"What should I do? Give Sophia the gold?"

"No, no, no. Forget about that. *Fly!* Fly to Jax! We'll meet you tonight at the Fat Crab!" She tugged off Polly's backpack and fastened it to her own with a compression strap. "The Fat Crab, got it? If you miss us, try again tomorrow. We'll be there, I promise." She slapped the pack. "Merry part, my dear, and merry meet again! Now *run*!"

The rubble and brambles slowed her until she came to a narrow trail through the speargrass—wheel tracks and hoof prints—where the way was clear. She paused to catch her breath. The fence was not in sight, but the trail headed in the right direction. Farther along, beyond a rise, she could see the tops of tallow trees riffling on the other side. That would be a spot where she could take her bearings.

But a minute later she caught sight of a small brown face peeking up over the rise in the trail. Her triquetra burned.

She left the trail and plunged into the speargrass. Soon, though, down through the greenery, she could see scraps of slow-moving water—a drainage ditch. Gator habitat. She turned around. Polly could outrun almost anybody, that she was sure of, but not with all this weight on her back. She shrugged out of the straps and propped the two packs against each other three paces off the trail.

With loose-fingered hands she swept a quick circle. "Heed me, spirit forces. I summon a cone to forbid and contain, that all threats without may encroach in vain." She recited the same protection spell she'd been using at Wendell's for the grimoire—two phrases, five words each. Done.

After that she bounded west along the trail free as an antelope.

Mrs. Hacker would be angry, but she would have lost the gold for sure if she hadn't hidden it. Now all she had to do was keep running. Keep running until she got to the utility gate apron. There she could—

"*Arghhh!*" She went sprawling.

A tripwire. Strung low across the path. Before she could regain her feet, two scavs had her pinned down, one straddling her legs, the other on her chest.

Dark-skinned, hairy, smelling like pee. The one on her chest found her triquetra through her jacket and pulled it out by the chain.

"Ha! Nice!"

They jerked her up, wrenching her sore shoulder.

"There's no need to hurt me!"

The smaller one pulled her close to snort at her neck.

The other one yelled at him. "*No lastimes a la puta, estupido hijo de puta!*"

Just two of them. Stay alert. First chance, she'd pull loose and be gone.

Through the rustling melaleuca, she could see the broad, open area along the security fence just 50 yards away. Two crawlers idled on the access apron waiting for the others.

The light-skinned scav had cankers on his arms and a fan of dried blood across his belly. He took Polly by the hair and tipped her face for the other one to see. "Nice? *Tu y yo, ahora la vamos a chingar.*"

The other one shook his head. He had no teeth. "*El Jefe tiene que verta.*"

Her scalp burned. "Let me go! *Please.*"

She heard a high cackle behind her. Another one.

She spun around. The third scav was Polly's age, with nut-brown skin, long whiskers, and a machete on his belt. The coiled-snake tattoo on his bare chest looked infected. His canvas shorts were stiff with dirt.

He looped a length of hot-pink plastic rope around her neck and cinched it tight.

Polly pulled at it. "I can't *breathe,* damn it!"

The scavs all laughed.

"What's your name?" she asked the young one.

The boy licked his lips and rubbed his crotch, grinning. If they attacked her, she would bite. Claw their eyes out.

"Please let me go! I'm just a poor traveler on my way home."

"Shut up," the biggest one said, shoving her.

She stumbled sideways. "What do you *want* with me?"

He shoved her again. "*Cierra la boca!*"

They marched her toward the coast, the boy with the rope prodding her in the back to keep her moving. Polly concentrated on slowing her breathing, retreating to a place within herself where the terror couldn't follow.

5

TICKA-TICKA-TICKA-TICK. *Ticka-tick.* A stick clacked against the mesh.

"*Te estan picando las pulgas alli adentro?*" A girl's voice.

The distant rustle of the surf.

She opened her eyes. She lay in a small oblong cage with a plate steel floor. Her neck was chafed and sore. Her bruised ribs throbbed. The tongue in her mouth felt like a dead toad. It was dusk. She could smell manure and smoke.

"*Tu quieres algo de comer?*" the girl piped.

She groaned and rolled onto her back. "Water?"

A goat bleated.

"Piece o' meat?"

She sat up. "Let me out," she whispered. "Please, my little friend, open the door."

The scav held her cupped hand close to the mesh. The lump she was offering looked like a dirty piece of soap.

"Water," Polly said. "*Agua*. Please."

Her eyes brightened. "*Esperate aqui.*"

Polly felt for the triquetra. It was gone.

She gritted her teeth. They hadn't raped her. What did they *want* with her? Scavs were gleaners. "Two-legged coyotes," Wendell called them.

The girl came limping back on a padded crutch, dragging one leg behind her like a leathery tail. A short man with a black beard followed. Some distance beyond them she saw two battered fiberglass caravans with slot windows. One had ragged pennants fluttering from its antenna. A couple of dogs. A cow. A dozen scavs crouched around a fire pit, jabbering and eating.

The girl stopped outside the cage. She had a plastic bottle in her free hand. "*Jugo?*" Her eyes shone.

"Thank you."

The adult scav watched her with his hands on his hips. He was wearing a stained canvas apron and leather shoes without laces.

The girl set the bottle in a shallow pan at the end of a bamboo pole, then pushed the pan beneath the cage to an opening in the floor, an eight-inch hole cut by a torch, for drainage.

The bottle was grimy. Polly unscrewed the cap and sipped. Warm and tangy—some fruit juice. Rancid.

The girl said something to the adult.

He stared at Polly. "*Te encuentras bien ahora?*" he asked in a rough voice.

Her throat tingled. She wiped the juice from her chin. "Please, I'm a free woman. I'm trying to get home to my family."

"*Tu ves?*" he said to the small one. "*Ella no tiene nada de malo.*"

Her stomach turned. "*Habla English?*"

"*Si, bonita paloma.*"

"Please. Let me out, let me go."

The scav muttered something to the girl, then turned and walked away.

The girl slung herself back around. "*Quieres comer?*"

"*Let me out!*"

"He sol' you," the girl said.

"What?"

She grinned. Her front teeth were broken. "He sol' you."

"He *sold* me?"

"*Si. Si. Ziegler viene pronto.*"

Polly doubled over and retched.

The girl screeched and whacked the cage with her crutch.

A woman yelled, "*Leena! Quita tu trasero de ahi!*"

After that, Polly was alone.

Sometime in the night a soft whistle woke her. Balthazar. He was inside the cage.

The sky was starless, the winds rustling the treetops. Soon it would rain.

"B?"

"Hello."

He hopped closer and dropped the triquetra into her lap, chain and all. Her heart swelled. The carving and the frame were intact.

"Oh, *thank you,* Balthazar, thank you!" How had he found it? But there was no point in asking—familiars didn't tell stories. "What do you think I should do now?"

He grawked. *Condense.*

Maybe. She had cast a contraction spell only twice, though, in training, and both times she'd had trouble with the release, she wasn't sure why.

"I'd rather not, Balthazar. Not unless I have to. Anything else?"

He looked away and said, "Be sick."

"Be *sick*?"

Trick them.

Right. A sick slave was worthless to a trader.

He spread his wings and settled them. *Be sick. Wait. Run.*

You'll stay with me?

"Aye."

"All right. Peck me. My face and my throat. Peck me hard, B. Can you do that?"

☾

By dawn the wind had stiffened. The surf was loud. She heard a baby crying.

She lay back, breathing slow and deep, balanced on the crest of the moment.

Commotion in the camp. A motor in the distance. Hooves. A wagon rattling.

A horn. *Ta-rahhhhhh.*

Laughter. Many voices, coming closer.

The salt in the mist stung the sores on her sunburned face. Her eyes burned, too. *Come, rain.*

"Pull her out of there! Can't see nothing inside that box."

A bolt clinked. Hinges squeaked. Scavs took her by the ankles and dragged her out. She let her head and arms thump onto the hard sand.

"*Oh, Dios! Mira ahi! Esa pinche muerta!*"

"Hell. She ain't dead. She's *poxed,* you goddamn fool!"

"*Cristo salvanos!*"

A woman moaned. Someone jabbered a prayer.

"She was frisky as a squirrel last night! Swear to God, Ziegler."

"I believe you, Julio. Know why? Because you ain't smart enough to cheat me, and you ain't stupid enough to try."

"Kee, *largate de esa plaga asquerosa!*" A shrill voice.

"You fucking *owe* me now, Julio," Ziegler said. "You drug me down here *three hours* out of my fuckin' way. For nothin'. For a poxed exile."

"She wasn't poxed last night! I'm tellin' you!"

"Don't be an *idiot.* Why you think she's walking around in the Wastes? She got lost pickin' flowers? *They threw her out here to die*, you ignorant fucking cannibal."

"But she—"

"Shut your mouth! Let me tell you what you got here. You got a *disease* problem, Julio. You understand me?"

Polly slitted her eyes. Ziegler had a stubbly beard, ski goggles on his sunburned forehead, tangled black hair past his shoulders, a sweat-stained leather vest, chaps, and a gun in a shoulder holster. The bare-chested man next to him had bleached whiskers, iridescent red sunglasses, and a black assault rifle on a sling.

"My gator box is *arruinada*," the scav said. "*Esta toda pinche contagiada!*"

"You be damn lucky if that's all you lose." Ziegler looked around. "*Escuchame a mi!* Any of you touched this girl, you go scrub your parts with sand. If you *took* anything off her, I don't care what it is, burn it. Burn *everything*. Including the girl."

"*Back! Back! ¡Atrás!*" somebody shouted.

The scavs shrank back, talking to one another.

Now?

She could feel Balthazar overhead. *Rise when I call. Rise and follow.*

Which way?

Cool raindrops brushed her cheeks and lips. There was no one close to her.

Which way?

Wait.

He whistled a rising note. *Now.*

Polly opened her eyes wide. Balthazar was holding steady on the wind 20 yards above her, silver needles of rain slanting in between. Polly jumped to her feet and set off at a trot down the lane.

No one raised an alarm. All she could hear was the slap of her feet on the hard sand and the regular, whistling wingbeats of her raven.

6

IT WAS MIDDAY BY THE TIME she reached the side of the raised highway she had been been plodding toward for what seemed hours. She crawled up the embankment and stood at the edge of the roadbed, dizzy and swaying. People in wagons and on horseback stared down at her but didn't stop.

She started trudging eastward, toward the low-hanging smoke and squat buildings she could see in the distance. Jacksonville.

A cart-driver whistled to his mule and steered his stake bed to the side of the road just ahead of her. He was very black with ash-colored hair. He had a canvas sunshade rigged above his seat, but the cart was uncovered otherwise, empty wooden crates stacked in the back. *Polkinghorne Fruits and Greens* burned with an iron into each middle slat. The mule was a round-bellied gray.

"Need help, sister?"

"That's Jax down there, isn't it?" Her voice was a rasp.

"You look like you about to drop where you stand."

She closed her eyes. "Do you have any water?"

"Surely. Hold on . . . "

He reached into the bin behind his seat for a jug with beads of moisture on the sides. Carefully he poured some into the turtle shell he was using for a cup.

"Take a little, swish it, spit it out, then take a little more. Hear?"

He set the shell on the running board. Polly slurped it in. It ran cold down her throat and chest. She choked and coughed.

She held the shell up for more.

A Southern Swift passenger coach with a fringed canopy thundered past. They turned their faces away from its loaf of dust.

"You headed some place special?"

"What?"

"In Jax. Where you headed?"

"I'm meeting some friends at an inn called the Fat Crab. Can you tell me how to find it?"

He gazed back behind him. "Take you right to the door. 'Cept the Fat Crab ain't no inn. It's a saloon."

"You're going the other way, aren't you?"

"Gert turns around sharp if I ask her."

She looked around for Balthazar. He was not in sight. "I— I—"She began to cry.

"Come on now, climb up here. I ain't gonna touch you." He pointed to an iron step below the running board. With the last of her strength Polly hoisted herself over the cart's varnished rail.

She thanked him and told him her name.

He was Brother Darius, he said. He lifted the reins and whistled two notes. Gert's ears swiveled, and they turned toward the jumble of structures on the horizon.

"I figure you for a runaway," Brother Darius said.

"I'm not a runaway." She was wiping the dirt from a limp carrot she'd found on the floor. "I'm a traveler trying to get home to my family."

He nodded toward the buildings ahead. "Who these friends of yours?"

"Two exiles. They said they'd help me book passage on a sea ferry."

He clucked. "Anybody lets you step foot on a *sea* ferry, they ain't your friend. Where's your home at?"

"Vermont. My family's there."

"Can't be. That's all radioactive up there, ain't it? Been zoned off for years."

Back at St. Mike's Polly had never mentioned Vermont. The other girls and most of her teachers understood that she was a refugee from the purge, but they didn't ask her about it. No one down here had any interest in the Regions or in the primitive, heathenish lives people led there.

"Most of Vermont's north of the zone," she said. "It's clean and peaceful up there." It was once. The Permanent Exclusion Zone was a rough triangle stretching from the end of Long Island west to Philadelphia and from there north almost to Albany, the capitol of the Third Dominion. From the Dominions, if you wanted to get to the northeast Regions, you had to traverse the Adirondacks, then cross the water at Ticondiroga. There were no airports in the Regions. No power plants, no shopping centers, no military bases, no hospitals, colleges, or factories. There were about 200 self-governing villages, a few north-running rivers, small lakes, wooded hills, and the rugged, ice-worn mountains. In the valleys there were sheep and dairy farms, orchards, vineyards, and woodlots. Vacation homes. Hunting camps. Summer retreats for the wealthy. Anyone could live there with no fear of another person's judgment. The Regions was the last free territory in the Protectorates. Until the purge. Now she didn't know what it was.

Darius leaned back. "Tell you what you *should* do. Take the Maglev to Richmond. Don't you be messin' with no sea ferry, you hear?"

She could hardly hold her head up. She cleared a space

among the crates, lay down, and slept until she felt Darius poking her hip with his whip handle.

"This is the place."

A redbrick building with boarded-up windows. Over the open doorway hung a painted wooden sign cut in the shape of a crab's claw holding a mug of beer. The other buildings on the sandy street looked vacant, at least at first glance. She heard the commotion of voices, music, and somebody hammering on something. There were people and dogs and horses, and the pungent smell of marijuana. Farther down she could see a bit of the harbor. Rotten wharves and listing freighters.

She jumped to the street.

"Want me to sit out here while you look for your friends?"

"No need. If they're not here, I'll just wait. But thank you, Darius, very much."

"Lord keep you. Wished I could do more."

The stout mule wheeled the cart around. Polly waved, but Darius didn't glance back.

The saloon looked empty at first, but as her eyes adjusted she could make out a few patrons back in a sunken lounge watching some kind of ball game on a big screen. No Mrs. Hacker, no Lascomb. The tables and booths were unoccupied. It was early.

A heavy-chested barmaid with red hair backed through a pair of swinging doors carrying a tray of glassware. "I help you?" She set the tray on the end of a long bar.

Polly described her friends.

The barmaid broke into a smile. "Sure, they been expectin' you, Sweetheart. Little CivSide runaway, right?"

"They're here? Really?"

"Ain't too far off. Grab a perch and I'll go tell Ronnie. He'll get 'em a message."

☾

In the dingy mirror over the bar she spotted Lascomb standing backlit in the doorway, squinting and scanning the room. He wasn't wearing his eyeglasses. Mrs. Hacker lumbered up the ramp behind him. They were dressed in loose sacks that reached to their knees.

Polly turned on her stool. "Lascomb!"

They hurried over, zigzagging among the tables. For the past hour the barroom had been filling with a rough crowd.

Mrs. Hacker clutched her by the hand. "Polly! You clever child, it's *such* a joy to see you again! Lascomb said you were a gone goose, but I told him, 'No, no, no! Polly's too smart to let those gargoyles get the jump on her.'"

"How'd *you* guys get away?"

"Does it look like we got away?" said Lascomb.

"Where are the packs, Polly?" Mrs. Hacker asked.

"I don't have them. I couldn't run with them, so I left them in the vegetation belt."

"You don't *have* them? What do you *mean* you don't *have* them?"

"I hid them in the grass. They're OK. They're protected."

Lascomb moaned. "Shit and damn, that's it! It's *gone*! After all we been through and all for nothin'!"

Mrs. Hacker was red-faced. "In the name of Hecate . . .! You hid the packs in the *grass*? *In the grass? What* grass?"

"You're drunk."

She took a wild swing at Polly's head.

Polly ducked and slid backward off her stool. "They're near the utility gate! I know *exactly* where they are."

Mrs. Hacker's face crumpled. She plonked her forehead onto the bar top. "My jade and alabaster! My *herbs* and *roots* and *amulets*. My seashells, my feathers and oils . .

.How will we get back to our sanctuary on the boulevard? How will we *survive*?"

"Be quiet!" Polly whispered. "It's a good thing I did what I did, because the scavs caught me, too. They tried to sell me to a slaver named Ziegler."

"They *caught* you?"

"Yes. But I *escaped*."

Four men drinking beer and eating mussels at a nearby table were eavesdropping on their wrangling—shipbreakers, Polly guessed, by their blackened clothes and faces.

The barmaid leaned in. "I get you folks something?"

"Three vodkas," Mrs. Hacker said.

"And a cheese plate," Lascomb added.

Polly ordered a sausage. "So the scavs took your clothes?"

Mrs. Hacker nodded.

"We bought us some clothes last night," Lascomb said, "but they had bugs. The girl is washing 'em for us." He glanced out the doorway. "Should be about dry by now."

"Where did you get money to buy clothes?"

Mrs. Hacker gave her a weary look. "Credit, dear girl, credit."

The barmaid brought three filmy tumblers and a saucer of sliced lemon. Polly said she didn't drink vodka. Somebody would, Mrs. Hacker said. She took the register punched in her code.

"Out of cheese," the barmaid told them. "Got yogurt, if you want that."

Lascomb said, "Just bring us that sausage and some relish, then."

"Want it heated up? The sausage?"

"Yeah, heat it up."

"Want to pay for it now?"

"No, we want to see it first."

The barmaid winked at Polly.

"So you had to walk all the way here without any clothes on?"

"No shoes, neither," Lascomb said. "First fella sees us, he says, 'Sure looks like the scavs give *you* the old howdy-do.'"

One of the shipbreakers leaned across and put a blackened hand on Polly's arm. "You look half-scav yourself, girlie. Got a boyfriend?"

Mrs. Hacker glared at the shipbreaker. "Ignore him."

Polly took a swallow from her glass, forgetting what was in it. "Blahhh!" She spat onto the floor.

The shipbreakers laughed and stomped their feet.

One of them rose and leaned over her. "You wanna dance?"

"Leave her be," Lascomb said.

"Who you givin' orders, monkey-face?" the shipbreaker said.

"Comin' through! Look out! Comin' through, boys." The barmaid sidled between the tables with a ring of sausage and a knife and fork on a serving board.

Mrs. Hacker turned to the shipbreakers. "How about if I stand you gents to another bucket of beer?"

They looked around at each other and shrugged.

Mrs. Hacker motioned to their table.

The barmaid leaned in for their bucket. "Be right back."

Lascomb passed around chunks of sausage on the end of his fork. Gristly but delicious. They ate fast. Mrs. Hacker downed her vodka and sucked air through her teeth. "Dusk descends," she declared, "and it would be unwise of us to linger in these iniquitous confines. Let's see about our laundry, shall we, Las?"

Lascomb urged Polly and Mrs. Hacker ahead of him.

The barmaid swooped in with more beer for the salvage workers. Soon they were out on the darkening avenue making briskly for the harbor mall.

☾

After reclaiming their clothing at a shop, Mrs. Hacker bought tea and bread for tomorrow's breakfast from an Asian man in a booth. They hurried past ruined wharves and smoky hovels, dodging wagons, dogs, and beggars, until they arrived at the rundown clapboard boarding house where Mrs. Hacker had taken a room. The stairs were dark and gritty with sand, but once they were inside the room Polly felt relieved, even grateful. There were four beds, a washstand, LED illumination high on the walls, and a real toilet in a stall.

Mrs. Hacker went for some hot water, while Lascomb inspected his shirt and trousers. He was especially pleased with his new boots, which sported fiberglass toecaps and red curlicue stitching up the sides.

Polly stretched out on a sagging bed and immediately fell asleep.

Not much later she awoke with a start at the sound of others in the room. Men, talking in low voices. They smelled.

She got up on her elbows and stopped her breath. Great Mother, it was *Ziegler*, the same sweat-stained vest, same rubber-handled pistol under one heavy arm. And his partner, the sunburned one with the automatic rifle across his bare chest. How did this happen? They'd sold her out, that's how.

Ziegler sauntered over, looking her up and down. "Gonna have to wash her, Eleanor."

"I can wash myself," Polly said, trembling.

He nodded toward his partner. "Best hobble her, Stuart. She's a slippery little fish." He whacked her leg with his hand.

Lascomb moved to block the door.

The stocky slaver took off his rifle and propped it in a corner of the room, then pulled a length of chain from a pouch hanging from his belt.

"Listen to me, Stuart," Polly said in a shaky voice. "Don't you dare put that thing on me, or—"

"It's no *use*, dear!" Mrs. Hacker sang, hurrying to her side. She had tears on her cheeks. "*Please* don't resist. You'll only get yourself *hurt*. Polly, you must forgive me. An old woman has to live."

Ziegler shoved Polly back onto the bed and held her arms while Stuart wrapped the chain around her ankles, locked it, and heaved himself up.

Mrs. Hacker helped Polly shuffle to the washstand, wiped her eyes, and turned to give Ziegler a look. "If you wouldn't mind? In consideration of a maiden's modesty?"

The door closed.

Polly wrenched herself free. "You're despicable!"

"Wait!" Mrs. Hacker hissed. "*Damn* it, this isn't what you think it is!"

"You were going to sell me right from the beginning. That was your plan all along, wasn't it?"

"Shut up and pay attention," Mrs. Hacker said under her breath. "We have a *swindle* in the works. Do you know what a swindle is?"

"I *knew* it was a mistake to trust you."

She took Polly by the shoulders and squeezed. "*Listen to me!* We're getting ten grand for you, Polly, *ten grand*! And *half* of that's yours! *Half*, do you hear me? That's money enough to get you back to Vermont."

"I don't want your money!"

"We're *counting* on you, Polly! Those bounty hunters think you're just another CivSide runaway. Ziegler won't lay a finger on you, don't worry about that. He intends to trade you to an auctioneer—untouched and unharmed. Do you understand? So here's what you're going to do. Tomorrow morning, first chance you get, you just *fly,* all right? *Fly!* Fly to the utility gate. We'll wait for you there until sunset. You give me back my pack, we give you the five grand, and you'll be free and on your way. Pretty slick, don't you think?"

In three fast hops Polly got hold of the assault rifle. She leveled it at Lascomb and Mrs. Hacker.

Lascomb cried, "No! No, don't! *Don't shoot! Please!*"

She couldn't shoot if she wanted to. She didn't know how the thing worked.

"No, Polly!" Mrs. Hacker warbled in panic. *"No!"*

The door flew open and crashed against the wall. BLAMMM! Ziegler fired a deafening round into the ceiling.

Polly cringed, blinded by the flash.

Ziegler yanked the rifle from her grip and rammed his hard fist into her belly.

TWO

7

LEON GUIDED HIS TRAVEL CART to the side of the muddy road to make way for a government vehicle closing fast behind him—a cream-colored rig, its teardrop-shaped dome streaked with rain. It was escorted by two horsemen in chaps, waxed riding cloaks, and closed vid helmets. They paid him no attention, though a leggy hound with a fighting collar trotted over to nose his leg. Leon held his breath until the dog moved away again.

The morning's rain had made the going slow and sloppy. Even the high road was criss-crossed with ruts. He had already missed the 11 o'clock ferry, and now it looked as if he'd miss the noon boat, too. Under the cabin in the cargo compartment he had a load of dry, split oak to sell, and in the bin beneath that he had twelve boxed pies his sister had baked the night before, six eel and six pork. He could smell them, even through their cotton batting. If he'd taken the coastal path, he might have made better time, but Tina wanted him to stick to the Old Dixie highway, so he'd be safer among the other travelers. "You should reach the Spartina shuttle by eleven. Soon as you get off the barge, you'll see the food concessions. You're looking for Sammy's Savories. Sammy and I agreed on twenty-five apiece, but that was back in March, and he's a money-grubber. If he goes *fifteen,* you tell him I said *twenty-five* and make like you're looking for another vendor.

He'll go, 'Twenty.' Tell him, damn it, these pies are worth *five dollars a slice*, but if he won't budge, settle on twenty. After that you're on your own. Just be sure you're back on the shuttle by four or you won't make it home before dark, and you'll have us all worried." It was already noon by the time he caught sight of the old airport across the water. There wasn't going to be much time for fun.

The Spartina shuttle was no more than an open barge attached by cables to a pair of steam-driven winches, one on either side of the grassy shallows. It left on the hour. From the top of the spur, you could judge from the line of waiting passengers whether to hurry or wait for the next crossing. Today there was no line.He drove right onto the waiting barge. The passengers were mostly CivSide tourists, the men wearing sidearms and the women with clean faces and shiny hair. The sleek, cream-colored vehicle that had passed him earlier was at the bow with its escort and their mounts.

In spite of the time, Leon let the others on the barge go on ahead of him up the landing ramp, the tourists, some vendors, and a couple of young pickers with push-carts heaped with machine parts to sell. Organ music drifted down the peninsula.

After delivering the pies and selling his firewood, he thought he would buy a ticket to the freaks and oddities, depending on what they had in the tent. Last year they had a live turtle with an arrow through its shell and a preserved squid as big as his travel cart. He wanted to check out the girlie shows at the end of the midway, too. And on the way back to the shuttle, if he had time, he hoped to cruise the tables in the firearms and tools tent.

He guided his cart up onto the packed sand of the midway just as the sun broke through the clouds. His leggings were caked with mud, his feet clammy in his wet shoes.

The breeze was intermittent and the mosquitoes pesky, but he'd bathed that morning and didn't feel like stopping to smear on the tarragon paste he had in the cabin.

A bald man without legs was juggling knives for coins outside the entry gate. Leon had to tap his horn to get the onlookers to let him through.

The food concessions offered fruit cakes, cheeses, meat and veggie roasters, tortillas, French fries, lemonade, tea, beer, nuts, sausages, taffy, and hard candy. Sammy's Savories was supposed to be a wood-slatted booth on a wagon with seats that folded down, an insulated basin for ice, and a yellow and purple Sammy's sign overhead. When he reached the arts and crafts tents without finding it, he turned and drove back past the food concessions on the other side of the promenade. Hot Stuffers, Pedro's, Oona's Honey Cakes, Sassy Lassie Cold Drinks, Buster Beef's, El Gaucho, The Fry Boy, Merrilee's, but no Sammy's.

A fat grill man in a red apron sat on the rim of the horse trough in front of Buster Beef's. Leon watched him snuffle some drug off the back of his hand. "Yo, pequeño, you wanna smooth the action? Five bucks a pop."

"I'm looking for Sammy's Savories."

"Don' know no Sammy," the guy said. "You want a job?"

Further down, Leon stopped at a Sweetie-Pie's. He and Malcolm sometimes used to get lunch at one of these on the street back in Tallahassee. Meat tarts, tubs of peaches and oranges, displays of cheeses, cookies, breads, and pastries. A simple-looking girl sat at the cashbox. The booth had eight stools at a narrow counter where two men sat slurping out of bowls. Pickers, by the looks.

The proprietor was a woman with red eyes and coarse hairs on her ears and cheekbones. She stood at one end of the counter, tearing glossy pages out of a large book to use as food wrappers. When she paused to blow her nose, Leon presented her with one of Tina's pies in its box. The top crust was a buttery gold, flecked with chives, and vented in a flower-petal pattern.

She sniffed it. "Fish?"

He nodded. "My sister baked it last night. She's a professional."

"How many you got?"

"Six eel, six pork."

"No rabbit?"

He shook his head.

"Give you twenty bucks for the pork."

"Apiece?"

"No, dumb ass, twenty for *six pies*."

"You're crazy! Eight slices to a pie, five bucks a slice—you'll be gettin' forty bucks a pie!"

She rubbed the corners of her mouth with her fingers. "Lunchtime's over. Who knows how long you been on the road with them things? Like as not, they'll go bad by suppertime. I buy 'em, I'm taking a big risk."

"If they go bad, you can have your money back. Twenty a pie. That's *dirt cheap,* and you know it."

"OK, listen. You want a hunnert-twenty? I'll give you a hunnert-twenty—for all twelve."

"You want the fish, too?"

She snapped her fingers. "I said all twelve, didn't I? That's my offer—twelve pies, ten bucks apiece. Take it or get the hell out of my establishment."

Tina would be disappointed in him, but Sammy wasn't here, and he didn't want to spend all his time shopping his goods up and down the midway. "I'll take it."

The woman tapped the plank countertop with a horny fingernail. He lifted the pies out of their boxes and placed them in front of her, one by one. The pickers rose from their stools to see.

"Jinga," the woman said, "pay this kid a hunnert-twenty dollars and write him out a receipt."

The girl had oily hair and a nubbly rash up the length of both arms. She counted out the money, snapping the coins down without meeting Leon's eye. The slip of paper she pushed toward him read, "12 pie, 120 $$." He tucked the cash and the receipt into the leather purse he kept inside his waistband.

"Boy!" the woman called out as he was leaving. She stuck three fingers into one of the pies and scooped out a mouthful. "Mm-*mm!* Tasty!"

Jinga and the pickers laughed.

He felt his face redden. She didn't have to humiliate him—he knew he'd been taken.

But after striking a deal with a potter for his stovewood and purchasing a stick of warm salt bread, a cup of orangeade, and a ticket to Dr. Whitney's Collection of Natural Horrors, he felt much better.

☾

By the middle of the afternoon a mustard haze had masked the sun. The mist creeping in off the ocean carried the stink of garbage. He sat on the deck of his cart with his eyes closed, tired and half-sick with disgust. The Spider Girl was a naked, dirty, brown person with four spindly arms and four legs attached to her hump-backed torso. The carny kept prodding her with a pole to make her move, and the crowd laughed at how she rolled in the shredded bark, waving her limbs like a beetle. Two scavs took turns spitting at her. Tina would have been outraged. Despite the ominous sky, he was determined not to leave the bazaar without having a look at the sex-show dancers. When would he get another chance?

On his way to the show tents, he stopped to watch a

snake swallower named Esmerelda. She wore red satin pantaloons with gold piping and two gold, snake-shaped coils around her fat breasts. Her nipples were gold, too. When she met his eyes, the green tail of a serpent waggled between her lips.

Frolicking Fillies was the only tent with a crowd in front of it, but the music stopped before he got close, and now the crowd—all men—was lining up at the ticket booth for the show inside. That he wasn't going to waste his money on. He headed back toward the center of the midway, cutting across a lot where a few scavengers had their junk spread out on the sand. A boy about Leon's age with a barrel of golf clubs poked him in the arm with one of them. "Hey! You like games? Five dollar! You pick! For you, three dollar."

He hopped to the pilot deck and sped up. The way that storm was building in the west, he figured he'd better skip the guns and tools and head straight for the ferry. The chain fights had started down in the bowl behind the pony rides—he could hear people cheering. That would be worth watching, but if it was going to blow a gale he had to get off this open peninsula and find a protected spot where he could tie the cart down.

A shrill scream cut the heavy air. Coming from the commission sales ring down on the flats. All he could see down there were scrawny cattle in pens near the livestock barns and a livery stable where horses rested out of the sun. And in among the idle wagons he noticed that yellowish government rig with the glossy black canopy.

"*Tock-tock-tock-tock.*" A hollow, musical sound, like wooden blocks. Then a honk. "*GRONK. Tock-tock. GRONK.*"

A bird. A black bird coasting toward him along the hard, sandy flats, low to the ground. Not an anhinga and not a cormorant. A large, husky glider with a beak like a scimitar. When it reached him, it looped twice around his cart. "Elper. Elper."

A *rook.* That's what it was. An acrobatic rook. Speaking to him.

"Urry!" The bird spiraled up and shot off downwind toward the sales barns. *Help her. Help her. Hurry.*

A girl. He could see her somehow—in his mind. Blond, bleeding at the mouth. Without another thought, he steered after the big bird down across the washboard incline.

The arrowing rook reached the empty bleachers around the sales ring and tumbled in the air right above one of the pole sheds. *Grawwwwk.*

He locked the rear tie-downs to a truck-frame sticking out of the sand, took his father's carbon-steel cane knife from its slot under the console, and trotted across the flats toward the rear of the shed.

About 40 men in chairs—all CivSiders wearing sidearms and snake boots. He found a place to stand behind the last row.

"My apologies for the outburst, gentlemen!" a bushy-bearded man was saying down front. A pitchman, he had on loose trousers with braces and a white shirt open to his belt, the sleeves rolled up to show off his thick, sun-burned arms. "Let's start over, shall we? We'll begin this afternoon with Number Two—Bobby, the boy. Bobby. Pretty Bobby—Number Two on your cards. Bobby, gentlemen!"

With a pink laser-pointer, he motioned to two men behind him. They picked up a wooden frame like a litter and set it up on end.

Strapped to it was a small child, chest and legs bare, with shaggy brown hair on his lolling head. He was unconscious.

"Heavensent Charity Auctions and I are pleased to offer this afternoon, from a good Christian family fallen on hard times, a sturdy boy of mixed race. Bobby is five years old, weighs a healthy fifty-two pounds, possesses all of his natural faculties and a docile temper, and is guaranteed free of any diseases or developmental defects."

Three or four men made their way to the stage for a closer look. "He baptized?" one called out.

The auctioneer looked amused. "Now that I couldn't say. But if he is not baptized, sir, will you bid for the privilege?"

Someone laughed.

The auctioneer surveyed the crowd. "Who will start us out this afternoon at twenty thousand dollars? Twenty thousand—just to get the ball rolling. Do I hear twenty?"

Leon had never been to a bondservant sale. He didn't like the idea of bonded servitude, but he wouldn't call it "an abomination," as his father and Tina did. They were dead-set against slavery. Malcolm used to speak in favor of abolition at campus demonstrations. But his grandparents, Tom and Yolanda, and their pastor, Clayton Gould, and his schoolmates, and every one of his friends in the Youth Guard regarded Malcolm's position as sentimental and backward. And the truth was that all the bondservants Leon had ever met seemed gentle and content. Besides, servitude had the sanction of the Gospels, and that was that. His tutor out at the dig, Mr. Olson, said that slavery was as beneficial a social institution as agriculture or education. The master-servant relationship was too often abused, of course, but when that happened the individual was to blame, not the institution.

On the far side of the shed, five more young people lay on their backs in a flatbed wagon. They looked drugged. Two attendants with black batons stood by, guarding them. One of the slaves had a bloody gag in her mouth. He held his breath. That was her. The one he had to help.

"Ten!" someone called out down front.

The auctioneer laughed and said, "Twenty! Do I hear twenty?"

"Ten-five," the bidder cried.

"Nay, now *twenty*!" the auctioneer said. "Twenty will open the bidding on this healthy, well-formed boy. Do I hear *twenty* now?" He scanned the buyers' faces, his teeth shining through his beard.

"Eleven in gold," another bidder said.

"Eleven-two," the first one countered.

"Three."

The auctioneer grimaced, waving his arms overhead. "Gentlemen, please! Look into your hearts as well as your wallets, won't you?" He stroked the boy's hair with the pink laser beam. "This Bobby is a clear-eyed, unblemished, male child of very tender years. Twenty thousand dollars is a *fraction* of what he would bring in Singapore, I don't have to tell you. What's more, this is no—"

"We ain't *in* Singapore!" the first bidder barked. "Nowheres close."

"You know what I mean, sir! This is no rough-trade exchange! This is a corporate-sponsored, faith-inspired benefit auction! The *entire winning bid* goes to the child's family! Good people fallen on hard times! Corinthians thirteen: 'And now abideth faith, hope, charity, these three; but the greatest of these'—word of God now—'*the greatest of these* is charity!' Christian charity, my friends. Heavensent. Let the Lord's compassion guide your heart and hand! This sweet Bobby deserves a *home*."

"Here's your twenty, sir!" a man in the last row called out. He was wearing a white silk blouse with puffy sleeves buttoned at the cuff, and he had a thick gray ponytail hanging between his shoulder blades. The carriage dog sitting beside him was the same dog he'd seen on the highway—with the fighting collar. The blue vid helmet the man held under his arm was the kind Security used.

The auctioneer flicked his laser in the man's direction. "Praise the Lord. Gentlemen, we have our twenty-thousand-dollar floor. Do I hear twenty-five?" He paused. "Twenty-five? Twenty-five for darling Bobby?" He cupped his ear. "Twenty-three?" He waited, fists on his hips. "Twenty-two-five? For this beautiful boy? Very well, then . . . Once more? Twenty-two thousand? No? Twenty-one? Twenty-one, I say?" He slapped his thigh. "All right, twenty and done! Number Two, Bobby, placed with the *very* fortunate gentleman in the back row." He nodded to his assistants.

"Bring up that Number One!" somebody shouted. "That princess you got laying back there!"

The auctioneer held up one hand. "Boys? Has she recovered herself?"

Some of the men in front were clapping in rhythm. Others craned their necks to see. There were a number of scavs looking on, too, out near the stables.

"Very well! Heavensent Auctions and I are very pleased to offer for your generous consideration a bonded female, Number One on your cards this afternoon, gentlemen—Cassandra, the Pagan Princess!"

The handlers trundled her onto the stage and tipped up the frame she was strapped to. Her clothing was stained and torn and her hair was a tangled mess. She was the one, but how in the world was he supposed to help her?

"I can't tell you what a rare pleasure it is to offer a prime virgin—healthy, white, and beautiful, and just fifteen years of age. Don't let her appearance deceive you. It's nothing that a good meal and a warm bath won't cure. Cassandra is exquisite. Blue-eyed and strong, with excellent teeth and posture. Yes, she's a heathen, that's true. She has a fiery, unbroken spirit, a spirit in need of discipline and forbearance—along with a few weeks' coddling and patience. But dismiss all that from your mind for the moment. Instead, feast your eyes. Examine her . . . the long-fingered hands, the head of thick yellow hair, the straight, smooth legs and square shoulders, the youthful breasts and high round buttocks, the clear line of the brow and jaw. Princess Cassandra is as rare a gem as I've ever had the pleasure to—"

"Fifty thousand!" boomed the well-dressed bidder who'd bought Bobby. Heads turned.

"Fifty-one," a fat man in front said in a high voice.

"Fifty-three!"

"I have fifty-three thousand. Do I—"

"Fifty-three-five!"

"Sixty thousand!" the well-dressed man shouted.

The bidding stopped as a torrent of wind ripped through the shed, followed by a storm of hail that thundered like stones on the metal roof.

"Sold, by God!" shouted the auctioneer. "The Pagan Princess, sold to the gentleman in the rear for sixty thousand dollars!"

Cows started bawling. Horses screamed. The scavs were keening.

Somebody yelled, "Oh, Jesus! Run! Run!" The air was roaring.

"*Torcedor!*" a scav wailed.

The woolly sky was black. Chairs tumbled away as the crowd scattered, yelling. Scraps of paper, auction cards, ribbons of kelp, grit, feathers, paper cups, and hats flew past.

Coachmen scrambled to save their panicked animals. A siren sounded in the distance. Leon hugged one of the shed's timber posts, the cane knife against his chest. He wanted to run, but that would be crazy. You could get knocked down and trampled. And there was nowhere to run to. CivSiders, scavs, carnies, cows, hogs, horses—they were all trapped together on this spit of sand.

Leon had seen many twisters, but he'd never seen one as monstrous as the one raging now over the high ground, a sinuous, blue-black vortex of water and debris. The noise was deafening, like a train in a tunnel. The wooden post he was clinging to shuddered as the wind howled overhead. If the roof went, the posts and their concrete footings would go with it, and so would he, but as long as the core of the storm kept to the north he would likely make it.

Two wild-eyed horses, yoked together, splashed by toward the ocean. Muddy water churned past his ankles. "*Please, God!*" he shouted. "*Let me live!*"

The whirlwind roared down the midway, pierced by shrieks and shouts, gunshots and bellowing animals. Through bursts of blinding rain, he caught sight of a gang of scavs making off with the auctioneer's flatbed, pulling it by its tongue and yoke. Four slaves were still in it, strapped to their racks.

The girl wasn't one of them. They'd left her to drown on that low-lying stage. He slogged his way toward the front of the shed, one arm shielding his eyes against the gusts.

There. Her litter had slipped half off the stage. And she was no longer attached to it. He felt sick.

But no—the wind had flipped the thing over. She was suspended beneath it, her hair bouncing in the frothy water.

He sloshed his way to her and righted the litter, bracing its upper end against his thighs. She was breathing. He sliced through the gag in her mouth. A CivSider—he could tell by the teeth. “Easy. You’re all right,” he shouted through the wind. “Let me help you!”

With the knife under his arm, he pulled the gag out of her mouth, holding her by the hair so her head couldn’t roll. Her eyelids fluttered open. The rain had rinsed the dirt from her skin. Her left temple was bruised, and her face and throat— God. She had sores. Was she poxed?

He rubbed his hands on his shift.

She was trying to speak.

He leaned over.

“Please. Don’t— Don’t—” She touched the torn corners of her mouth with her tongue.

“It’s OK,” Leon said. “I won’t hurt you.”

“Don’t be afraid—” she coughed— “of me. I’m not truly sick.”

“You’re all . . . “

“I know. It was a trick.” She swallowed. “It hurts to talk.”

“You don’t have to. The bird came to me—the rook. It spoke to me.”

“Where is he?”

“I don’t know. But we have to move. Soon as this blows over they’ll be back here looking for you.”

Her eyes closed.

“See if you can keep your feet under you. I’m cutting you free.”

He slipped behind her and sliced through the nylon strapping, arms first, then her thighs and chest. The girl sank to her hands and knees in the water. He caught her and drew her left arm behind his neck.

They walked that way for a distance until she could support herself.

His tethered cart lay on its side, festooned with seaweed and grass, two wheels slowly spinning, the other two buried in muck. Luckily, he'd had the sheathing drawn down over his solar chargers.

Up on the peninsula, the annual Augie Bazaar—flag-topped tents, game booths, mechanical rides, animals, transport vehicles and carriages, lacquered signs, flashing lights, prizes, handicrafts and curiosities, foodstuffs, leather goods, hand tools and firearms, the pawnbrokers' booths, the beer and gin stands and the body-art practitioners, the snake swallower and the spider girl and the rambunctious crowd—was gone. All of it. There was nothing left, only wet sand, wreckage, and corpses.

The storm now blackened the eastern horizon, and the rain came in lashing sheets. The temperature was dropping as the sky brightened to the west. Humans and animals were crying out. Twice he heard gunshots. A woman screamed, "*Theresa!*" over and over.

He shoveled. Water and sand kept oozing into the trough, defeating his gains, but finally he was able to push up on the frame with enough force to heave the cart free a wheel at a time.

He stopped to catch his breath. His arms ached. His mind was numb. He put away the shovel.

Everywhere people were weeping, yelling, screaming. The gulls sounded jubilant. The scavs were yipping to one another, too, as excited as the gulls. Their simple happiness seemed almost touching.

On foot and on horseback, stunned survivors plodded toward the far side of the peninsula and the shuttle dock. But if the shuttle had been destroyed, the only way off the peninsula would be to the north, through the marsh. He'd have to abandon the travel cart.

The girl was in a crouch, hugging her knees and shivering. He lifted her chin so she would look at him. "Come on, Cassandra. We need to get you out of sight."

She rose to her feet, saying, "My name is Polly."

"Mine's Leon. Leon Krauss."

They shook hands.

He showed her where to place her foot on the sill. "It's clean and warm inside. There's a featherbed and a fan and water to drink, and some oat bread. And there's a waste vent."

She hesitated. "Where are we going?"

"I'm going back to our camp. My dad's doing research there."

"What kind of research?"

"He's an archeologist."

"TwiceBorn?"

"No. He's a scientist."

"Everybody down here is born again."

"Not my father. He's a freethinker. He's against slavery and censorship."

"So you're not CivSiders?"

"Not anymore. It's a long story."

"I'm not either," she said. Then she smiled. "It's a long story."

"I figured. Why don't you come with me? Our camp's straight up the coast three or four miles."

She studied the travel cart. "You don't have a horse."

"Don't need one."

"You push it?"

"You can. It has self-charging motors. Solar auxiliary, too. Moves right along on a hard surface. Go on, climb in." Malcolm had bought the cart before they left Talla, a brand new Kia Nomad with custom composite wheels, an eight-by-fourteen-foot cabin on a tubular steel frame, with running lights, a computerized autopilot module, a driving deck, and screened air and waste vents. The cabin was made of oil-sealed bamboo, and the rubberized cargo compartment underneath had removable shelves and a tool box.

"You can lock it from the inside," he told her.

Even with independent traction, it wasn't easy maneuvering the rig back up to level ground. A couple of pickers dragging a collapsed tent eyed him as he struggled with the cart. At least the scavs wouldn't make trouble. They were gathering around a bonfire down at the chain-fight ring. Already they'd rounded up a number of stray animals—horses, goats, pigs—and they'd seized a wooden water tanker. And the auctioneer's flatbed wagon. No sign of the four slaves. Some scavs ate human flesh, but only when they had nothing else, and this band had more meat than they could consume in a month's time. They'd settle in for a while now, salvaging goods, curing skins, making jerky.

At the west end of the midway the road surface sloped down toward the old shuttle landing. It was gone, roadway, pier and all. So was the entire spartina tidal basin. In its place, a broad sandbar strewn with puddles and glistening cord grass formed a causeway to the far side, along which a ragged procession of people and horses was slowly ambling.

8

He eased the cart over the hump of the old stone culvert crossing the path into the dunes. The acrid tang of Tina's mosquito torches on the night air reached him before he could make out the lines of the camp's bunkers under the bluffs of sand and beach grass. The outdoor oven cast a red glow. Mooch woofed and bounded up to greet him, shoving his square head against his hip.

He thumped the dog's chest.

Tina hurried up, lantern swinging, and hugged him. She raised the light. "It's a joy to see you, Leon. Are you OK?"

"I'm fine. But all I could get for the pies was ten dollars apiece. Sammy wasn't even there."

"Well, at least they didn't go to waste. A big storm blew by to the south this afternoon. You must have seen it."

He nodded. "It was really terrible. A lot of people got killed." Up on his hind legs, Mooch was snuffling at the cart hatch. "I rescued a slave. She's in the Nomad. Down, Mooch." Leon rapped on the roof. "Polly? We're here. It's safe."

The hatch rose on its pistons.

Tina gasped. "Dear Lord! A *child*!"

"She isn't poxed. She did that to herself to scare off the slavers."

They helped her out of the cart. Tina brushed the hair

out of Polly's eyes. "Food's on the table," she told Leon. "You go get something to eat. I'll take care of your friend."

He followed the path to the main shelter, one of two steel shipping containers half-buried in the dunes. The other one housed his father's field lab. He was working—light filtered through the curtains.

At one end of the big table he found a cross-hatched loaf of sourdough bread, a dish of diced beets and carrots in vinegar, half a grilled chicken, and a jug of mint tea. He made himself eat slowly, pondering the bazaar, the tornado, and the girl. Polly. He was a different person from the one who'd left the dig that morning. Older. Bigger, in a way. Sadder. Last week, Mr. Olson had told him and Nando that their last writing assignment of the year would be a formal essay of personal reflection, a true story about the self. He had his topic.

At his sister's end of the shelter Tina and Polly were going through Tina's wardrobe, choosing things for her to wear. Talking and laughing. He couldn't make out their words. After Tina left to put Polly's clothes in the washtub and check on the hens and rabbits for the night, Leon found some classical music on the radio.

He served Polly chicken and beets. "There's more of everything."

"This must be the most wonderful place to live," she said.

"I don't know about that. It's pretty remote. We used to live in Tallahassee—when my dad taught at the university. I liked it there."

"Is he retired?"

"They cut him loose. He didn't really mind—except we lost our health coverage."

"So this is an archeological dig?"

"Well, it's not far from here. Tomorrow I can show you."

The mounds and middens that Malcolm and Nando's mom, Giselle, were excavating were a quarter-mile north of the bluffs, where coastal erosion had exposed them.

"It just seems so peaceful."

"The weather gets pretty ferocious sometimes." In the lamplight, the calm in her washed face made him feel like he was seeing her for the first time. "You look a whole lot better than you did this afternoon."

"Thanks to you, Leon."

Embarrassed, he asked, "What was it like when the scavs caught you? Did they hurt you?"

"They didn't rape me, if that's what you mean. I was worth a lot more untouched."

"Thank *God*."

She smiled. "Did you say your dad's a freethinker?"

He nodded. "That's basically why we're out here. What are you?"

"I'm a witch."

He almost laughed. "No, really?"

By the way she nodded he knew she meant it. The hairs on his arms tingled. That explained the talking rook! There used to be witches, he knew that much. He'd read about them, but supposedly they were all imprisoned or exiled. Or burned. Long ago now, too, before he was born. "So can you cast spells?"

"A few."

"Any time you want?"

"No, not exactly. Anyway, I had to hide all of my things, including my book of spells, so I'm kind of incapacitated at the moment."

"Where'd you hide them?"

"Out in the green belt. I only hope I can find the spot again."

"I'll help, if you want, when you're ready to go look. If

you go out there again, you're going to need some protection."

She looked surprised. "Thank you, Leon. But I can't go back for a while yet. They'll be looking for me."

"The scavs? Nah, they forgot all about you."

"Not the scavs—the slave dealers, the people who drugged me and sold me."

"Those guys? They *abandoned* you! You're nothing but sea wrack now. Anybody that finds you can claim you."

She stared at him.

That was the wrong thing to say. "*I'm* not claiming you, if that's what you're thinking."

"'Nothing but *sea wrack*'?"

"Technically, I mean."

"You *accept* that? Humans as property?"

"I don't *accept* it—it's the *law*." He felt like an idiot.

"Those men *abducted* me!"

"And that's a crime! *Obviously*. But servitude is legal, that's all I'm saying."

"Immoral laws are never accepted by moral people."

"Sometimes they are. Come on, you go to *prison* if you break the law."

"I can think of worse fates."

After a short silence, he pushed up and left the shelter. There were lots of bad laws, he knew that, but nobody wanted to go to jail.

The night was thick. The noise of surf cloaked the thin sound of the two clashing radios, the strings behind him and a clarinet on the jazz station his father had on in the lab.

He heard the screen door slap shut, but he didn't turn around.

"I'm sorry, Leon."

After a moment, he said, "My father's an anti-slavery

activist. That's the reason he lost his position at the university."

"Is he over there working?"

"Yes. At night he transcribes his notes."

"My familiar's name is Balthazar," she said after a time. "He's the raven who spoke to you."

Raven, that's what he was. "He's really amazing."

"What's amazing is that he managed to find *you*."

He turned to her. "So when you got away from the scavs, then what happened?"

She told him how two people she'd thought were her friends sold her to a couple of bounty hunters, who then drugged her and sold her to the slavers. God. No wonder she wasn't ready to go back for her belongings.

"Polly, if you can describe for me where you left your things, tomorrow I'll take the cart and see if I can find them. I know the Wastes pretty well."

She placed the tips of her fingers on his forearm. "Thank you for offering, Leon. You're generous and brave. When I need your help again, I'll let you know."

He nodded. Not *if*. *When*.

9

ONIONS FRYING.

The salt-encrusted roof window over her head framed the sky. Every morning when her eyes opened she expected to see the silhouette of Balthazar looking down at her, but once again the skylight was a milky blank.

"Morning, Polly!" Tina was at the cookstove.

"What are you making?"

"Texas eggs. And red-pepper cornbread."

Polly slipped out into the sea air and crossed over the grassy dune to the outhouse. Nearby in the lab, she could hear Leon and Nando's tutor scolding them in his nasally voice. She didn't know how the boys could stand it, listening to that Mr. Olson day after day.

Except for Balthazar's absence and one heedless plunge into the jelly-fish-infested surf, Polly's few days at the dig had been pleasant. Mornings she gathered driftwood for Tina's stove, helped with the washing and the rabbits and hens, and weeded the gardens. Evenings she helped the boys transport artifacts from Mound One down to the lab for cataloging.

After breakfast, Tina asked Polly to walk back to the marsh to fill a pack basket with sea asparagus for pickling. She was almost there when she heard running feet on the path behind her. She froze, then ducked into a stand of reeds, holding her machete with both hands.

It was Leon, out of breath. "Your bird! Your rook! He's here!"

"Where?"

"At camp. But I think he's hurt."

"Oh, Great Mother. Here—" She took off her pack basket and shoved it into his hands.

☾

"Balthazar won't go inside if Mooch is in there, too," she said.

"Stay," Tina told the dog, pointing.

Mooch lowered himself to the sand, whimpering. Polly stepped around him, the nervous raven on her shoulder. He was dusty and thin, with mites and swollen feet. He hadn't preened in days. He couldn't fly, not actively. He'd been hopping along the ground and gliding when he could, all the way here.

Polly set a cup of water before him.

"Open your wings for me, won't you?"

He tried. The right was lower than the left.

Polly gently probed the bones and joints. "I don't think anything's fractured, but I'm going to have to immobilize this wing."

No.

"Do you ever want to fly again?" But sarcasm was lost on a familiar. "Balthazar, when you move, you can't help using both wings. The bad one won't heal unless we make you rest it."

"You'll want some diatomaceous earth for the parasites, too," Tina said. "I dose my chickens once a month."

Leon slipped in through the screen door.

"Is he hurt bad?"

"I think he'll be all right, but he's weak. He hasn't eaten much since the storm."

"There's some crab in the cooler," Leon said.

"Perfect."

Polly rubbed his chapped feet with fish oil and gave him a sponge bath. From a piece of gray felt she fashioned a sleeve and taped that to his wing and shoulder. He wouldn't eat with anyone near, so Polly carried him outside again into the shade behind the lab.

He gulped the meat.

She said to him, "I want to thank you for getting the boy to help me—back at that auction. If you hadn't found him, I'd be dead."

He is keen.

"He's sharp-witted and sensitive. And he's kind. That Mrs. Hacker, though— I'm sorry, but *she* was a bad choice."

She was keen, also.

"I'm not blaming you. I never should have put my trust in those two. You were right about that."

She was tricky.

"Yes. Takes one to know one, I guess."

Leon came up behind her. "So you two can talk to each other?"

"A little. Balthazar's unusual, though. Most familiars aren't able to vocalize."

"But you can communicate without talking, too, right? Like telepathically?"

"Most of the time. It's iffy, though. Familiars don't think the way people think."

"I've been wondering," he said after a moment. "Would you mind telling me sometime how you connect with a familiar? And just, you know . . . what it's like being a witch?"

"Not at all. Come on." She took his hand.

They followed the winding path out among the sandy bluffs through the beach plum and sea rose to the surf. The first thing to understand, she told him as they walked, was that all witches were endowed at birth with a sense of the enclosing energy of the universe—its texture and pressure. Some witches felt it more keenly than others, but with training and practice, all witches could learn to make some transformative use of the Spirit Braid, it was called. Or just the Braid.

"The Braid?"

"Yes. My father thinks of it as an infinite fabric—the tapestry of awareness. To me it's more like a gas, or like skin, sort of, because it has warmth. But what it is most simply, I guess, is the field that connects all of life."

"And familiars can sense the Braid, too?"

"Oh, yes—much more acutely than witches can, too. That's how you bond. When an animal in synch with the Braid crosses paths with a witch, if the witch is alone in the craft, the animal will offer to entwine its consciousness with the witch's. They don't always want to, either—it's almost like they can't help it."

"And so that's how witches cast spells? By using their connection to the Braid?"

"Well, not exactly. Access to the Braid makes magick *possible*, but a witch's skill in the craft depends on how good she is at actually *influencing* the Braid. Both in the moment and over time."

Leon nodded slowly. "So, the Spirit Braid . . . is that kind of like the soul?"

The tide was out. Rills of seaweed, driftwood, scrap plastic of a thousand kinds, and a gummy mat of dead jellyfish blanketed the sand for miles in both directions. On the horizon a two-masted sailing ship slid north.

"No," she said. "Spirit is the spark of life, and while we live, the Braid is our own personal connection to the field of consciousness. When we die, that spark goes out."

"So the difference is that *all* animals have spirit, but only people have *souls*."

"I wouldn't say that. The universe isn't much more than matter and energy joining together and falling apart over and over, forever. And spirit is the name of the spark that animates each point of consciousness, whether it's in a flea or a hippopotamus."

"So it's like the breath of *God,* then. And matter, *without* that spark, is seaweed and clouds and the sand and the ocean. The physical world."

"Matter *is* all that, that's right, but it's *more* than that, too. And most of it can't be seen or felt. By anyone. And it's always changing."

After a moment he said, "Change is the only certainty. That's what my father says. Everything has to evolve."

"That's true. Does that frighten you?"

He looked at her. "No. Why would it?"

"Change means death. That frightens most people. That's why they seek comfort in stories."

"What stories?"

"You know. Myths. About how the earth and the stars came to be. About angels and heaven and what happens when you die. Adam and Eve. Reincarnation. The Devil. Why people have to suffer. Those stories."

"Have you read the Bible?"

"Most of it."

"But you're not an atheist. Because witches have gods and goddesses, don't they?"

"We have gods and goddesses, but we know they're not real."

"I don't get it."

"Gods and goddesses are ideals. They're just projections of ourselves."

"Like super-heros?"

She smiled. "Sort of, yeah. Gods *look* like humans

because they're supposed to stand for the things we admire in humans. Also the things we're afraid of."

"Did you learn all this stuff in school?"

"I didn't go to school. My parents were my teachers."

"Are they witches, too?"

She laughed. "Leon, when I was little, I thought *everyone* was a witch."

He was digging in the sand with a curved piece of glass. "I never knew my mother," he said.

"No? How come?"

"When I was just a baby, she took a trip north to visit a sick friend of hers. In New York."

New York, sixteen years ago. There was nothing to be said about that.

They watched the foaming waves. The schooner was out of sight.

Leon leaned back on his elbows and tilted his face toward the sun. Eyes closed, he said, "Here's what bothers me. If it's all just *stories*, the Bible and the Quran and all those, and if there's no heaven or angels or anything, and no god-given purpose to life . . . then what are we *doing* here? I mean, I hate to think we're just these random blobs of cells that sprang into existence for no reason at all."

"But, Leon . . . " She swept her hand along the horizon, blue on blue. "*This* is the reason. Awareness. And if you want purpose, well, we create our own purposes, each one of us, for ourselves."

He stared out across the water. "Then our lives don't actually *mean* anything."

"Who says they're supposed to?"

"I know, but if our lives don't *mean* anything, then . . . Then people might as well be jellyfish. Or *seaweed*."

"That's true."

"And some day we're just going to go extinct, like the woolly mammoth and the stegosaurus."

"Some day the sun will swell up and consume the earth. So? We're just specks, Leon. Tiny specks in an ocean of space and time."

He sighed. "Mr. Olson says it's ridiculous to think about humans going extinct, because we're God's chosen people, and when Jesus comes back, all the Christians will be raptured and taken up into the clouds."

She shook her head. "If anyone's going to save us, Leon, it'll have to be us."

"Then we're doomed."

Polly looked over at him.

"That will be a very sad day," he said, "the day human beings go extinct."

Polly laughed. "Oh, yeah? Who'll be sad? The moon?"

"The mosquitoes," he said.

She laughed again and jumped to her feet. "You know what? I really like how your mind works." He was smart and sincere. Brave. Trustworthy. Funny. A friend. A true friend. She had never had a true friend her own age. Till now.

☾

Polly put up with Balthazar's complaints for three days before finally giving in and removing his wing wrap. He flew for a bit with the aid of the shore breeze before settling on the edge of the cistern to preen.

Much better.

"But not a hundred percent."

Enough to leave this place. It is time.

"He looks *good*," Leon said.

Nando and Mr. Olson were standing behind him, watching from the landing outside the lab door. The tutor was a bony, hollow-chested young man with crooked teeth, long, wispy brown hair, and black-framed eyeglasses. Malcolm and Nando's mother, Giselle, had hired him to come out from Tallahassee to see to the boys' schooling. When he wasn't here at the encampment, where he used the lab for a classroom, he mostly kept to himself in a rundown travel cart up behind the garden.

"What kind of bird is that?" Nando asked.

"That is the common raven," Mr. Olson said. "Also called the wolf bird. This specimen is quite some distance from its normal habitat, I'd say. No doubt we can blame a storm for that. Ravens belong to the Corvid family. As birds go, they're quite intelligent, and they have superb eyesight. They subsist on insects mainly—though they relish carrion and fruits."

The boy snorted. "Doesn't sound too intelligent to me."

"Oh, he's intelligent, all right," Leon said.

"A raven's sex cannot be determined by external appearances, Leon," Mr. Olson informed him.

"His name is Balthazar," Polly said in spite of herself. B was right—it was time to leave. "He's been a friend of mine for more than ten years."

"*Really?*" Nando said.

"Yes. He travels with me."

"Good heavens, that's *extraordinary*," Mr. Olson said. "He follows you, then?"

"When he wants to."

"You see, Nando? A very intelligent bird." He turned to her. "Polly, Nando tells me you're on your way to a farm up north of the Exclusion Zone. Way up in the Regions. Can that be right?"

Leon gave Nando a hard look. But he wasn't to blame. Mr. Olson was the prying sort, and Nando was young.

"Yes, that's right," Polly said. "My family lives there. My father runs a tennis camp."

"He might have once. But not anymore. The Regions have been purged. Surely you know that."

Polly said nothing.

Nando turned to the teacher. "She got kidnapped by *scavs!* And they sold her to these bounty hunters! And *they* sold her to a *slave* dealer!"

Mr. Olson pursed his lips. "My, my, how colorful."

Polly turned away. First chance he had, maybe tonight, Mr. Olson would be reporting her to Security.

☾

Over supper at the outdoor table, Polly delivered her announcement. Now that Balthazar had recovered, she would be resuming her journey north. Tonight.

They all looked startled, even Leon, who already knew.

"But why tonight?" Tina asked.

"You've all been wonderful," Polly said, "but it's time."

Malcolm sat back. "This seems sudden. Did something happen?"

"It's because of Mr. Olson," Leon said.

"Mr. Olson?" Giselle asked. "What do you mean?"

"He's a jerk."

"Archie Olson's harmless," Malcolm said. "What's he done to deserve this?"

"Don't blame me." Leon glared across the table at Nando. "*I* never told him *any*thing."

"You're a *masturbator*!" Nando shouted. His eyes filled as he glared around at the others. He pushed up and beat his way out through the mosquito netting.

Giselle sighed and rose to go after him.

"Mr. Olson thinks Polly should be in school," Leon said.

"No, he thinks I'm a witch. And it's true, I am. It's not Nando's fault."

"Even so, Polly," Malcolm said, "witches can't travel.

Not nowadays. You'll be lucky just to make it out of Florida."

"Well, I have to try. I'm not safe here any longer." She fingered her triquetra through her shirt.

Leon was whispering to Malcolm. Malcolm listened, nodding. Earlier that afternoon when she told Leon about her decision, all he'd managed to say was that he would miss her. Since then, no doubt he'd been thinking about his options.

"Polly won't have to cross the Wastes alone," Leon said. "I'll go with her—as long as she wants me to."

Tina turned to Malcolm. "He *will*?"

Malcolm patted her hand. "It's not such a bad idea. He's got to travel to Talla, anyway, to pick up my medication, and I'm sure they'll be safer together than each alone."

"Does that sound OK to you?" Leon asked.

"That sounds perfect," she said.

☾

"This is a road map from the Oil Age," Malcolm said, unfolding it on his dusty lab bench. "The Southeast Coastal States." He smoothed out the creases. "It's surprising how many of these highways are still passable. On foot, anyway. And whenever you can identify intersections and old towns and whatnot, the mileage is very accurate."

With his finger he traced a line north to Atlanta and an inch or so beyond. "The trail begins here. Amicalola Falls." He tapped the spot. "Used to be quite a popular pastime. People would hike all summer long, all the way to Maine."

"Really?" Leon asked. "Why?"

"Just so they could say they'd done it, I suppose."

Polly gave Leon a nudge. "Have you ever gone hiking in the forest?"

He shook his head. "Never."

"It's the most wonderful thing." Whatever the trouble awaiting her in the north, it was a long way off. This leg of the trip, at least, if she could share it with Leon, might be a jolly adventure.

Tina presented Leon with an oblong metal box. "Here's something for you to keep on your person—just in case you should get separated from the cart."

She showed them what was inside: matches dipped in wax, a lens and a sheaf of tinder, a tiny LED flashlight, a compass, water purification tablets, folded plastic bags for storing water, four packets of antibiotic ointment, butterfly bandages, a bobbin of fishing line, fish hooks in two sizes, split-shot weights, and a wire snare for rabbits.

They packed the cart with rain slickers, blankets, towels, tools, five jugs of good water, a mule whip, a solar stove, a carton with a few loaves of sourdough, a crock of lemon marmalade, waxed cheeses, hard-boiled eggs, some olives, dried fish, sea rocket, salt, flour, rice, honey, and tea—enough to see them to Tallahassee and beyond.

Malcolm took Leon by the shoulders. "If you decide to go on with Polly to the trailhead, you have my permission. But promise me you'll send the medication out here to me by bonded courier. And send us word when you can."

"I will."

In the glow of the cart's headlamps, Polly noticed the sheen on Leon's cheeks. They hugged everyone. Tina said solemnly that the world was a hard place, but she had every confidence that Polly would find her family, whatever it took, as long as she did nothing on impulse and watched out for herself. "I hope our paths will cross again some day," she said, her voice cracking.

"Oh, they will," Polly said, "I'm sure of it."

It was a sad parting.

10

The Wastes were no trouble to cross, Leon told her, as long as you kept to the high road and within sight of the security fence. There, patrols and security cams monitored the traveled way. Elsewhere, if you were accosted by scavs, you had to remember that they were cautious by nature. They had pack-like instincts. As long as you stood your ground with a rifle or a shotgun, usually you could count on them to back down.

"Do we have a rifle or a shotgun?" Polly asked.

Leon leaned forward on the pilot deck and patted the stock of his lever-action carbine in its leather scabbard. Malcolm had bought it for him when he joined the Youth Guard. "I can put ten rounds into a teacup at fifty yards. Do you shoot?"

She shook her head. "Witches have no need for guns. My father says they're crude."

"*Crude*?"

She nodded.

"I guess if you're a witch you can think like that. But the way the world is nowadays, regular people have to protect themselves. Seriously, people need firearms."

"I don't doubt that," she said.

They made good time on the mostly empty roadway, giving a wide berth to any campfires they spotted by the wayside, until they got to the raised thoroughfare. Occasional vehicles rumbled by.

The banked-up route took them around the brown murk that hung like fog over Old Jax. After a long descent, heading south, they came to a wooden barrier with a hand-painted sign on it, reading, "End." Here the graded surface stopped, and the flood plain spread out before them. Cart tracks fanned off in three or four directions. In the distance they could see slow-moving carriage lights. He chose a path that veered toward the vapor lights that marked the security fence, a mile or more to the west.

"That's it, Polly. Main gate to CivSide."

"Looks busy," she said.

"It usually is. Didn't you say you hid your pack in sight of the gate?"

"Oh, but not that gate. The *utility* gate—where the pickers come through. Do you know the one I mean?"

He leaned back against the push bar and rubbed his forehead. The utility gate was miles away. They wouldn't make it tonight.

"I'm sorry, Leon. Is it much farther?"

"Well, not really. The trouble is after dark it's too hard pick out a route through the refuse plain. Too many obstacles."

"So what do we do?"

"I could cross through by myself up ahead, then come back by the utility gate in the morning. But how would I find your things?"

"You couldn't. They're coned."

"What's that?"

"They're protected by a cone of magick."

"Could Balthazar find them?"

"Sure, but he couldn't release them."

A motorcycle with three jiggling headlamps rumbled up behind them and pulled to a stop alongside the cart. Two men in sky-blue Security vid helmets, one seated in a sidecar. The cycle was chrome and black with yellow fenders and a blue-and-white CPA governmental license plate. Its dusty saddlebag had the CPA Security shield embossed in the middle—the sword and the cross.

The driver lifted his visor. His read-out flickered in the curved glass. "Everything all right here?"

"Fine," Leon said. "We're taking a breather." Just a border patrol checking them out.

The slump-shouldered passenger groaned and got out of the sidecar. "So. What's in the cart, kiddos?" He nodded at it.

"Clothing, bedding, provisions. We're on our way to Tallahassee."

"Tell me, did you happen to see a brawny black man on horseback pass you on the highway, oh, golly, some time within the last two or three hours? Either of you?"

"We haven't seen any riders at all."

He scratched his jaw. "Mind if I take a peek inside the cart?"

Leon cocked his head. "What's your reason?"

"Routine inspection." He stepped out of the sidecar, hitching up his trousers with his thumbs. Polymer semi-auto on his duty belt, along with pouches for his mags, cuffs, tactical baton, and pepper spray.

"Don't you need probable cause?"

"Well, listen to you. Bet you're one smart schoolboy. Kind that likes to sit right in front, always got his hand up."

"We haven't done anything wrong."

"Hope not. You're Leon Krauss, I have that right?"

"Yes, and the cart belongs to my dad. It's registered."

"So I see. You have an address in Talla, is that right?"

"Twelve hundred-and-eight Madison. We live there."

"You live there. With your grandparents. You have a sister, Tina, twenty-three. Your father is Professor Malcolm

Krauss. Blew off an FTB inquiry last year. Some kind of rabble-rouser, looks like. Your mother was Carole Pierce, a weaver, disappeared in the holocaust."

"Yes."

"You're enrolled in the New Florida Christian Schools."

"Yes."

"And you're a team leader in the Junior Guard."

"Last summer I was."

He turned to Polly. "And your name is . . . ?"

"Polly Lightfoot. Why?"

"Because, Polly Lightfoot, for some reason I am not picking you up on my screen here."

"My chip failed."

"Guess it must have. Where do you go to school, Polly?"

"St. Michael's Academy. In Orlando."

"Long way from home, aren't you?"

"My home is in the north."

"Where in the north?"

"Upper Duxton, Vermont."

The other officer shut off his engine.

"That makes you a refugee. I'm going to have to see some external ID, I'm afraid. Church card, cash card, DNA portrait, what have you."

"Last week I was robbed by scavs. They took everything I had."

"That's the truth," Leon said. "She got jumped trying to cross the flood plain."

The driver spoke up. "Found her, Bix. Missing juvenile. Ward of Wendell Houghton, residing at Eighteen Coconut Way, The Ponds, in Orlando—*Captain* Wendell Houghton of the New Florida Home Guard, Twelfth Reserves. Wayward Youth has a BOL out on her."

"Why, thank you, Frank." Bix clucked. "So. A refugee, a

runaway—*and* the ward of an officer in the Home Guard Reserves."

"He's my uncle. I've been staying with him and my aunt since December. Now it's summer vacation, and I'm on my way back to my family."

"So what are you doing way out here in the Wastes?"

"I was thinking I might book a ferry from Jax to Boston, but I changed my mind."

"Smart move. Let me guess. Last winter, your parents—Jews or pagans of some kind—they sent you away to safe haven in a solid Christian community, where your uncle protected you and supported you, until you decided, all on your own—"

"Excuse me," Leon broke in, "but since you have no reason to detain us, if you don't mind, we'll be on our way."

"Excuse *me*, smart boy, but '*missing juvenile*,' no identification? *And* a BOL from Wayward Youth? You call that 'no reason'?"

The motorcycle driver dismounted and unfastened the flap on the bike's saddlebag. He pulled out a flashlight and a pair of gloves.

"Open your main compartment for me, will you?"

The driver stood by, one hand on the butt of his pistol. Officer Bix, holding his torch beside his ear, leaned into the cart. He took out one of Leon's school books, *The Science of Life*, and tossed it back. "OK, kiddos, here's the plan. Sergeant Michaelson and myself will escort you to the Jax gate. After that, Leon, you can either continue on your merry way *or* you can accompany the sergeant and I to the Osceola barracks, along with your friend here. First thing tomorrow we'll be contacting her uncle and the New Florida Guard. See what they have to say. Any questions? Good. Lead the way!" Bix made a bow.

Leon pushed off toward the fence and the floodlit gateway apron in the distance, Polly beside him on the pilot deck.

"This is bad," he said. "Could be they're just looking for a bribe, I don't know." They had cash, but most of it was for Malcolm's medicine.

Polly looked at him. "No, no bribes. But thank you, Leon."

The motorcycle burbled along about 30 yards back, keeping them in the wobbling funnel of its headlamps.

"Here's an idea," he said. "Next bend in the road, soon as we're out of their sight, you make a break for it."

She glanced behind them. "I like that idea."

"I'll stop and wait for them. I'll say you're answering a call of nature."

"Then what?"

"Meet me in Talla. Twelve-oh-eight Madison—Tom and Yolanda Pierce."

She made a sharp nod. "Let's do it."

When the roadway dipped around a curve toward the open plain bounded by the endless, illuminated fence, Leon came to a quick stop. He drew Tina's oblong tin from his pocket. "Better take this."

"No, no. You may need it."

"*Take it.* Anything can happen out there. You should know."

She accepted the tin, then leaned in to kiss him. "Wish me luck, Leon."

"You'll have Balthazar," he said. "You'll be fine."

She skipped like a goat down the slope. The orange wash from the vapor lights along the border cast the littered plain into ragged relief. He watched her cover the ground at a trot until she was out of sight.

11

THE SMELL OF RAIN had been on the wind for some time. Now she could see it, a long, blue-black squall line against a reddening eastern sky. The wind was gusting.

Balthazar. Come.

Whooh, whooh, whooh. There he was, high up, a dark fleck gliding among the currents, sailing down and down. He circled her once, read her concern, and then veered away, beating out toward the sea to get a better read on the storm.

The sun broke above the horizon, red and swollen.

A row of careened freighters and tankers along the strand loomed over the shipbreakers' fires. The furnace sheds gave out ingots of light. Half a mile away, on the flats, she could see their scrap-metal-roofed shanties. A few livestock pens. A long carriage shed. Scrap heaps spread across acres of grassy sand. Beyond that lay the vegetation belt, a vivid green under the leaden sky. The spot where she'd hidden the packs wasn't very far off, two or three miles.

She was parched, but there were storm channels out in that jungle, and she had the purification tablets.

Balthazar set himself beside her on a concrete outcropping.

"How's that wing?"

Mended.

"That's wonderful."

He fluffed and whistled. *Bad.*

The coming squall. "I know. I guess we'd better find a place to ride it out."

Wait. He hopped into the air and flapped away.

She sat in the shadow of the reeds, huddling out of the cold wind. The gulls were making a racket. Far below, the salvagers' cutting torches sent cascades of sparks down the flanks of the freighters. Their shouts and the clang of their hammers reached her on the rising wind.

Balthazar returned. *Follow.*

He led her down the long, grassy hillside toward the salvagers' sprawling camp. He would not be taking her there, of course, but it made her nervous to be within sight of the camp, even at such a distance. After a time, he guided her into a shallow ravine and toward a small, reedy pond. At the pond's edge she discovered a ship's overturned lifeboat, long buried in the ground.

Balthazar landed on its keel piece. The transom and a few feet of the fiberglass hull were exposed, scraped down to the fabric.

"Hello?" She rapped on the hull, then knelt to peer under the rail. "Anybody in here?"

She bellied halfway in but couldn't see much. She smelled mold and rot. A burst of rain came splatting down. She crabbed the rest of the way in.

The overturned boat formed a long, sloping cavern with a ribbed roof. There was plenty of room. She could half stand, at least at the stern end.

B hopped in through the entry. "Dead."

"What's dead?"

A man. Long ago.

As her eyes adjusted, she could make out a low, scrapwood platform toward the bow. A sheet-metal cabinet. A porcelain wall-sink without its fixtures. A collection of bottles.

Rain pounded the hull. Balthazar stood just inside the lifeboat's rail, looking out. Polly waddled up beside him with an unfolded plastic water bag. She held it out in the lancing downpour until it was half full, then cinched it closed.

"Food?" he asked.

"I'm sorry, B, I haven't got a crumb."

He preened. *Hard weather.*

"Just a squall. It'll blow over in an hour."

No. "Long."

"Long-lasting?"

"Aye."

She sighed, thinking of Leon warm inside the Nomad having a bite of breakfast. Hard-boiled eggs, olives, and oat bread. Unless those border guards had arrested him. But he'd done nothing wrong.

With her arm for a pillow, she slept.

Hours later when she woke, the storm had not slackened at all. She rubbed her chilled arms and kneaded her legs to get the blood moving.

Balthazar was silhouetted against the commotion outside, still as a weathervane. She crawled to the entry. Rivulets of bright water coursed over the ground a few feet from them.

She was so close to her belongings. The unattended cone had been weakening day by day, but unless someone actually tripped over the packs, they would probably remain safe. It was frustrating to be stuck inside this stinking hovel. She wished she could just fly there. Two or three minutes through the rain, that's all it would take. She'd flown in rain before.

You can.

"What?"

You can fly.

"You don't mean now. Do you?" Her ointment was at the bottom of her sewing box, which was in the pack.

"Aye."

"How?"

By your will.

"Are you saying I can *will* the Dispersal?"

"Aye."

"The ritual isn't necessary?"

Not always.

"What about the spell? And the ointment?"

The words hone the mind. The unction fuses the senses.

She looked closely at him. Refined skill in the craft depended on ritual for consistency and precision. That was why most witches relied on grimoires.

The magick's in the mind. Not the ritual.

He was right, strictly speaking. Adepts could cast spells by the force of their minds, without invoking the aid of the elements, without even language. Adepts were rare. There were six among all the witches Polly had known—her father, Tessa, Glynnis the Gray, Nyx, Ophine, and Lil. The youngest of them, her mother, was almost 50. "I'm only a novice, B," she said.

He pivoted away, rocking on his feet. He would not debate her.

Polly opened the water bag and drank. It was a little salty, and it tasted like plastic.

She crabbed back down the length of her shelter to the edge of the platform.

Corked bottles covered in dust as thick as mouse fur. Canned goods in wooden crates. She took one and rubbed the dirt off with her thumb. Pinto beans. Too old to trust.

She played her tiny light over a scabbed row of metal lockers, four of them, with vented doors. On the raised platform lay a heap of blankets and some clothing. An oil lamp and a fishing rod.

The platform sagged under her weight. The first locker held plates and bowls, forks and spoons in a mug, a chef's knife, a ballpoint pen, a claw hammer, a can opener. She took the knife and wiped it clean.

In the second locker were books, 20 or more, swollen, with crumbling spines. In the third were a hairbrush, a withered cake of soap in a dish, and two worn toothbrushes.

Inside the last locker she found eight styrofoam bricks of cartridges, 50 to a brick. And a blue plastic case. She unclasped the lid. Inside, wrapped in an oily rag, was a blue-black revolver with wooden grips. Also a small bottle of gun oil and a brass-bristle brush. Rust freckled the frame and cylinder. It said "S. & W. 357 MAGNUM" on the side of the barrel. She was surprised at the weight of the thing. She pushed the tab on the frame, and the cylinder swung out. It was empty.

She snapped it closed and pointed the muzzle toward the back of the shelter, holding the gun with two hands. It felt unwieldy. She pulled the trigger. *Clink. Clink, clink, clink, clink, clink.* It worked. She polished a cartridge on her sleeve. "WIN 38 SPL +P." Well, as long as this ammunition was still good, she had herself a firearm. Leon would be impressed.

She crawled to the rag heap at the boat's bow and shined her light around. Two pair of men's shoes with their upper parts eaten away, a red life vest, a five-gallon bucket, a casting rod, a salt-corroded shotgun. With the casting rod she poked at the blankets. They slid away like ashes, and she flinched at the sight of a splotchy leg bone. How terrible it must have been to have to live your last hours alone in this dark hole.

She took the bucket and crawled back to the edge of the platform.

The triangle of daylight in the transom was brighter, but the rain had not let up. It beat like gravel flung against the hull.

“Will it end soon?”

The raven didn’t reply.

She cleaned the patina from six of the cartridges with the chef’s knife and the rag, loaded the gun, and returned it to the blue plastic case. The case fit edgewise into the green bucket with two bricks of bullets on either side. That was all the weight cared to lug around.

The rain fell in veils.

Oh, Balthazar. Are we going to make it? Are we ever going to see our families again?

He watched her cry, his head tipped to the side, until she stopped. Then he blinked and turned away.

12

THE DAY DAWNED CLEAR AND CALM. Balthazar was off searching for something to eat. She crawled out and stood to stretch and take in the rain-washed air. The landscape was bathed in a soft, yellow light. The gulls sounded exuberant.

Tendrils of mist rose from the flats below as the sun chased the haze. The shipbreakers' fires were out. The whole settlement was flooded halfway to the greenbelt. She could hear shouting over the heavy crashing of the surf. She hoped no one had drowned.

The pond just below her shelter was rich with cattails. She looked around for gators, then undressed and waded in. She rinsed her face and arms and spent some time harvesting cattail shoots. She peeled them with her chef's knife and fingers to get to the core. It was crisp and mild. She stripped several more for another meal.

Once she was dry, she set off across the landfill toward the greenbelt at a fast pace, trying to warm herself.

Off to the west, she could see bands of pickers with their carts and wheelbarrows already working the hills of refuse. In the middle distance a caravan of scavs rolled along toward Augie. With the brilliant sun at her back, they wouldn't likely spot her, but she was glad when she reached the shelter of the tallow trees, brambles, melaleuca, and speargrass.

She pushed into a thicket and trampled out a space where she could sit and wait for her familiar. After a time, he dropped into the clearing.

"Find something to eat?"

They attack me.

The gulls, he meant. "I'm sorry to hear that. Why do they have to be so mean?"

They are that way.

"Yes, I suppose."

I killed one.

"You *did*?"

A crazy one.

"Are you OK?"

They fear me.

"Well, they should. You're twice their size."

They are many.

"No kidding. The sooner we can get ourselves out of this awful place the better."

He opened his wings and refolded them. *One place is like another.*

No place was safe, he meant. True enough. "What did you find to eat?"

I ate the one I killed.

She laughed in surprise. But of course he would.

After she'd reached the denser growth, her progress was slowed until she came upon an occasional cart path. That she followed at a good clip in the direction of the utility gate. Now and then she could glimpse the fence through the trees.

Soon she began to feel the fine vibration of her magick. There was still some strength in it, too.

But something wasn't right.

Balthazar glided into a melaleuca and descended to a limb just above her head.

"We're very close," she said. She rubbed her sore hands together. She had wrapped the bucket's wire bail with rags, but it would be good to have the use of her pack again.

"Aye."

"My cone is holding, but it's gone brittle for some reason. Do you feel that?"

Not yours.

"Not my magick?"

"Aye."

She stood. "All right. What's going on?"

A dome.

A guardian dome. "*Really?* Whose?"

The raven had no answer.

And why would anyone alarm her things? It wouldn't do much good, not unless the witch who'd cast the spell was waiting nearby. Was that possible? And who would have the wherewithal to dome her things? Not Mrs. Hacker. Maybe the border guard. That had to be it—the lapsed witch, Sophia. Hoping to get her hands on Mrs. Hacker's gold.

Her familiar awaits you.

"You mean there's another familiar?" But as she spoke, Polly realized she could feel it, too, the tightness. From a new direction.

She does not know we know she's here.

Who does she belong to? Sophia?

No. Another one. A bad one.

"Somebody Sophia knows? Or Mrs. Hacker? Is that what you mean?"

"Aye."

"This familiar . . . is she dangerous?"

Very. She would kill you.

"And she's close. Waiting for me to dissolve the cone."

"Aye."

"All right. Keep watch. I'm going to lift the protection. If this familiar wants Mrs. Hacker's gold, she's welcome to it."

He flapped up into the trees.

Three steps. Another. One more. Now she could pick out the fuzziness of the cone in the grass. She set down her bucket, swept a circle with the backs of her hands, and stepped into it. She spoke the four-word release. "As this be my will, so be it done."

They came clear, her ratty green backpack and Mrs. Hacker's large framepack, just where she'd left them. Hers was scarred and damp. She loosened the flap cords to check its contents. Everything seemed intact and undisturbed.

She took the time to tie the four bricks of ammo together, two by two, with lengths of fishing line so the bullets wouldn't fall out of their trays, and she made room for them at the top of the pack. She opened the gun case, took out the revolver, and placed it beside her on the ground.

She went through Mrs. Hacker's pack, pausing now and then to look around. Poncho, altar pieces, candles, wand, vials and pouches, a few oranges, three tins of Ocean Blue sardines. In the side pockets, she found the spotting scope, a water bottle, a pair of reading glasses, a flashlight, and a lovely jade athame. But no gold. She felt carefully along the pack's seams and frame and squeezed the padding in the straps and hip belt. No gold.

Her triquetra burned.

Watch. Watch now. She comes.

A chuffing snort.

Polly lifted the revolver and pointed it toward the noise, elbows on her knees. "Whoever you are, know that

I'm armed. Do not make me hurt you." She saw nothing, just dappled sunlight on the foliage.

She took a deep breath. "Show yourself. I demand it."

Ten feet off, a hooked paw parted the tall grass. A black bear, upright, with small, stony eyes. Her rusty chest and shoulders were flecked with brambles. She was shorter than Polly, maybe five feet, but she was three times her weight. Insects circled her ears.

"Who do you belong to?" Polly held the gun's muzzle up to ease the strain on her forearms.

The bear stared, wet nostrils flexing.

"If it's Mrs. Hacker's pack you're after, you can take it. Go on, take it."

"No," the bear rumbled.

"Suit yourself. I'm leaving this place. If you come toward me, I will shoot you."

"Nooo!" she groaned, twisting her thick neck. The bear was in pain. Polly could feel it.

"Balthazar? Can you reason with this poor animal?"

He swooped down to a branch and settled his wings.

"She's supposed to identify her partner, isn't she? Why is she resisting me?" Familiars owed every witch a good measure of respect. It was a fixed trait.

She fears you.

"She should."

She is in thrall.

"She is? That's terrible."

The bear swayed foot to foot in anguish. For a witch to crush a familiar's will was not only rash and cruel, it was reckless. An abused familiar could turn on a witch in a blink. Though, barring that, a determined familiar in thrall to a malevolent witch could cause a lot of trouble.

"Tell me your witch's name."

"Theldred," the bear said, groaning.

A name she'd heard before, she was certain. Where? From one of her parents probably. "Why has Theldred sent you here?"

The bear groaned again.

"Let me see her."

There. Tall, straw-haired, broad-shouldered, almond-eyed, face dull and white as parchment, lips like worms, thin and liverish.

"OK, what is she after if it isn't the gold? Tell me!"

The bear yawned and shook her big, dusty head.

"What should I do, Balthazar?"

Shoot her.

That she couldn't do. Killing a familiar without provocation was forbidden. She turned to the bear. "Do not follow me. You should know that I won't hesitate to shoot you if I have to."

She could feel the bear's hesitation—yet the driving menace in her heart was unmistakeable.

Polly shouldered the pack by a strap and backed away, gun in hand, glancing around her so she wouldn't trip and fall.

The bear growled and shuffled her feet in frustration.

A flight of ducks whirred overhead. When she had put enough distance between them, Polly spun around and ran headlong through the shrubby trees, her pack bouncing, clutching the big handgun by its frame.

Minutes later she stopped atop a rise to catch her breath. From here she had a view over the treetops all the way to the coastal berm. Behind her, she could see to the fence. No sound but the wind, the bugs, and the gulls.

She took out one of Mrs. Hacker's oranges. Balthazar settled into a tree just beyond her.

"Like some fruit?"

He glided down and thumped onto her left shoulder, then to the ground. He smelled like smoke. She bit off half a section and gave him the other half.

"She isn't about to give up, is she?"

She follows.

"That's not good. How far back is she?"

Not far. She waits.

"For what? Darkness?"

For your sleep.

"Well, she's out of luck. Soon as it's dark I'm going to take to the sky. How does that sound?"

Kill her first. He swallowed.

"You're a hard one, Balthazar. I feel *sorry* for her."

Her own will is gone. The raven fluffed his neck. *Only death will stop her.*

☾

Saturn glowed bright in the west by the time she was ready. With a broom of grass, she swept her circle. "Render the place herein a place apart, the locus of my lifting energy and my dispersal. Let nothing untoward intrude."

She called the quarters, paid her respects, and then pronounced the eleven phrases.

The seven:

Bone beon waeter,
water beon aesch,
aesch beon ethm:

ethm unstrength,
aesch unswimrth,
waeter unthicceth,
bone unbindeth.

And the four.

Swa sunne slaecceth
bone to waeter
swa swegel uncnotteth
ond ich lyftlich.

She spread a dab of ointment in a line from below her belly to the hollow at her collarbone. The icy flame climbed through the middle of her being, her focus narrowed, and, faster than she ever had before, she ascended, knees and ankles airy, toes pointed.

13

TOWARD DUSK, Leon was held to a crawl by construction crews on the highway outside of Talla so that by the time he was finally rolling down Madison it was long after dark.

He steered the cart down the alley behind the shabby, yellow-brick condominium cluster where Carole's parents leased a small apartment and locked it to a curbstone. The year after Malcolm was forbidden to hold classes but still permitted to keep an office at the university, the five of them had shared Tom and Yolanda's four rooms. Rough living compared to what they'd been used to. On-and-off electricity, no air conditioning, no hot water, and no civil services—not even police. Local volunteers kept watch for trouble. Great neighbors, though. Everyone looked after everyone else. A lot of Jews. Some Muslims. A few Buddhists. Freethinkers like Malcolm. All gone now, of course—the FRA had seen to that.

Many of the apartments were now unoccupied. It seemed quieter than he remembered. Sadder. But the same old gas sconces lit the stairwell landings. The smells of someone's cooking—garlic, roasting meat—made his mouth water.

He knocked on 303 and called in, "It's me! Leon!"

Yolanda threw back the bolt, opened the door, and

pulled him into her arms. “Oh, Leon, thank God you made it! We’ve been worried about you!”

“You were expecting me?”

“She got here this morning, Leon. Your friend! Polly!”

His heart melted at the sight of her standing in the kitchen doorway, relaxed and smiling, with Tina’s Siamese, Gwendolyn, in her arms. “Hi, slowpoke,” she said.

His ears were hot. Polly set Gwendolyn on the sideboard and opened her arms to him. She smelled like sandalwood.

“Leon!” his grandfather called from his chair in the living room. “God bless you, Leon!” He was yoked to the canister of oxygen next to his chair.

Leon took one of Tom’s dry hands in his. “How are you, Grampa? You doing all right?”

“Not too bad, praise Jesus. Just thankful to be alive.”

Yolanda served Leon tortillas, beans, tomatoes, and grapefruit juice.Polly sat across from him in the dining nook, watching him eat.

“So you *flew*?” he asked in a low voice.

She nodded. “I almost lost it, though.”

“What do you mean?”

She shrugged. “I got tired. My focus went off.”

“It’s hard to believe you can do it at all.”

“I know. I can hardly believe it myself sometimes.”

“And you found your pack and everything?”

“Right where I left it.”

“Great!”

“Yeah, that was a huge relief.” She looked away. “So I’ll be on my way tomorrow.”

“Tomorrow?”

“Soon as it’s dark.”

All along he’d been hoping she would ask him to go with her to the mountains. Even so, he wasn’t really surprised that she hadn't. It wasn't his journey. It was hers, and obviously she could travel faster alone. Still, it wasn't unreasonable for him to imagine she might invite him to meet her at the trailhead. From there they could hike the forest trail together. *The most wonderful thing,* she called it. All he'd have to do was hire a courier to take the medication back to the dig, and he'd be free. If she wanted him. Maybe she would change her mind. But he was not going to invite himself. It had to come from her.

☾

The next morning, on his way out to the Walgreen's at the Tomahawk Plaza near the highway, he decided to take the long route through the heart of the university. How he'd missed this place! He used to like riding his bicycle on the smooth, well-kept walkways. Not nearly as many students about as there used to be, but it was a pretty place, still. A mule driver and his team pulled a gang of rotary mowers across Landis Green. The flower beds around the fountain were lush with red and gold pansies.

He skipped up the steps to Strozier Library the way he used to do, even though the building was closed and locked. Just a few years ago, before the *Guide to the Written Word* was handed down, you could go in here any time, day or night, and read whatever you wanted to read. You didn't even have to be a college student. Of course, there was a lot left to read, Leon reminded himself, but you had to order it at a store or online. Most of the bad stuff was restricted. Malcolm had been outraged by the loss of the libraries. His was a prominent voice. Every weekend he spoke at some demonstration against the censors. At the invitation of the government, he attended the Written Word hearings in Atlanta and Dallas, too, where he gave passionate testimony. For all the difference it made.

Not even Tom could remember the days when Old Downtown had been a crowded, built-up cityscape. North of church row and All Saints Hospital, today it was just a patchwork of vineyards, market gardens, and feedlots. The city kept up the main roads, most of them lined with wild pea, beach plum, and stubby palms, making it a very pleasant walk to the Tomahawk Plaza.

His business with thin-lipped Mr. Espinosa took less than a minute. Leon slipped the note and the cash under the lucite window, and Mr. Espinosa passed him the pills in sealed boxes along with a Walgreen's bag to carry them in. He asked how Malcolm and Tina were doing and wished them all good health. He'd felt bad when they lost their benefits, but even if Malcolm had been eligible for ChristianCare, he could never have afforded this prescription. Mr. E was cutting them a very good deal.

Outside on the plaza, he bought a slice of mushroom pizza from a vendor at an open-air oven. He sat on a bench and watched the shoppers and the beggars, the kids in school uniforms, a wealthy couple in a wheeled sedan chair propelled by a shirtless, sweating servant. A cardinal was singing in the live oaks.

Slouching against the door of a booth outside the walkway to a First CommonWealth Bank kiosk was someone he knew—Derek Larsen, his Youth Guard team captain three summers ago. Had to be 21 or 22 now. He was wearing a gray uniform.

"Excuse me, officer," Leon said in a deep voice, "can you tell me where I might find a rep for a courier service?"

Derek grinned. "*Leon!* By the *Christ*, Leon!"

They shook hands, laughing, while Derek took his measure. Leon knew he looked rough in his patched canvas field pants and hand-made rubber sandals.

"What are you doing back in Talla?" Derek asked. "Y'all got banished, I thought."

"We didn't get banished. My dad's on sabbatical."

"That right? Where's he at?"

"Research station out on the coast. It's a peaceful spot."

"Funny, I heard he got exiled. Your dad's the atheist professor, isn't he?"

After a hearing, Malcolm had been censured by the Trustees for heresy. His computer and all his books and papers were seized, and he was forbidden to teach or to speak in public. A few months after that, before the FTB could take up his case, a colleague of his arranged with the Sciences dean for the sabbatical on the coast.

Leon changed the subject. "This what you do now?"

Derek looked around at the booth. "What's wrong with it?"

"I just figured you'd be at college."

"It's *vacation*, numb nuts. What you got in the sack?"

"A prescription. I have to get it delivered to my dad. Do you know if there's a courier service around here?"

Two Security officers leaving the banking kiosk with their vid helmets under their arms gave Leon a close look.

Derek said, "Private parcel, you mean?"

"Yeah."

"How come? You don't trust the regular mail?"

"Out to the coast?" Public services didn't extend into the Wastes.

Derek nodded. "I know a guy does stuff like that. If you want, I could call him."

On the other end of the crosswalk the two officers had stopped to talk. One looked back toward Leon. This wasn't good.

"Is he bonded?" Leon asked.

"I think so. Name's Jerome. Him and a buddy of his got a motorbike."

He told Derek to make the call, though he wasn't sure he ought to trust Derek, much less Jerome. He'd have to size the guy up for himself.

He ambled quickly downhill toward the highway rest area, hoping to put the two Security officers behind him.

Garrity Brothers Carriage & Ironworks looked busy, so he ducked in under the canvas awning to mingle there and stall for time, watching a glassblower fashion tumblers out of old beer bottles. Tina would love this.

After a while, he meandered back around through the used lumber and brick yard along the paved road that led out to the old football stadium. Our Savior Daycare's sandy lot and seesaws were empty, the kids inside having lunch. Further along, in a live-oak grove he spotted a concrete-block building with a corrugated metal roof and six garage bays. The sign on the fence read:

A-1 AUTOMOTIVE
RESTORATION AND REPAIR

Three of the bays were occupied by motor carriages in for maintenance. One looked like the cream-colored vehicle he'd seen at the Bazaar—the fancy rig that belonged to the bidder with the gray ponytail and the escort, the one who'd bought Polly.

He walked through the gate. Derelict gas cars stood in a long row in the shade of the live oaks, blanketed by dead leaves and road dust.

Two brown-skinned mechanics were eating at their workbench when Leon stepped in out of the sunlight. They wore green, short-sleeved coveralls with A-1 stitched on the back. One had a gray beard.

"You the kid from Gallagher's?"

"No, I— Sorry, I don't mean to bother you, but I think I saw this same vehicle out on the highway a few days ago. OK if I take a look?"

The one with the beard wiped his mouth. "Something, ain't she? Brand new Brilliance Atomic, custom-built in Macao."

An Atomic. He'd read about these. Powered by an helium-cooled pebble-bed reactor—safe and small. These cars never switched off, and they drove themselves. "Whose is it?"

"Belongs to the Dominion Secretary, if you want to know," the first mechanic said. "Clyde Morton Trumble himself."

"No kidding. What's wrong with it?"

The mechanic shrugged. "Got banged up in a blow. Good as new now. Take a look, if you want, but don't touch. She bites."

"It's beautiful."

"That baby's built for *speed*. Waste of money, if you ask me."

The other one laughed.

"Pretty expensive, I suppose."

"Ain't that. Where you gonna drive the damn thing?"

He was right. This wasn't China. The speedway corridor was always crowded. Whenever they had to get somewhere fast, rich people took the Maglev or hired a helicopter.

The vehicle's sloping deck and flanks almost seemed to glow. In front, in small gold letters low on each side, was the word *Brilliance.* There was no other embellishment—no sensor bulges, no lenses, no vents or latches or handles, just the glossy, curving shell of pale yellow enameled titanium, its door seams barely visible, and the teardrop dome on top, reflections of the shop's overhead lights curving in the dark glass. He couldn't see anything inside.

This was the bidder's car. But no dominion secretary would ever go out into the Wastes to check out the bond-servant auctions. The six secretaries were the most powerful and pious men in the Protectorates—the Executive Branch. They were elected every four years by the Council of Parish Representatives in each dominion. The Chair of the EB was Lloyd Ferris, from the First Dominion up in Richmond, the nation's capitol. The five others were Keith Chu, of the Third, in Albany; Oswald (Spike) Robitaille, of the Fourth, in Dallas; David X. Blackmore, from the Fifth, in Chicago; Graham Kissel, from the sprawling Sixth, in Vancouver, and Clyde Morton Trumble, of the Second, in Atlanta. Along with the 422 members of Legislative Branch (one from each parish) and the Judicial Branch, the EB governed the Protectorates, which included the Outlying Regions of the northeast and the great deserts and mountains far to the west.

"What does the Secretary look like?" Leon asked.

"Silver hair. You ain't seen him on TV?"

"I don't remember. Does he have a long, gray braid?"

"No. That's Yuri who you're thinking of."

"Who's Yuri?"

"Works for the Secretary. He's the one brought her in here."

Leon reached out to stroke the side of the Atomic. In the next instant he was on the floor, hugging his hand to his chest, his yell ringing in his ears.

The bearded mechanic knelt beside him. "Told you. You gotta keep your hands off this baby."

His arm throbbed.

"You'll be OK. First jolt's just to get your attention."

Leon sat up, dizzy.

The mechanic set the Walgreen's bag in front of him. "Thing of it is, now she'll be running your particulars. Hope there's nothin' messy in your file."

"I'm not too worried," he said.

But closer to campus he caught sight of the two officers again—or maybe different ones, he couldn't tell—across Academic Way. They were standing on a little rise with their visors up. Watching for him. He jogged to the east at the end of Dewey Street and darted up between the telecommunications building and a rose arbor. He hid behind a notices board and waited a minute. From there he sprinted for a few yards and ducked through a side door into long, low building. He watched through a sidelight as the helmeted officers hurried on by toward Landis.

What did they want with him?

A banner suspended from the corridor's ceiling read, "*Fertility Conference!!! June 18-20.*"

He stopped at a fountain for a drink. His arm still tingled.

This was an ag building—he'd forgotten the name of it—but he'd been here once before, with his Natural Life class. There was no one around. He decided to hang out in the greenhouse till the officers gave up, then make his way back to Madison by the low road. Close one.

He'd been sitting on a bench in a corner between two banana trees for less than a minute before the door at the end of the center aisle opened and a white-haired campus guard stepped into the greenhouse. She marched straight toward him, her rubber soles creaking on the damp concrete. "Leon Krauss?"

"Yes?" His heart pounded.

"Come this way, please."

"Why? I haven't done anything wrong."

Into a mike clipped to her collar she said, "You're very welcome. Yes, sir, right away."

"Are you arresting me?"

"You've been detained for questioning, that's all. Come along with me, Leon."

"What for?"

"You're a PPL. That's all I know."

"What's a PPL?"

"Pre-empt Priority Locate. We get a PPL, we drop everything till we apprehend the individual."

The guard ushered him outside, down a sidewalk, and into an older building. They descended two flights of stairs and entered a windowless room containing only a long table and a few metal chairs. The table was bare except for a Bible and a remote. The vid panel on the wall displayed a glowing cross with a spray of beams all around it.

"Sit here." The guard pulled out a chair.

A chime sounded. "All set, sir," she said.

The vid panel blinked. Two older men in their shirt-sleeves, one of them holding an unlit cigar, were seated on padded chairs in another room somewhere. They eyed Leon for a moment.

Finally, one leaned forward. "Thank you, Officer Wainwright. Stand by, please."

Wainwright nodded at Leon. "Good luck."

"Leon Krauss. Second child of Malcolm Krauss and Carole Pierce?"

"Yes."

"Very good. I'm Senior Agent R. W. Rasmussen, FTB investigator, and next to me here is Mr. Jose Galt, Chief Prosecutor for New Florida, Tenth Parish, Second Dominion. Mr. Galt and I are looking into a felony grand theft which took place at the Augie Bazaar on the afternoon of May 18. Will you answer a few questions?"

"What was stolen?"

"We'll be asking the questions, Leon, if that's all right."

Leon nodded.

"Thank you. Place your right hand on the Bible before you, if you will."

He did.

"As Jesus Christ is your witness, will you swear to answer all of our questions as fully and truthfully as you can?"

"Yes."

"And do you now so swear?"

"I do."

"Very good. May the Lord guide us to the truth." The FTB agent sat back. The room they were in had blue draperies across the back wall. That was all he could see.

The prosecutor, a swarthy man, lit his cigar, puffing. "First, where is Cassandra?"

"Who?"

"The bondservant girl. The two of you were stopped together one-point-four miles east of the Jacksonville gate three days ago. She identified herself as Polly."

"Polly is not a slave."

Galt shook his head. "I'm going to advise you to be straight with us, Leon. Your freedom is on the line here."

"Why? What did I do?"

"Class-A felony, conspiracy in the commission of a felony, obstruction of justice. If the Dominion brings charges, you'll be looking at six to ten years in a federal work camp. Is that clear?"

He nodded.

"Very good. Where is Cassandra?"

"She ran away."

Galt leaned in closer. "You visited the Augie Bazaar on the afternoon of May Eighteen. Isn't that right?"

"I don't know the date. The day the tornado struck."

"Thank you. May Eighteen. Were you alone?"

"Yes."

"And why were you there?"

"I had pies to sell."

"To sell pies." He puffed on his cigar. A fan somewhere in the room drew the smoke away from the men. "And what brings you to Talla, Leon?"

"I had to pick up some medicine for my father." Leon held up the Walgreen's bag.

"Show us, please."

Leon opened it and took out the two boxes of pills. He rattled one of them.

"Do you have a receipt?"

"I think so."

"Place it on the table."

Leon unzipped his leather wallet. The only receipt he had said, "12 pie, 120 $$." He set it in front of him.

"He's an exile, your father. Isn't that true?"

"No. He's on sabbatical. He's excavating two paleo-indian sites out on the coast."

"*Professor Krauss?* Come on. Your father supports every heretical cause there is—abortion-on-demand, Darwinism, repeal of indenture, freedom from faith . . . Doesn't he?"

Leon said nothing.

"Doesn't he?"

Leon shook his head. "He thinks people should be free to say and think whatever they want, that's all."

Galt glanced at Rasmussen. "That day at the bazaar. You were there to spy on the bondservant auction. Isn't that true?"

"No. I wasn't spying on anything. I thought it was a livestock sale."

"And you were in the market for livestock?"

Leon said nothing.

"I remind you, Leon, you have given your word before God. Admit it now. You were collecting information on slave dealing in the Wastes, isn't that right?"

"No! I went there to trade goods for cash, and that's *all*."

Galt sighed. He twirled his cigar ash against the arm of his chair. "All right. I want you to think back now. Think back and relate everything you witnessed at the charity auction. Will you do that?"

"I saw two bondservants get auctioned off to a man in a white blouse and a vid helmet. First a small boy and then Polly. Right then this giant tornado blew in, and everybody ran for it. A lot of them got swept away and killed."

"What happened to the bondservants?"

"The scavs took them."

Galt leaned into the cloud of his smoke. "And the girl?"

"I cut her free. I had to, or she would have drowned."

"And after that?"

Leon told them how he took Polly to the dig in the cart, how she recuperated, how she set out to walk with him to the Jacksonville gate, and how she made a break for it after the border patrol stopped them. He figured they already knew all this from the patrol's report, but that's all they knew or he wouldn't be here. They weren't hunting Polly just because Wayward Youth had a BOL out on her. They were after her because Yuri wanted to get her back.

"What was the girl's plan when you two left the coast?"

"She was going home. To Vermont. I don't think she had a plan."

"And who is helping her?"

"Nobody, not that I know of."

"Come off it, Leon. An unescorted female with no money and no ID? She can't travel by herself, not freely—

you know that. She wouldn't get anywhere without someone's protection. Who's helping her and where is she?"

"I *told* you. She ran off into the flood plain. Maybe she went back to Jax."

Galt sat back. "He's lying."

"Let's give him a little time to ponder his predicament," Rasmussen said. He gave Leon a long look. "Covering for that girl will land you in prison, Leon. Just as sure as lying before God will land you in Hell."

His cheeks burned.

Galt turned to Rasmussen and said something he couldn't hear. Rasmussen nodded.

"Enough of this," Galt said. "We're going to keep close track of you over the next few days, Leon. So you behave yourself, all right? Officer Wainwright? Activate a Trace-let, will you?"

The campus guard approached him holding a length of metal ribbon with a small black knob at each end. "Wrist or ankle, your choice."

14

"I CAN GET RID OF THAT for you," Polly wrote.

"How?" he wrote underneath.

He passed her the notepad. His Tracelet communicated sound, motion, body temperature, and pulse, so they couldn't speak.

"De-integration. It focuses the will on the bonds that hold an object to form. It's like Dispersal, but looser. And it only lasts a few seconds."

Leon wrote, "You mess with it and they'll know."

She wrote, "But not right away."

They sat on either side of a ring of unlit candles on the floor of the room he used to share with Malcolm—two cots, a painted bureau with a tilting mirror, a keyhole desk and chair, a rag rug, Malcolm's rowing machine, and a window that looked out toward a scattering of lights—the rough settlement people called Ticktown.

"Think we can make it into Georgia before they figure it out?"

She lifted her wide eyes his face. Then wrote, "You want to come along? To the falls?"

He nodded. It was either that or stay here without her. Which he couldn't bear to do. And if he tried to go back to the dig, they'd arrest him at the border. He wrote, "I take the Maglev to Atlanta. You fly. We meet at the trailhead."

"I like that," she wrote. She shut her eyes and waved him out of the room.

☾

He and his grandmother sat out on the balcony. The air was thick and still. She had a pot of cattail fluff burning on the table to discourage the mosquitoes. Dogs barked far off.

As they talked, sitting in her dusty plastic chairs with mugs of hot lemonade the way they used to do on so many evenings the year before, Leon realized how much Gram had missed him. Tina and Malcolm, too, even though she resented Malcolm's pointless apostasy. They chatted about why anybody would want to study ancient Indians, how his own studies were going, whether he and his sister were sad or afraid to have to live in exile and when they might be coming back again, the unending dust storms in the west, the sickness and suffering of so many everywhere, and whether the Legislative Branch might lift the cap on wheat prices before adjourning for the summer. How long would he and his friend be able to stay in Talla? They could go to the zoo, if he wanted.

He hated to disappoint her. "Oh, four or five days," he said, "maybe longer. I still need to get batteries, tea, flour, sugar . . . " On the pad he wrote, "Leaving tonight." Definitely, now that Gram had said the words "your friend." Would they catch that?

Her eyes filled. She was thinking she'd never see him again.

"I love you Gram," he said.

Polly walked onto the balcony, her chin high, lips and cheeks flushed. She smiled and beckoned to Leon.

Leon kissed his grandmother on the cheek, then followed Polly into his old room.

She led him by the hand into a ring of dried palm fronds spread out on the floor. Their shadows trembled in the candle-fire as they stepped into the circle.

"Render the place herein a place apart, to shield and contain our words and thoughts." Her book of magick lay open on the cot beneath the window, its corner pieces catching the light. Gwendolyn sat next to it.

They closed their eyes.

After a silence, Leon felt three sharp taps on his wrist. Polly took the Tracelet in her fingers.

"Now I would loosen the bonds that hold this singular object to form." She spoke a few words in another language, then a firm command that sounded like "*Nu. Feran.*"

The Tracelet swelled and blurred in his sight. Polly lifted it from his arm like a loop of crepe. Then turned in the cat's direction. With a push, she slipped the loop over Gwendolyn's ears and whiskers.

"*Geendian.*" It closed around her neck. She was purring.

Polly carried her out of the bedroom.

"Now. Show me where they put your chip."

He turned away, feeling his blood rise into cheeks and ears. He had nothing on under his trousers. He lowered them, just on the left side, and touched the tip of his finger to the undercurve of his buttock. "Here."

Her hand followed his. "This may hurt."

"It's OK."

She spoke a short phrase.

The chip burned under his skin.

"There. Cooked it."

He retied his waist cord. "They'll make me get a new one as soon as they figure out mine got fried."

"That'll be the least of our worries."

Right. "How come you're not chipped?"

"I was. Right after I got off the plane in Orlando some Customs guy pulled me aside, and they inserted one right there at the gate. Here." She tapped the back of her neck. "It died in about three minutes."

☾

At first light, rumbling along a clay track through pastel stands of redbud, hickory, and longleaf pine, they crossed the line. "Welcome to Grady County, Georgia," read a small sign on a pole with a cam on top. Leon was piloting the cart, while Polly rode in the cabin. Security wasn't watching for Leon. Not yet.

He coasted down a long incline with the brakes pulsing, holding the cart at a steady clip until the trail flattened out through a stretch of waist-high wiregrass. The May morning broke around him. Wildflowers—pink, white, blue, yellow. He didn't know their names. The air was cool and piney, the sky a soft blue.

He rapped on the cabin roof and pulled over to the side of the road. Time for a little breakfast. Polly climbed out and stretched. "Satellite says we're in Georgia."

"About seven miles," he said. "How long do you think it'll take them to realize we tricked them?"

"That's hard to say. By the signs, you're very sick. You have a hundred-and-three fever, terrible chest congestion, you've lost your voice, and you're sleeping all the time." She was combing her hair with her fingers. "Couple days, I'd say."

"If they catch us, we'll go to jail. For a long time."

"I know. That's not very funny, is it? I'm sorry I got you into this, Leon."

"I wouldn't want to be anywhere else." It was true. He

felt wonderful, free and brave, out on his own, traveling, all the world's possibility before him.

He opened Yolanda's basket and took out two cottage-cheese sandwiches and two carrots.

"How delightful," Polly said.

Hoofbeats. A cargo wagon with wooden sides approaching from the north, slowing. The driver was bearded young man with a rifle across his back. The horses were lathered up and mud-spattered, the wagon heaped with split stovewood bound for the market in Talla.

Leon pulled his carbine out of its scabbard and laid it beside him in the tall grass.

"Ho-ahh!" The driver came to a stop alongside the Nomad.

He had passengers seated up behind him on the canopied bench, an elderly couple, the woman with a blue bandanna over her nose and mouth.

The gaunt horses blew and shuddered and rolled their eyes, smelling food.

"This track still lead on through to Old Ten?" the driver wanted to know. He sounded older than he looked. Leon didn't like him.

"Yes, it does," he said.

"No wash-outs or nothin'?"

"Didn't see any."

"Praise God for that. You come from Talla?"

"From the coast, actually."

He spat into the road. "If you ain't been up to Thomasville in the past year, you best pull off when you get to the Magnolia Vale Inn. Ask somebody to direct you around the sinkholes."

"Thank you. How long a run is it to Valdosta, do you know?"

The driver looked behind him. “Sir?”

The man leaned down. He was very old, Leon saw now, with white whiskers and milky eyes. “You fixed on Valdosta for some particular reason?”

“Hoping to catch the Maglev to Atlanta.”

“Don’t stop there no more.”

“How come?”

The woman bent forward. “Me and mister, we lived up in Valdosta our whole life. Never been this bad. Over a thousand dead since Christmas.”

“The flu?” Polly asked.

The woman nodded. “Everything’s broke down. Power’s been out since February. Hospital’s shut down. Whole west side’s gone to looters and vigilantes . . . Him and me barely got out before Security come in and quarantined the town.” She sucked a breath past her teeth. “It was just by the grace of God we got out alive.”

The old man raised a hand overhead. “‘And they journeyed. And the terror of God was upon the cities that were round about them, and they did not pursue after the sons of Jacob.’”

“Well, thanks again,” Leon said.

“Truly,” the woman said. “Y’all best head on up to Tifton. That’s where the good Christians is at.”

“And don’t be settin’ up camp where nobody can see you from the right-of-way,” the driver said. “God bless you and keep you safe!” He clucked his tongue and slapped the reins. The poor horses lurched ahead.

“Well, that was cheery encounter,” Polly said.

They unwrapped their sandwiches.

After a minute it was quiet again, just the wind high in the pines and a nuthatch tooting somewhere far off.

Leon’s good mood was gone. The sleepless night was

catching up with him. "You know, I haven't seen Balthazar for days. Have you?"

"Oh, he's been close most of the time. I feel him now."

Leon scanned the trees. "Is that him?"

"Never point," Polly said without looking up.

"Sorry." Leon finished his sandwich.

In grade school and at church he'd been taught that God created the animals of the earth for our benefit and enjoyment. Animals endowed our worldly lives with wonder, variety, service, and nourishment. But, like rocks and trees, animals had no souls. They belonged to us, to people. They were gifts of God. Something he'd never questioned. God gave us dominion over the fish of the sea and the birds of the air. He made man in *His* image. Not in some animal's image. Weird to think of the Creator of the Universe as a tiger, or a flamingo. Or even as a woman. He looked up from his sandwich at Polly. She'd finished hers. Now she had her tanned face tipped back in the warm sunshine.

"I never realized your dad was an exile," she said.

"Who told you he was? Yolanda?"

She nodded.

"He isn't an exile. We left before he was supposed to appear before the Faith and Truth Board."

"He can't come back, though, can he?"

"He *could*, but then he'd be arrested. If he was an exile, they'd never let him back in in the first place."

"Not much difference, then."

"Well, you have to be *exiled* to be an *exile*."

She shook her head. "You're a stubborn one, aren't you?"

"My dad says I take after my mom." Carole had eloped with Malcolm the day her parents told her she could not keep seeing him. As a rebel sympathizer back during the Uprising, he wasn't fit for any Christian's company. Never mind marriage.

Balthazar thumped onto the roof of the Nomad and settled his wings.

"It's good to see you," Polly said. "You must have been worried about me back in the city."

"Aye," Balthazar said. His voice fell between croak and a creak, but he could shape vowels well enough so you could understand him.

"Oh, no," Polly said, frowning now, in reaction to something the raven had told her without speaking.

"What's the problem?" Leon asked.

"I might as well tell you. It seems that some witch's familiar is stalking me. I have no idea why."

"A bear?"

She looked closely at him. "Yes, a black bear. You understood that?"

"So there's a *bear* after you? Really? Who's the witch?"

"Her name is Theldred. There were some witches long ago, after the rebellion, who agreed to work for the government in exchange for their lives. I suspect she's one of those."

"You mean she's a traitor."

Polly nodded.

"And she sent her *bear* after you?"

"The bear's in thrall. Her witch has apparently crushed her will. Terrible thing to do to a familiar—it destroys the relationship forever."

"So why would you do it?"

"To create a ruthless, totally obedient servant. Why you would do *that* I don't know."

"How did you find this out?"

"The bear was waiting for me near my backpack out in

the green belt. Oh! Here's another piece of news. I have a gun."

"You have a *gun*?"

She told him the story.

"That's great!" he laughed. "But aren't you the one who said witches think guns are *crude?*"

"Yes, and *you're* the one who said everybody needs protection. Turns out you were right."

"We're both right. Can I have a look?"

She tugged the case from the pack, popped the fasteners, took the weapon by the barrel, and handed it to him.

"One thing," he said. He unlatched the cylinder.

"What?"

"Before you hand a gun to another person, you *always* open the breech to show that it's not loaded."

"Oh. That one's loaded."

"I see. Here's another thing. Always keep the muzzle pointed in a safe direction. And never touch the trigger until you're ready to shoot."

It was a fine revolver—a big Smith & Wesson .357 with six-inch barrel and a ramp sight. He'd looked at revolvers in gun-shop display cases back in Talla, but he'd never asked to handle one. "This is a classic. Very good condition for its age, too. Have you fired it?"

She shook her head. "Haven't needed to."

"Just so you understand, this three-fifty-seven wouldn't stop a bear. Not unless you hit something vital."

"I had it aimed at her eye."

"That would do it. But you'll need practice before you can hit what you aim at, even at close range." He opened the cylinder and handed it back to her.

"You're a regular deadeye, I suppose."

"Not with one of those. My Youth Guard instructor used to say that all a pistol's good for in a gunfight is to get you back to your rifle, which you never should have left in the first place."

"So this is worthless?"

"No. It's just . . . *crude*."

They both laughed.

"Actually, revolvers are very dependable. Pull the trigger and it goes bang." He patted his carbine's stock. "And my Marlin here is also a three-fifty-seven, so we can use the same cartridge."

"Well, that's good, then. I'm glad." She placed the gun back in the case.

"How does this bear know where you are?"

"Black bears have excellent noses. And this one's a familiar, so all the more."

"Why didn't you just shoot her when you had the chance?"

"That 's what Balthazar wanted me to do. But I couldn't. Familiars are gifted beings. Besides, it's her witch that's the problem."

"And you have no idea why she's after you?"

"No." She looked at Balthazar. "What do you think?"

Power.

"Power?"

"Aye."

"What does he mean?" Leon asked. "Power to do what?"

She shrugged. "Power leads to happiness."

"It does? How?"

"Somewhere I read that people desire power because they fear pain. It's pretty simple. The more power you have, the safer you are. The safer you are, the less pain you'll have. The less pain, the more happiness."

"Do you think that's true?"

"For some, sure."

"But what *power* could this witch get by going after you?"

GRAWK. Balthazar flapped his wings. *Trouble.*

"Wait—" Polly rose to her feet. "Here comes trouble."

"Where?"

Through the trees, a flash of sunlight in the headlamps of a motor-assisted travel cart. They waited. It looked a little like his Nomad, but it was larger and less refined—made from a kit, he thought. It had an oil-cloth cover.

Beware. The raven flew off low to the ground, then up into the pines. Leon felt for the carbine's receiver and thumbed off the safety.

The squeaking cart pulled to the side of the roadway behind theirs. The pilot was a leathery-looking woman wearing a wide-brimmed felt hat and a wooden cross on a leather thong. She jumped down and nodded to them. The hair hanging under her greasy hat was coarse and wind-blown. "Everything OK here? Y'all ain't broke down or nothin' . . . "

"We're fine, thanks," Leon said.

She peered sideways at the hooded gauges on his cart's back panel. "Y'all like your Nomad?"

"Sure."

"Reliable?"

"So far."

"Got a new solar charger for mine, but I ain't hooked it up yet. Which way y'all headed? North?"

"Same as you, looks like."

"Bad shit up that way, brother, *bad* shit. Outlaws . . . plague . . . Vigilantes. S'posed to be."

Leon didn't answer. The woman had a low, knotty forehead, tangled eyebrows, and an upper lip that didn't cover her long incisors.

"How y'all fixed for food?" she asked.

"OK."

"Got any medicine?"

"Why, are you sick?"

"How 'bout weapons? Y'all got weapons?"

"We can protect ourselves."

The woman walked up to the side of the cart for a look inside. The hatch stood open, but the lights were out.

W*hooh whooh whooh*—Balthazar returned to a limb just above them. Leon caught Polly's glance. She gave him a shake of the head. What did that mean?

The woman gestured in Polly's direction with her chin. "She your girl?"

"We're traveling together."

"All alone?"

Leon didn't answer.

"School kids." She wiped her nose on her wrist. "Coupla runaways, I expect."

"Runaways with a travel cart?"

"Nice rig, all right. Betcha you hijacked it."

"You lose. It's my father's."

"That's OK, Leon," Polly said, rising. "We don't have to explain ourselves to these people." She had the revolver against her thigh.

The woman caught her breath as Polly leveled the gun at her middle. "Tell your friend inside, *no violence!* If there's any shooting, you'll die where you stand. Tell him! Now!"

"Raney!" the woman shouted. "Christ on a cracker, Raney, what y'all tryin' to do? Get us *killed*?"

Polly slipped around to the front end of the Nomad and propped her forearms on the cowling. "*Tell him!*"

"Whoa, whoa, whoa," the woman said, her arms high in the air. "Easy, hon, *easy*. Nobody's gonna shoot nobody. Swear. OK?"

"Polly?" Leon said. He lifted the carbine into his lap.

"There's a man in the cart," she told him, "and he's got a gun."

"You in the vehicle!" Leon shouted. "Open the door and throw your weapon out on the ground. *Do it.* After that, climb out and stand where I can see you."

"His back is broke," the woman said. "He can't stand. Not by hisself."

"All right, then, you go take the weapon from him. Take it and set it on the ground. *Now!*"

The woman sidled over to her cart without taking her eyes off Polly. She peeled the canvas back and raised the door. "Fetch it up," she said.

She nodded at Leon and Polly and laid the weapon in the pine needles—a matte-black machine pistol with a folding stock and a fat, brick-like magazine.

"I want to see his hands."

The woman said something to the man. Ten dirty fingers rose into the light.

"Polly. Get that gun, will you, please?"

She came around from the front of the cart and picked it up.

"Have pity, girl," the woman said. "That's all the firepower we got."

"It better be."

"We never had no evil intentions."

"Bullshit," she said.

"Old gal and a cripple all alone? Christ, out here can't trust *no*body."

"We noticed," Leon said.

"Hey, boy, I gotta ask. Y'all in the Youth Guard?"

"I was. Why?"

"'Cause maybe you know my nephew. Ike Lundgren?"

"Doesn't ring a bell."

"No? Listen, him and me, we're good people. That's all I'm sayin.'"

"You're highway robbers is what you are," Polly said.

A sharp whistle, low to high. *Watch!*

Polly dropped into a crouch and fired. BOOM!

BAOW BAOW BAOW! Polly grunted and fell.

The man in the cart had another gun—an auto.

In a single motion Leon raised his carbine and fired at the head he saw just above the cart hatch. KA-BLAM. He levered another round, but the head was gone.

Polly lay next to the Nomad's front wheel, hugging her leg and gulping air.

The woman slumped to her knees in the roadway, wailing. Her cart's canvas topside was covered in blood.

He knelt next to Polly. "Where'd he hit you?"

"Here," she breathed.

Inner thigh. Blood, but not a lot. "Feels like a through-and-through."

"What?" She was panting, eyes shut.

"The bullet passed out the other side." He smoothed her forehead. "What the hell happened?"

"He— He just popped up. He was looking to shoot you, so . . . ."

"He's dead."

"I killed him?" she whispered.

"No, I did."

"*You* did?" She sighed. "Well, at least we know the gun works."

He was too numb to laugh. He patted her hand. "Let me deal with her. Then I'll help you treat that."

The woman was beating the ground with her fists. "We was just goin' to the *clinic!* He was s'posed to see the *doctor*. At the goddamn *clinic*."

Leon boosted himself up to look into the cabin. It

stank. The man lay crumpled in a pile of blankets. The top of his skull was gone. "He your husband?"

She shook her head. "Forklift knocked him off the dock back around Christmas-time. He ain't been right since."

Leon leaned into the cabin and brought out a small, chromed semi-automatic, a nine mil. He hopped down and flung it off into the brush.

From the tool compartment under his cart, he took a spade and a pickaxe.

"We gonna bury him?" the woman asked.

"You want to take him with you?"

She took a deep, ragged breath, then shook her head.

Leon started digging. Polly had her pants folded down so she could hold compresses to her wounds, eyes closed.

The dead man was too heavy. Leon had to climb into the cart, hoist him little by little, and heave him over the side into the roadway. Long gray beard, white hairless legs, bare feet.

The woman was weeping into her hands.

Leon went off into the grass to throw up.

Together, they dragged him to the grave.

"He wasn't that good of a Christian," the woman said, "but seems to me a little scripture wouldn't hurt." She looked at Leon. "Y'all got a bible?"

Leon shook his head. "Just speak from the heart."

She took off her hat and thought for a few seconds with her eyes closed. "Lord, please have mercy on Raney Mitchell. He didn't treat me and Bonnie and them as good as he could have. But all the bad stuff he done, he knew it wasn't right when he done it, Lord, every time. What I'm sayin', he had good Christian morals. Only thing was he couldn't live up to 'em. So have mercy on him, Lord. He always feared y'all, too, Lord. That's gotta count for some-thin'.Lord have mercy on a hard man that just couldn't help it. Amen."

"Amen."

Leon didn't spend much time covering the body. The coyotes would find him before long.

☾

For the rest of the day, stoked on black tea, Leon drove while Polly rested in the compartment. She didn't wake until they had stopped for the night among many other wagons and carriages in a grassy field behind the famous Magnolia Vale Inn, a roadhouse with wrap-around porches and windows filled with lamplight. Dance music floated in the heavy air—a fiddle and a harmonica. People sang. He could hear horses. Goats.

Polly sat up, groaning. "Where are we?"

"The inn. It's safe. How do you feel?"

"Pretty sore. I think I'm going to work up a healing spell."

"Good. I'll go check out the menu. Want anything special?"

She shook her head. "Hand me my sewing box, will you, please?"

He watched her make a poultice of comfrey with egg yoke and tea. She pressed dark honey into her wounds.

He stood in the darkness at the edge of the yard behind the inn for a while, watching the kitchen through a wide screen door. At last a black woman came out to empty a box into one the inn's smoking trash barrels.

"Ma'am? Excuse me, ma'am."

The woman frowned at him. "We don't give out no scraps," she told him.

"Here," he said. He handed her one of Tina's 20-dollar coins. "There are two of us. We'd like a little supper."

In a minute she returned with a paper sack of barbecued ribs and wheat biscuits and a quart jar of braised greens and onions, still warm.

They ate with the hatch open to the stars. Polly looked calm in the cabin light.

"You must be feeling better."

"I'm mending. How about you? How are you feeling?"

Dizzy. With love. But he couldn't say that. "You know, you're lucky that bullet didn't hit an artery, or you'd be dead."

"I'm lucky you're a sharpshooter," she said. "How do you feel about what you did back there?"

"Can't tell yet. It's a good thing I could do it, I know that much."

Polly shook her head. "There is nothing good in an act like that."

This surprised him. "Seems to me if you can stop somebody from murdering you, that's a good thing."

"Well, it's the *natural* thing."

"You don't think nature is . . . naturally good?"

"No. I think living things just want to stay alive any way they can. Good or bad doesn't come into it."

"But *life* is good," he said. "So good or bad *has* to come into it."

Polly didn't reply.

He knew he was right, but he was too tired and jangly to explain why. Anyway, it hurt to disagree with her.

He stood to close the hatch.

They each managed to use the waste vent without making the other self-conscious, then undressed and slipped into their sleep sacks. They arranged themselves as they had been, head to foot, and Polly fell asleep in less than a minute.

What a person she was. The most amazing person he'd ever known. He lay awake for a long time, listening to the vent fan and the dance music.

THREE

15

AFTER A FEW DAYS, when Polly had healed enough to stand on both legs, Leon taught her how to pilot the Nomad. After that they spelled each other to make better time. Even so, according to Balthazar, the corrupted familiar kept pace with their progress. Leon offered to circle back and put an end to the bear's torment, but Polly would not sanction anything so cold-blooded. Besides, it wasn't necessary. Balthazar would make sure the bear did not surprise them.

They passed mossy swamps lined with tupelo, fragrant pine stands, and fields of well-tended beans and peanuts, squash and corn. Where the red clay road was flat, they averaged almost 30 miles an hour, rolling past hog farms, horse and sheep pasture, hardscrabble settlements, and the shells of old buildings and factories. Children stared as they cruised by. Venders accosted them, hoping to sell them cider, cheese, medicine, firewood, and friendly locals told them where to find good water, wild fruit, and safe places to pass the night. More than once they saw a police patrol, but the officers gave them no notice.

The still nights were lit by the waning moon, the days hot and thick. One morning they awoke in a grove of pecan trees gone scraggly and wild a mile or more from the rutted main road. After gathering nuts in the cool of the day, Polly convinced Leon to leave the cart for a while and hike further off, to forage and explore a little. They crossed two trails and a wooded ridge, gathering morels along the way, until they came to a good-sized brook between banks of glade fern. They rested and bathed, first Polly, then Leon, and they fished for a while with no luck.

That afternoon Leon asked if she might like him to teach her how to shoot a handgun, and she said that was a good idea. Leon set up targets made of flat stones, and they took turns, a cylinder at a time. He showed her how to stand, how to breathe, and how to hold a target, keeping the pistol aligned with her point of aim. She was good at it. "You have a very steady hand," Leon told her. He seemed surprised. What she didn't like was the noise. Her hearing was dull for the rest of the day.

☾

Leon gave her a nudge and nodded toward the jagged skyline of Atlanta, about five miles off. Three bright buildings towered over the rest, the tallest of them like a stack of giant coins supporting a platinum dome.

"The big one's the Crozier," Leon said. "Second Dominion capitol building."

"It looks enormous," Polly said. "Do people live there?"

"A lot of people—rich, important people. Clergy and government. Supposed to have their own gardens and everything."

The roads converging on the city were in better shape than the highways around Talla and Orlando. This one, the 75, had a speed lane for fancier vehicles, though they hadn't seen many of those. A few times they passed road crews in jumpsuits, shoring up banks, clearing culverts, collecting trash, patching holes. Because they were all shackled together, Polly took them for convicts, but Leon said no, they were slaves held by the governing authority.

Like the wars overseas and the Cataclysms, servitude was something no one talked about very much, even in the Regions. Years ago, fugitive slaves on their way north would show up now and then in the dooryard, hoping for a meal. That ended long ago. Once, at a Midsummer's Day picnic when she little, she heard the grown-ups talking about a group of slaves who'd come shambling up the Connecticut Valley, straight through the zone, the way people used to do before New York. They were all rad-sick and dying. And at Wendell's one night, she watched a FaithWays television special about some Sixth Dominion social workers in Oregon who opposed the subjugation of any of God's children, no matter what the Bible said or what God's divine plan for them might be. Their leaders were in jail for blasphemy.

Leon slowed the cart. The traffic ahead just crept along. A horn blared, then another. They stopped.

"Accident." Leon raised the bird glasses. "Nope. Checkpoint."

"Home Guard or Security?"

"Can't tell." He steered the cart to the shoulder. "Know any vanishing spells?"

She smiled and shook her head. "No such thing."

Leon scanned the terrain with the binoculars.

On their run up the 75, they had passed mostly woods and swamplands at first and then weedy fields and small farms with vine-covered hedgerows. There were more and more occupied dwellings after that, most with cisterns on their roofs and vegetable gardens in front, many with citrus trees, chicken coops, rabbit hutches, goats, horses, pig pens. As they got closer to the rail line, they had passed sawmills, shoe and tire factories, tanners, millers, furniture makers, grain merchants, forges, welding and wheelwright shops, windowless warehouses, nondescript office buildings, taverns and barbecue joints with illuminated signs, wayside chapels, cemeteries, fuel and battery dealers, travel and shipping agents, dry goods stores, electronics and computer outlets, and concrete plants. Now it was all freight and salvage yards. Polly could see the Maglev corridor half a mile to the east. Leaving the main road would pose its own problems.

"Emergency ramp up ahead," Leon said.

"Anybody getting off the highway?"

"No. We'll stand out, that's for sure."

"If we get stopped, you can tell them I'm sick and we're looking for a clinic."

"I could. The trouble is, neither of us has any ID."

Leon maneuvered the cart around an idling transport and up along the shoulder to the unmarked break in the guardrail. It gave onto a steep ramp with an open gate at the bottom. Two cams were mounted on the gateposts along with a red-and-white sign:

POLICE, FIRE, AND SECURITY ONLY

NO EXIT

A rough service road ran along the foot of the highway embankment, wind-blown trash littering the ditches. In a big lot on the other side of a chain-link fence she saw a multi-colored maze of stacked shipping containers and rusty 55-gallon drums with narrow alleys in between.

The traffic started to move. Two burly black men driving a team of mules and a covered cargo wagon pulled up alongside. One of them asked Leon if he needed help. No, but thanks.

The men rolled on, glancing back more than once.

"See the grooves in the weeds on the left?" Polly said.

"Right where it dips? Looks like somebody else squeezed through there to avoid the cameras."

"I think you're right," he said. "Worth a try." He hit a button on the console. "Better wait up here in case she gets away from me."

She hopped off the driving deck.

Leon pitched the cart down the bank. It nosed over the rim of the ramp and shot down the incline, rocking side to side, its stability mechanisms chittering. Leon brought it to a stop in the service road, turned with a grin, and waved.

☾

By sundown they'd come to a community of small, run-down houses, stables, a few wood-frame churches, and a busy marketplace. Fruit trees and patches of corn and melons. Scruffy playgrounds. Pasture. Trash dumps.

Wild dogs skulked in the alleyways. The people were all on foot, bicycle, or horseback. No sidewalks, no street lamps. The men carried guns. Everyone stared. Polly figured they rarely saw strangers rolling through with travel carts. Out in the countryside, few people ventured very far from home.

Leon stopped at a food stall in a square. He bought warm tortillas filled with shredded pork and onion with lime. About a dozen jabbering children were lined up to fill their water jugs at a spring—an L-shaped pipe set in a wall above a concrete basin.

"I hope you kids aren't drinking that water," Polly said to the oldest-looking one, a barefoot girl in a dirty sweatshirt.

She laughed. "Gotta boil it first, is all."

Leon approached a wiry, middle-aged woman and asked if she could point them toward the capitol. The woman flipped the hair out of her eyes and gave Polly a long look. “Back that way. Take the Seventy-five.” She was wearing sagging jogger’s pants and scuffed cowboy boots.

“There’s no other route?”

“Not with this.” She kicked one of the Nomad’s wheel rims. “Who y’all runnin’ from?”

“Nobody.”

She scoffed at that. “So what’s the story? She pregnant?”

“Go to hell.”

She laughed. “Listen. Gettin’ dark. Y’all want to spend the night in my barn, it’s real comfortable. I got a stock tank you can cool off in. Him and me don’t bother with animals no more, so it’s clean.”

“Thank you,” Polly said. “That sounds wonderful.”

“All right, then. You just follow me.”

They rolled down a lane between ramshackle homesteads and weedy lots till they reached her small, shady dooryard at the end of a narrow alley. Beds of azaleas lined her brick walkway. A dog barked inside the house.

“This woman’s not stupid,” Leon said under his breath. “She could sell us out in two seconds flat.”

“She’s not going to sell us out,” Polly said, though she knew she couldn’t be sure. She was tired, that’s all, and she really wanted a bath.

Her name was Candy. Used to work as a nurse and midwife at the women’s welfare clinic at Sheepshead Corner up until the health authorities shut it down. That was about 15 years ago. Ran a daycare for about ten years before that. Stabled horses, kept bees, used to sing in the choir Wednesdays and Sundays down at Saving Grace. These days all she did was read, knit, and tend her tomatoes. Her husband Rudy worked maintenance for the Peachtree Grand Express, the Maglev line between Atlanta and Orlando. The dog’s name was Gus. Both her sons, Philip and Henry, got killed in Saudi. She missed them every day. How would they like a cup of cherry wine? she asked before she went inside. It wasn't strong.

Polly told her they didn't drink.

"Suit yourself. Stock tank's around back. Sets in the shade all day, so it's cool. Soap and shampoo's in the chest. Couple decent razors, if you want one."

Candy's barn was actually a pole shed open along one side like the carriage shed at the farm, spare and clean inside, with a hoof-worn timber floor, two stalls, and an empty hay loft at one end. In the middle of the space, flanked by two large candles, stood a washstand and a double bed inside a net that hung like a big cobweb from the rafters. Leon went to bathe, while Polly walked back out to the Nomad to unload her pack and Leon's satchel.

Together she and Candy made up the bed, listening to Leon sing out in the stock tank. "Sweeter than all the roses . . . " He has a fine tenor voice.

"Don't mind me," Candy said, "but if I had to guess, I'd guess y'all ain't found Jesus. Am I right?"

Polly just looked at her.

"I ain't gonna turn you in, not in a million years, so don't worry about that."

"Thanks."

When they shook out the sweet-smelling yellow sheets, the candles fluttered and went out. Candy lit them again. Dairy cows mooed somewhere. It was milking time.

Candy plumped the pillows. "If I insulted y'all out there on the street, I apologize."

"How did you insult us?"

"About y'all being pregnant. Reason I said it, there was a time when they would come to me. And when I seen y'all, I don't know, it just took me back."

"Pregnant girls."

She nodded. "Me and Hannah, my partner, we helped 'em out."

"That was brave of you, to do a thing that."

"Huh. Greedy and sinful's what it was."

"An old friend of my father's does abortions." Bald, profane Bertine.

"No! In *Florida*?"

"Oh, no. I'm from Vermont. That's where I live."

"Vermont?" She sighed. "Me and Rudy, we always wanted to see Vermont in the *worst* way. Maine, too—that whole area."

"It's not as easy to get to as it once was, that's for sure."

"Can't get there at all no more. Half of it's contaminated, and the other half's been purged, praise the Lord."

"You can get there," Polly said. "You just have to detour around the zone, that's all."

"Be one hell of a detour." Candy looked at her closely. "Heaven's sake! Refugee pagans! That's what y'all are. I'm right, ain't I?"

"We're not refugees, no. I'm just trying to get back to my home—and Leon's my traveling companion."

"I know, but you said *Vermont*."

"That's my home."

"Like I said, hon, it's been *purged*. The pagans and heretics, they been drove out! Ain't nobody livin' there no more, if you watch the news. Just Security."

"My father's there. He sent for me."

Candy lowered herself to the edge of the bed. "Well, hon, even if he did, y'all can't just *walk* to Vermont. Just plain ain't feasible. No way."

Leon came into the candlelight wearing only his heavy pants, his wet hair combed straight back like an otter's. He hadn't shaved.

"How's the water?" Polly asked.

"Great. Perfect."

He looked fresh. Strong and glowing.

Candy shook her head."Must be some angel's watching over y'all," she said with a sigh. "Better pray she don't slack off." Polly saw tears in the woman's eyes. "Y'all like bacon for breakfast? Scrambled eggs and jalapeños?"

☾

The water in the tank came to her chest. Using a pail, she washed and rinsed her hair. She thought about shaving, but it didn't matter—she wasn't playing tennis anymore. Who knew if she'd ever play tennis again? She took her time working out the snarls under the starless sky. Candy's boxer trotted down the walkway and sat to watch her. She pointed back toward the house. "Gus. Go. Go inside." He did.

Not long after that, Balthazar glided in over the rooftops. He dropped with a faint whoosh onto a fencepost in a corner of the yard.

Hello.

"Where's the bear?"

She comes.

"Is she close?"

B ruffed his neck. Polly could see the bear ambling across a flat, rubbly surface, lights in the distance.

"Bad," he said. He spread his wings and closed them.

"What's bad?"

This place.

"How?"

As before.

Like Mrs. Hacker's makeshift shelter in the Wastes. "You mean Candy? Is she bad?"

You cannot trust her.

"I see. So I guess Leon and I shouldn't sleep together in that open shed. Is that what you're suggesting?"

Maybe.

"You think we should stay in the cart?"

"Aye."

She found Leon lying on his back, naked under the yellow sheet, his chest gently rising and falling. She just couldn't make him move to their sour-smelling sleep sacks in the cart. She wanted to lean in and kiss him. Instead she reached through the netting and touched his bare shoulder.

He cried out and pushed up to his elbows.

"I'm sorry, Leon. I wanted to tell you that I'm going to go sleep in the cart. It'll be safer. For both of us."

"Why? What's wrong?"

"It's Balthazar. He doesn't trust Candy."

"I *knew* it. You never should have told her we're going to Vermont. Polly, you can't keep blabbing to every old lady who offers you a free meal or we'll never get past Atlanta."

"I wasn't blabbing."

"You know what I mean."

She straightened and stood back, hurt. "Please, Leon—" She was going to remind him that Balthazar was *her* guide and she had to depend on his judgment—but it wasn't Candy he was angry about, she realized. He was angry because they wouldn't be sleeping together.

She lifted the netting aside. "Good night, Leon." She pressed her lips to his cheek, then his mouth. He reached up and dug his fingers into her smooth wet hair.

☾

Rain pattered on the roof above her. She sat up in a panic, thinking she was back inside that coffin of a lifeboat, but the smell of her shampooed hair brought it all back—Candy, the shed, the bear. Leon. Her triquetra felt hot against her skin.

She unlatched the panel and looked out. The sky was gray. Candy's pink azaleas gleamed in the drizzle. Men's voices, far off. Birds. She slipped her storm jacket over her head and climbed out.

Under an open window she stopped to listen, but she could hear nothing in the house. When she passed the open barn, Leon was snoring softly.

She rinsed her face at the stock tank, waiting for Balthazar. *B?* He was nowhere near.

A moment later she began to hear a mechanical hum out in the alley. Getting louder. She darted down the path to the compost bin behind the house, but she couldn't see the alley through the shrubs and fencing. She waited. Moisture dripped from the eaves into her hair and the pachysandra at her feet.

The humming stopped.

Polly slipped alongside the house till she had a view of the alley. Looming over the travel cart, its black canopy glistening, was the cream-colored government Atomic Leon had seen at the slave auction. Behind it, two officers in boots and vid helmets were walking their horses up the alley. One of them vaulted up onto the Nomad's side rail with a crowbar. He jammed it into the hatch frame.

She ran back to the barn.

"*Leon! Wake up! Now!*"

He groaned. "Why? What's wrong?"

"They've caught up with us. They're here."

"The Guard?"

"The government men from the auction—with the Atomic. They're breaking into the cart."

"The cart? But—"

"Come on, Leon! We have to *go*."

He was groggy. He swung his legs out of the bed, looking around for his pants and shoes.

Polly snugged her backpack closed and hoisted it onto her shoulders. Candy's boxer was barking now inside the house.

"Jesus, my rifle!" Leon whispered.

"I have the revolver in the pack. Come *on*, Leon!"

He was pulling his pants on. Candy's back door flew open and crashed against the outside wall. Boot heels thudded across the porch floor.

They weren't going to make it.

"*Hurry*, Leon! *This way*."

"You go!" he said. He was barefoot. "Go. It's you they want. Don't wait. *Go!*"

A rough rail fence separated the backyard from the community pasture. On both sides of the yard the houses were shielded by trees and vines. Across the pasture she could see a string of lights—the Maglev corridor. She looked back. No Leon.

She climbed the fence and jumped down into the pasture.

Leon wasn't coming.

She ran toward the lights.

16

ACROSS THE MUDDY PASTURE a metal gate in the fence opened into a lane bounded by a screen of bamboo. She unlatched it and slipped through. The rain dripping in the vegetation intensified the pre-dawn stillness. Far down the lane she could see a steel fence with a razor-wire skirt. Beyond that, about 15 feet off the ground, ran the Maglev line.

Looking back across the pasture, she couldn't tell which bungalow was Candy's. No sign of Leon. Cows and a few horses grazed in the distance.

She took off the backpack. All she had was the handgun, her bird glasses, her flying get-up, the sewing box, a water bottle, her knife, a flashlight, and *The Craeft*. Her extra clothing, all their food and water, the maps, the tools, the solar cooker, what money they had left, and half the ammo were all in the cart. She still had the survival kit, at least.

Slumped against the fence with her backpack across her knees, she let the tears come. What would they do to him? Where would they take him? She'd have to get word to Malcolm. But what could she say?

Balthazar was approaching.

She wiped her eyes. He glided in low and straight, whooshed up and over the screen of bamboo, and set himself down in the lane. *I did not see the horsemen.*

"It's not your fault, B. They probably caught onto us soon as we left the highway."

The bear is close.

"She's going to make me shoot her, isn't she?"

She cannot stop.

"What's it about?"

He didn't know, and he wouldn't guess.

"Oh, Mother. And now we've lost Leon. What are we going to *do*?"

You are free.

Free to leave? Was that what he meant? Alone? After all she and Leon had been through? She couldn't. "You like him, too, Balthazar!"

He is caught. You are free.

"Free to help him? Is that what you mean?"

Free to choose.

This was strange. She'd never heard of a familiar putting a witch's welfare at risk for the sake of some ordinary human.

The raven rocked around. Her ambivalence bothered him.

"Are you sure you could find him?"

No. He faced her again.

"So what do we do?"

"Try."

She sighed. "Did they take the cart?"

"Aye."

"Well, you could follow that, couldn't you?" Polly stood and brushed the dirt from her bottom. "You're right, B. If there's any chance we can save him, we have to try. OK, find out where he is. I'll wait here. When you—"

You must fly.

"You know I can't do that. Not in the daylight."

Above the cloud.

The cloud deck was low and thick. "What if someone sees me?"

Look. He tipped his head.

On the far side of the pasture one of the horsemen was riding toward them through the mist, his eyes to the ground.

She put on the backpack and cinched the straps. "Which way?"

Fly!

"That's crazy, B! There's no *time*!"

Speak the words. Force it.

Force the Dispersal?

Do it.

She swung the pack off and took out the ointment, ski hat, and goggles.

Hurry.

"Are you sure this'll work?"

No.

Great.

She spoke the seven phrases, then the four. She applied the ointment in one swift stroke. On with the pack again and the goggles.

The charge stopped her breath.

She rose. Fast and faster. Her fogged goggles left her blind, but she could feel Balthazar at her right shoulder.

She cleared the lenses with her sleeve. The murk soon thinned to cold white. They broke into a brilliant vault above the cloudscape. Droplets streamed from Balthazar's wingtips. All around them was a cushion of undulating vapor and blue air. Years ago, one afternoon in the fall when she was twelve and in training with Lil, they had flown above the clouds in the daylight. The wonder of that was unforgettable. This was just as wonderful. But the air was much colder somehow, and she wasn't dressed for it.

Stay here. Balthazar plunged out of sight.

She glided, teeth clenched. It was very strange, this ethereal, forbidding place, so thrilling and lovely and painful at the same time.

Balthazar returned. *Follow.*

They dove into the gray deck, not breaking into the clear again until they were just a hundred feet above the jumble of the city. The three government buildings she'd seen from the highway rose out of a central plaza far off to her left. All around, trees and rooftops lined the roads. She saw a rail yard, a horse-racing track, tennis courts, the lights of a big airport . . .Balthazar swung in just below her.

There.

A park. Walkways, grass, trees. A misty pond.

They slanted down.

Polly coasted in over the pond and thumped to the ground, stumbling on her numb legs. Nearby, at the water's edge, stood a roofed pavilion covered in ivy and framed by dogwoods and rhododendron. Nobody here, only a few mallards paddling fast up the reedy shore of the pond. Balthazar set down on the pavilion's pointed roof. Polly propped herself against a dogwood tree and worked to knead the sensation back into her legs and arms. They felt frozen. It was starting to drizzle.

A man.

"Where?"

On a path above them someone in an orange knit cap was jogging by. A shaggy dog trotted beside him on a leash. She slipped behind her little dogwood.

She couldn't stay in this place. The city was waking up. It was mostly government people in Atlanta, but there were military and clergy, too, along with anybody else rich enough to afford a life of privilege—no scarcity, no hardship, no riffraff in the streets. A scraggly-haired waif wearing a dirty backpack would be reported by the first person who happened to see her.

It was raining harder. She ran for the pavilion. It was sturdy and dry. Broken glass, leaves, and cigarette butts littered the stone floor. Why couldn't these people take better care of what they had?

B swooped in and lit on the half-wall. *Do not stay here.*

"I know. Soon as the rain lets up, I'll find a better place."

Do not wait long.

She watched him flap away, straight and strong, until he disappeared beyond the trees.

17

THE ROOM WAS HOT. Filled with harsh light. He was gazing up into a ceiling of formed concrete, patterned like a giant waffle.

He sat up. The far wall looked like a vid panel with a line of strange, purple disks sliding slowly across the bottom. But the wall was glass, and the disks were oblong clouds.

His head and back and arms ached. He looked around for his clothes but didn't see them. They had caught him and thrown him to the ground out by Candy's stock tank. A few hours ago. Or less. He couldn't remember anything between then and now.

The mattress was a thin, canvas-covered pallet. No pillow, no blanket, just a blue cotton sheet. On one side of the chamber, in a lit alcove, there was a waste vent. And a steel wash basin. On the opposite wall hung an ten-foot cross of gold-flecked timbers. It shimmered. The floor was polished stone.

Some monk's cell, that was probably what this was. He couldn't make out a door, but it had to be one of the panels in the wall opposite the window.

He went to the window with the sheet wrapped around him. That was Atlanta spread out below. Buildings, trees, criss-crossing roads. On the horizon, the cooling towers of a power plant. A high-voltage power corridor. Helicopters. He was higher than the helicopters.

They'd brought him to the capitol building. The Crozier. That's where he was.

He heard a panel sliding open behind him and turned.

A stocky man stood silhouetted against the brilliant, featureless space outside. "May I?"

He stepped in.

The aide to the Secretary—with the gray ponytail. Same wide cheekbones, same deep slots for eyes. White blouse with buttoned cuffs, loose tan trousers, black pistol-butt in a hand-tooled flap holster.

"I saw you at the bazaar," Leon said. "You drive that Atomic."

He gave a little laugh. "That Atomic drives itself."

"You work for the Dominion Secretary. Your name's Yuri."

"Very good!" He bowed. "Yuri Vasilevsky. Chief aide to His Excellency, Clyde Morton Trumble."

"So I've been kidnapped by a Dominion Secretary."

"Not at all. You've been *rescued,* Leon."

"From what?"

"Prison. Possibly worse."

"Prison for what?"

"The FTB agent back in Talla. Rasmussen—remember him? He'd like to see you sentenced to a camp for ten years. But you're safe here. For the time being." Yuri walked to the window and gazed out into the sky.

"Ten years for saving a girl's life?"

"There's worse news. Last week a team from Justice raided your father's slave shelter out in the dunes."

"*Slave* shelter? My father's an *archeologist*!"

"Not anymore, I'm sorry to say. Malcolm Krauss is currently behind bars in Talla awaiting arraignment."

"What's he charged with?"

"Aiding in the felony theft of human property."

"That's bullshit! That's *crazy*!"

"I need a little information, Leon. Help me out now, and I promise to do everything in my power to have the charges dropped."

"What information?"

"The slave girl. Cassandra. How can I find her?"

"She's not a slave."

Yuri turned toward the big cross. In a quiet voice he said, "Help me get the girl back. You do that and I'll make sure your father is released from custody and banished. If you refuse to help me, I'll make sure he dies in prison."

"Polly is just trying to get home to Vermont! I *swear*, that's all I know."

"You know she's a witch, don't you?"

"So what? Witches are just people with natural abilities you're too ignorant to understand."

Yuri turned around. "The girl is carrying a book of Satanic arts. Your grandmother's seen it. You've seen it, too, haven't you?"

He said nothing.

"Leon, please. Think of your father. *How can I find the witch?*"

"I honestly don't know."

Yuri stood waiting.

"Here's the truth." Leon didn't look at him, but he could hear him breathing. "My father had *nothing* to do with Polly. *Nothing*!" He clenched his jaw. "If any harm comes to him or my sister because of all this . . ."

He didn't finish. Yuri had left the room.

☾

For hours he lay in the hot cell, dozing and waking into the same knot of thoughts. He'd been a fool. Only a fool would run off with a witch. Only a fool could hope to have a witch for a *girlfriend.* A lover. If he'd just gone back to the dig, everything would be fine. School would be over and he could help at the dig and read books and play games with Tina and Nando and Giselle. And he and Polly would both be safe and sound. He fell in love with her, that's what happened. And love was one of those things that got people killed. From the night they left the coast all he had done was lead her into trouble, over and over again. Now, on her own, at least she could *fly* home. Or maybe she couldn't. Flying was quite dangerous, she'd told him. The truth was that without him Polly might not even have made it to Georgia. He sighed.

None of that mattered now. It was summer, just about. She was a day or two from the trailhead. Amicalola Falls. From there, if she followed the spine of the mountains, she could walk all the way to the edge of zone in eastern Pennsylvania. And from there she could fly.

But whether any of that happened, whether she made it back to her people in Vermont or got killed by the bear, he was never going to find out. Polly was over.

☾

He woke at daybreak. Sitting up, he realized the wall window responded to his movement. Its dark tint broke into horizontal strips that slowly faded to let in the light. He used the waste vent, rinsed his face at the basin, took a drink from his hands, dried himself with his sheet, and went to the window. Under the wash of the sky stretched a dusky horizon of wooded hills. Lines of green stood out here and there—trees and shrubs marking the boundaries of walled communities and commercial centers. To the west, beyond a barrier or some kind, alleyways meandered through smoky slums.

He was so hungry his gut hurt. He made himself drink

more water, then lay on his side with his knees tucked up, trying to quiet his mind by slowing his breathing. The giant cross glimmered. The quartering sun pounded through the glass.

At some point, a rush of cool air made him lift his head. The portal slid open.

He sat up, dizzy.

A husky blond woman wearing a lavender short-sleeved top and creased white pants stood there smiling broadly. She had a cardboard box in her hands. "Good morning, my boy. How are you feeling today?"

"Hungry."

"I should say! How would you like some breakfast?"

"Sure—anything."

"Okra and grits?"

He hated okra. "I'd rather have eggs. Or bread and cheese. Some fruit, if you have any."

"Nice hot Brazilian coffee?"

"Tea. With honey."

The woman's laugh whistled in her nose. "Smoked salmon and cream cheese?"

"You have *salmon*?" No one had salmon.

"Banana muffins with ginger marmalade? Strawberries and sweet cream? Apple-pecan crumb cake? Oysters on the half-shell?"

His ears burned. "Go to hell."

The nurse chuckled, setting the carton at the foot of his pallet. In it were a folded towel, a wood-handled toothbrush, a cake of grainy soap, and a foil-covered bowl.

"Who are you?"

"You can call me Sarah. I look after the menagerie."

"Sarah, let me ask you. Is the dominion secretary in this building? Secretary Trumble?"

"The *secretary*? Goodness, I don't know. Why?"

"I need to talk to him. In person."

"Oh, do you? In person?" Her eyes danced.

"It's about my father, and it's really important. But first I need to have my clothes back."

"Eat, Leon. I brought you a tub of nutriment. Eat that and your spirits will spike in a jiffy, I guarantee."

Before the panel closed, he'd opened the foil-covered bowl at the bottom of the box. Warm mush. With a bamboo spoon, he scooped it into his mouth. It was thick and sweet and nearly tasteless. He ate it all.

As he washed with the cloth and the rough bar of soap and brushed his teeth, he could feel a luscious calm welling up in him.

The panel opened. There stood Sarah again. She was radiant. "Ready to boogie?"

"You didn't bring my clothes."

"You're right. Are you ashamed of your nakedness?"

He wasn't ashamed. Not at all. He was serene. He was happy. There was a strip of velvety shade on the other side of the room. It looked soft and cool.

"You can leave now," Leon said.

"Oh, I know!" Sarah said in a piping voice. "I can do anything I want, as long as I leave no mark on the skin! Ha ha!"

So there were others, he realized. Others like him. *I look after the menagerie.* What a relief! He would not be alone here. He might have friends.

The shadow on the opposite side of the room was breathing, pulsing. So was the glittery cross. The tender air itself. The room. Everything glowed with soothing, living light. It was almost too much.

"Stand up now, Leon," Sarah said. "Come now—come walk with me."

"Where are we going?"

She sang a verse from a hymn about a "heavenly home." Her voice came in concentric waves that broke like bubbles against his face. Like kisses. He could feel them.

"What did you give me?" It didn't matter. He was only curious. His palms were wet. His powerful heartbeat felt like the engine at the center of the universe. And it was!

"Do you feel the love around you?" Sarah asked. "Are you finally at peace with the world?"

He did. And he was. He truly was.

18

As soon as the clouds began to lift and break, Polly ducked out of her shelter and ran toward the far side of the lake across a ragged lawn and through a copse of redbud until she reached a thick, sandstone wall—the park boundary. An iron gate, chained and locked, gave onto a cart path. She wriggled underneath, shoving the pack ahead of her.

On the other side of road lay a broad, sunny swale covered as far as she could see in green, undulating kudzu thicker than a mattress.

She walked along the quiet thoroughfare for some time, crouching down into the roadside growth whenever a vehicle passed, keeping an eye open for a spot where she could wait for Balthazar without being seen. Whether any of the nearby kudzu-cloaked mounds would do for cover she couldn't tell, not without wading through the overgrowth for a close look, and that she knew was a bad idea.

Where the park's sandstone wall ended the road forked. The traveled way was paved with crushed shells. It led uphill toward a distant highway and the capitol district. The lower route was a more a wagon track, skirting the jungle and heading toward the distant ruins of the old city. She could see vultures out that way among the gulls, coasting on the thermals.

She climbed the bank to peer through a barricade

of stout planks bolted to pilings, built to keep the jungle from overwhelming the tended properties on the other side. Between the planks she could see mowed lawns, pine trees, rhododendron, magnolias, and the sun-bright windows of houses. She could hear motors and traffic.

She chose the lower road to the west. In that direction she could see nothing but vine-covered buildings, half-visible road signs and fencing, and rows of power poles sticking up through the green like the bones of a huge skeleton.

After a time, as she came to a steel-grid bridge spanning a narrow ravine, she heard a jangling wagon closing in behind her. She left the road to hide beneath the bridge. The pitch of the bank was steep, but there was a concrete ledge between the abutments. She sat there.

Two pair of horses and four big rubber-rimmed wheels passed overhead. The rumbling transport rained dirt down through the gridwork.

A short while later a boy driving a team of mules and a rotary mower came clattering up from behind her—a city worker keeping the jungle off the roadway.

Polly raised her arm.

He reined in, beaming his crooked teeth her. "*¿Quieres una vuelta?*"

"*No hablan español.*" Her Spanish wasn't very good.

"Where you go?" The team quivered in the traces.

"I'm going to look for a friend."

"Ah, si. Een jail?"

"What jail?"

He grinned again and jiggled his eyebrows. "You no from here, *chica linda*." He nodded ahead up the puddled road. "*Nada más que la cárcel en la selva. ¿No sabes que?*"

The way to the jail. "Is there any other shelter out this way, do you know? Out in those ruins? Where a person might rest for a few hours?"

He looked in the direction she was pointing. "Si . . . si . . ." he said, rocking his head from side to side. "*¿Usted es vagabundo, muchacha?*"

No. I'm a traveler."

"Come. *Justo aquí. Paseo conmigo.*" He slid to one side and patted rig's single seat.

"Thank you, but—"

She turned to look toward the rumble of wheels and jingling harness fittings on the road ahead. A four-horse team and a bullet-shaped van painted red and white came into view, its red composite wheels splashing in the ruts.

"*Subir! ¡Ahora!*"

Polly set her foot on the step and jumped up beside the mower driver.

The van rumbled past. Black letters across the doors read, "*Georgia Department of Corrections. Serving Justice, Jesus, and Georgia.*" Two men in the open cab, one driving, the other leaning back.

The boy nodded to them, but they paid no attention. "*Hola, bastardos!*" He spat.

"Where's the jail? Out there?"

"*Si. Para el insano y poseidos.*"

They started up again. She flinched when he put an arm around her, but he only meant to keep her from tumbling back into the blades. Soon the mower's regular slap and whir made her sleepy and she had to work to stay awake.

The big American cities today, the ones that remained from an earlier, voluptuous age, when cities spread for miles, held a small fraction of their Oil Age population. In the wake of the Cataclysms, the cities' sprawl had fragmented into rough, insulated communities. And way out here there was nothing. Nothing to salvage, nothing to live on. Just junk and ruination. The reclamation efforts had ended long ago—no one had a use for the land, and there was no point in moving debris from one dump to another.

The driver reined in and nodded toward a prominent, craggy ruin. A sort of path seemed to lead toward it, a seam in the vines. He pantomimed climbing a ladder. *¡Suba para arriba!*

"Si, climb up."

"*Guárdese de serpientes,*" he said.

"*Gracias, amigo.*"

"*Adios, muchacha.*"

She took out the revolver and marched toward the lowering sun, pushing at the vines with her shins. Dozens of small, pale-blue butterflies flitted around her like confetti. Some kind of animal scurried away from her—a raccoon and her young.

The zigzagging footpath branched off in more than one direction. Polly followed made her way nimbly toward what looked like a wide apron of granite steps at the foot of the facade the boy had pointed out. Tiers of window openings against a hazy sky. She climbed the vine-choked steps and paused to survey the interior of the ruin. A shadowy jumble of weeds, rubble, clay, and junk. A large scummed-over pond on the far side. Frogs chirping madly. Pigeons fluttering through the sunbeams. Dragonflies. Flycatchers. Swallows.

A utility pole stood propped at an angle against the near wall. At its upper end, 30 feet off the ground, a remnant of an old floor extended from the wall to make a freeform balcony almost the size of a tennis court. The pole had galvanized rungs on either side. Up she went.

The balcony was pasted with dirt and guano. Inside a fire ring near the back wall was a pile of rusty cans and charred sticks of wood. Someone had rigged a pulley to a stub of girder overhead so you could raise the butt of the pole off the ground for safety. The rope was gone.

She sipped from her water bottle and watched the sky. *Balthazar?* He wasn't near. A while later her heart leapt as a dark bird came angling in just above the far wall. But it was another bird. A falcon. A pair of them had a nest up there. And a brood. She wouldn't see Balthazar tonight. He wouldn't intrude on a raptors' nest site if he didn't have to.

Stars—Spica, Regulus. Bats. Insects. The frogs' ear-filling chorus.

She swept a circle to the edge of the shelf and called the quarters. She mixed a bit of rue, vervain, and valerian root in a small saucer. Mostly for the reassuring smells. *Grant me protection, spirit forces, from all harmful creatures and conditions.* She pinched out the candles. She set the handgun on floor beside the grimoire and stretched out with a groan.

The night was mild and still. The mosquitoes let her be, but the hard surface kept waking her. By daybreak she was sore everywhere.

The falcons creaked to each other. Bullfrogs glunked.

She was almost out of drinking water. She rinsed out her mouth, sipped a little, and repacked. When she stood up, she felt so light-headed she had to sit again. She needed food. Balthazar would find her something. Where was he? Where was Leon?

She dissolved the cone. As she began to back down the pole, rung to rung, at first she felt heat, then a jab at her breastbone, like a splinter.

The triquetra.

She turned. The bear was standing down in the shadows at the foot of the pole, burning to have her.

She scrambled up onto the shelf.

The bear huffed and started to climb.

Polly grasped the pole in both hands, squatted, and heaved it sideways with a scream.

The bear crashed to the ground. The bounce of the pole echoed through the huge, roofless cavern, *donk, donka-donk,* silencing the frogs. She dropped to her knees and looked over the edge.

The bear was on her haunches moaning and rocking her square head, her tongue a scroll in her mouth. She'd damaged her hip—Polly could feel it.

How long had that beast been down below, unmarked, waiting for her to leave her sanctuary? "Bear! You listen to me now. Your witch has done a terrible thing to you. I think you know that. And I *hope* you know that I mean no harm to anyone, not you, not Theldred, not anyone. If you promise not to attack me, there's a good chance I could lift your ensorcellment. Will you let me try?"

The bear moaned again. She saw two yearling cubs. They were curled up together in a dim stall with straw bedding. Then she saw Theldred herself, tall and straight, standing with her back to the room and gazing out through a narrow, diamond-paned window, her hands high on either side of its carved stone frame, her sinewy arms bare. Her fall of hair reached to the small of her back.

With a grunt, the bear stood. She tested the air. Her alarm was sharp.

Off on the sunny side of the ruin where a stand of bamboo masked the pond, a heavy animal came thrashing out of the water. Alligator.

She swung off the pack.

The bear ruffed her neck and bobbed her head in that direction, growling low.

Polly watched the reptile lash its way through the vegetation until it crested a mound of rubble 20 yards off. It wasn't a gator, but a crocodile. Huge and muddy green with a thick, yellowish chest and a long snout full of crooked teeth.

"You'd better run, bear! You can't fight that monster."

The bear kept sampling the air. She couldn't run. Her hip.

The croc plunged off the hummock, shoving hard through the scrub.

The bear shuddered and snarled.She would die here if it had to be.

Polly stretched out on her stomach. She held the gun in both hands, muzzle up, elbows on the hard terrazzo floor. The frogs were singing again.

The croc paused, then thrust himself ahead with more speed. The bear roared.

She wouldn't waste a round, but if she got a clear shot she would take it.

The giant crocodile closed in. He looked about 20 feet long, and he had to be three times the bear's weight.

The bear roared again, twisting her head.

Polly lowered the muzzle.

If the croc managed to sink those teeth into the black bear's hide, she'd be finished. He'd drag her back to the pond and drown her.

The croc lunged, jaws wide. The bear slugged him in the throat with a forepaw, lifting his scaly chest off the ground.

The croc lunged again and took another hard cross to the neck. He slid left, lashing his tail. The bear quartered with him.

Polly cocked the hammer and picked out a spot just behind the croc's bulging yellow eye. The croc hesitated, watching for an opening . . .

BOOM. Echoing through the ruin.

The croc sank to the ground, shivering, tail out straight. The bear dropped to all fours and moaned.

Polly's ears rang.

The bear stared up at her. *Why?*

The frogs were still. "Because I wasn't going to just sit here and watch him tear you to pieces."

The bear sagged and shook herself. She humped away, limping, toward the outside.

"Let me help you!" Polly cried.

The bear roared, "*Noooo!*"

Faintly now, she could feel her own familiar, high above her.

She pulled on her hat and goggles and applied the ointment.

Soon as she'd intoned the spell, the charge climbed through her like steam.

She leaned out away from the ledge and jumped. She picked up speed. Balthazar waited far overhead.

When she cleared the heights, the landscape spilled away all at once, a lumpy canvas, the low morning sun highlighting the endless man-made geometry beneath the green shroud. She could only hope no hunter would catch sight of her.

Balthazar fell in at her shoulder.

I need to find food. Soon.

Follow.

He urged her along fast and straight, just a few feet above the stumps of the buildings, to an industrial lot near a small settlement on the outskirts of the capitol district where the kudzu had been burned out or poisoned. The lot held piles of building materials long abandoned—girders, lumber, pipe, sheet metal. In the neighboring yard, beyond a screen of sumac and jewelweed and a broken fence, was someone's kitchen garden. The house it belonged to seemed quiet. Polly helped herself to a cucumber and a hatful of cherry tomatoes. Balthazar watched from above, then dropped into the lot to share the tomatoes. She could hear a snorting horse and a radio not far off.

I found Leon.

"You *did*? Where is he? Is he all right?"

He is imprisoned.

"Where?"

A building.

"Is he hurt?"

They cloud his mind.

"How's his body?"

He heals.

"Which building?"

The bird swung his head toward the domed silver cylinder, the only structure visible above a steep, tree-covered slope.

"Great Mother, the *Crozier*?"

"Aye."

"How will we ever get him out of that place?"

They will.

"They will what?"

They will get him out.

"How? Explain."

He will trick them.

"Oh, Balthazar. You and your tricks."

If they hate him, they will get him out.

"Why would they hate him?"

They keep the ones they love.

Polly thought for a moment. "I understand. He has to make them *not* want to keep him. Is that what you mean? So they'll send him away."

"Aye."

"Like what I did out in the Wastes. When I pretended to be poxed."

"Aye."

"But how will he know what to do? Can you get him a message?"

We must go to the cart.

"The cart? Why? Where is it?"

Follow.

"What for? I can't possibly drive it, not here."

Follow.

☾

B guided her trotting and walking down the settlement's zigzag byways, past orchards and fields of melons and corn, and at last into a leafy, landscaped park. By mid-afternoon they had reached the foot of the vast capitol plaza's smooth palisade, a sloping concrete wall 20 feet high. Here a tiled chute for storm-water ran down the side.

Climb?

The lip of each four-foot tile made a hand-hold. "I think so."

Wait. Balthazar flew up to survey the plaza. *Now.*

She scrambled to the top. Beyond a low brick wall just at the boundary, beds of marigolds defined a crushed-shell walk. Off in the wavery distance a number of people and horses were moving about, but there was no one nearby.

Go to the stables. Find the cart. Get the knife.

The cane knife, he meant.

He glided off. She vaulted over the wall.

Far across the plaza, the three Second Dominion government buildings dominated all the others, although from here the all-glass Cathedral of the Virgin stood out, too, gleaming orange, white, and gold, like sculpted ice.

Open spaces toward the center of the plaza were interspersed with vendors' booths, various statues, and gardens, with lamp posts and benches along the walkways. Off in the distance people drifted about like herd animals on a prairie.

She tagged along with a tour group for a few minutes, then hung back beside a souvenir-seller's display wagon as the tourists trooped down into an amphitheater. Cams were all over the place.

"You lost?"

A pudgy Chinese man sat in a ratty armchair under the wagon's scalloped awning. He wore one of the purple and yellow baseball caps he had for sale along with religious icons made of wood, leather sandals, lacquered seashells, slabs of slate engraved with scripture, and big posters of the crystal cathedral and the silver-blue Crozier against the night sky.

"I'm supposed to meet someone at the stables. Do you know where the stables are?"

He studied her. "Livery and carriage is down by Newgate. Transport level."

"Is that far?"

"Far enough. He work there, your friend?"

"He's a cart driver."

The man got up out of his chair with a sigh. He seemed neckless, like a cartoon character. "Other side of the square, down below. See that dip, like?"

"I think so."

"That's the trolley track. Follow that down to transport. Stables are past the hog pens—you smell 'em before you see 'em."

The dust veiling the transport yard sparkled in the heat. The place was crowded with commercial wagons and carriages, highway barges and shipping containers, livestock, tourists, bicyclists, food vendors, and Dominion police officers in blue shirts and white pith helmets. At the transport entry gates, winding lines of people waited to clear inspection.

In the midst of that, no one took much note of Polly, though she was aware of the looks she drew from the better dressed. A crowd milled about in the cobblestone courtyard among well-tended magnolia trees. Somebody played a lively accordion. She spotted a courier, a fresh-faced boy about her age wearing a black satchel with a gold cross embossed on it. She approached him and asked if he would point her toward the stables and carriage sheds.

"Storage or repair?"

"Storage, I guess."

"Long-term's down yonder," he said, nodding in that direction. "Just-for-the-day's back alongside the trolley shuttle."

The shingle-roofed storage stables, built in a long row against the district's outer wall, were mostly unoccupied. She paused at a fenced-in yard to look at a small display—a blacksmith's forge with a crumbling chimney and two rusted anvils, one on its side in the clay. A brass plaque on the ironwork said the tableau was a memorial in remembrance of Lucas Reynolds, father of Isaac Reynolds, the famous evangelical firebrand and theologian. Lucas, a blacksmith, had been shot dead on this spot during the Uprising long ago. Polly had never heard of him.

A little farther along, there it was, Leon's pretty travel cart. The sign tacked under the roof of the stall read:

POLICE USE ONLY.
La policía utiliza sólo.

☾

The damage looked minimal—broken running lights, hatch frame gouged and cracked by the pry-bar, wheel wells caked with clay. The wheels themselves looked fine. Even if it would run, though, she'd never be able to drive it out of this place. She knelt to retie her shoelace, glancing around, then slipped unseen into the stall.

She pressed the code into the console. *Click-clink,* the latch pins snapped back.

Leon's rifle and the solar array were gone, but nothing else seemed to be missing. The canisters of rice, cornmeal, tea, and beans were still snug in the compression rack where Tina had put them the night they left the coast. The computer's tiny charge light glowed green.

She took Leon's cane knife and fit it into its slot on the pilot deck, where he kept it while they were on the move, then climbed inside. The ventilators began to whir when she lowered the hatch.

19

LEON DIDN'T HAVE TO OPEN HIS EYES to know what they'd done to him. When he sobbed, it hurt.

A few years ago his father told him that before he was born his mother had promised she would not allow their son to be circumcised, and, with the help of a sympathetic midwife, she'd succeeded in keeping the birthing team from snipping off the end of Leon's penis.

Sarah had fixed that.

He couldn't remember where she'd taken him, but he had a hazy recollection of soft air, flowers, sand and water, music, baskets of fruit, lounge chairs, leafy groves, red-faced men in straw hats and sunglasses. And kids. Lots of kids, like at a playground, none older than ten or twelve, all barefoot, wearing light smocks and swim suits.

He turned onto his side. The pain was bad. The portal opened.

"How are you feeling, Leon?" Sarah.

He said nothing. He was furious. He wanted to jump up and punch her in the face.

"It's sore now, I know," she said, "but you'll be good as new in a day or two." She set a box at the foot of his pallet. "I brought you something to eat and some antiseptic salve."

"*You had no right!*" Shouting hurt. He drew up his legs. "Why did you *do* it?"

"Leon, Leon, Leon. You're a child of God. Genesis seventeen, 'This is my covenant, which ye shall keep: Every man child among you shall be circumcised.' It's as simple as that."

"But that doesn't give *you* the right to cut me!"

"Oh, for heaven's sake. What's done is done. And all to the good! For cleanliness, health, and a more pleasing appearance."

Appearance? He pushed up on his elbow, shocked. He got it. What this place was about, the grove, the men, the children, what it was all for. A wave of disgust made him want to puke.

"Eat and rest," the nurse said. "You need time to heal. Just be still now. Eat and rest."

The portal slid closed.

☾

Thwapitta-thwapitta-thwapitta.

The light in the chamber was a deep blue.

Thwapitta thwap.

Bruised clouds and splintery stars. In a corner of the window wall he saw a black wedge. *Balthazar*. How? Polly! She hadn't left him! If her familiar was still here, then so was she. Where?

Not far.

He saw her. Sitting cross-legged on the ground near a heap of salvaged lumber, her scuffed backpack in her lap and her wild hair tied up in a head scarf.

But this was no good! What could she do for him? Nothing! She should have been in the mountains by now. On her way home. If she got caught here and killed on his account . . . .

He got up, clasping the sheet around him.

The raven paddled the air to hold his perch on the narrow window ledge.

"Balthazar. Please, go to her. Tell her there's nothing she can do for me."

You.

"Me what?"

You will do it.

"Do what?"

Trick them.

"How? They're *watching* me all the time."

The bird turned his head sideways. *Eat nothing. Drink nothing.*

"Nothing at all? Not even water?"

See. Hear. Wait. The bird tumbled from the ledge and disappeared.

☾

Someone—Sarah—was stroking his hair. "Dawn of a new day! How you feeling, my lad? Better, I hope."

"Leave me alone."

"Still cranky? Awww. Listen, love, you wash up now. Here's your breakfast. Back in a jiffy!" She set a cardboard box at the foot of his pallet and left the room. Warm, cinnamon-flecked oatmeal in a bowl, a roll of gauze, and one of those loose cotton smocks. Nothing else. His was beige.

He pretended to eat, plopping the cereal into the basket before lifting the spoon to his mouth.

He washed himself and changed his dressing, then slipped into the beige smock and sat on the pallet. He kept watching for Balthazar, but the raven did not return.

It was cloudy. Nothing moved in the sky.

After a while, in a mumble, he started singing a song Tina used to sing to him when he was little. "'When the red, red robin comes bob, bob, bobbin' along . . . "

The portal whirred faintly.

He rolled his head side to side. "'When he starts throbbin' his old, sweet song . . . '"

Sarah. And Yuri, his flat face and little eyes. Rolling a gurney between them.

Sarah touched his throat with two fingertips. "Hmm. I don't know . . . "

"He's gone." Yuri lifted Leon's head and fitted a suede collar around his neck.

They moved him onto the gurney, legs and then shoulders, and rolled him out of the cell into a column of up-rushing air.Leon couldn't distinguish a single thing around them. It was all a luminous fog.

"You ever feel bad for them?" Yuri asked.

"Who?"

"Who do you think?"

"Why should I? They're happy. You don't think they'd rather be slaves, do you?"

Yuri didn't answer.

"So, do *you* feel bad for them?"

"I feel bad for this one."

"How come?"

"He's different."

Sarah chuckled. "I heard that one before. Buy a loving share."

"I don't mean that."

"What?"

"He's not here for the jollies. He has information, but he won't talk. If the treatment doesn't soften him up, they'll start in torturing him."

"That's hard to believe. What information?"

"He ran off with a slave girl that belongs to the Secretary. The Secretary wants the girl back, whatever it takes. He's sure the boy knows how to find her."

"Good God. Trumble's obsessed with a *slave* girl?"

"So it seems, and as it happens, this one's a witch."

The nurse snorted. "Witches can't be slaves."

"That's what I mean. Buying her wasn't my idea."

A chime sounded. The gauzy air thinned, revealing a vast, sky-lit plateau. Palm trees in the distance. The smell of the sea. He could hear a calliope and high-pitched voices. Kids playing.

Sarah opened one of his eyelids. He blinked. "I just don't know, Vasilevsky. I don't think he's there."

"Give it time. Show him around a little bit. We'll meet you on the terrace in ten minutes."

The nurse clipped a leash through a ring on his collar and tugged him to his feet. "Come along, my pup, how about a little walk? Sound fun?"

"Fun," he said.

"Make a bark for me, will you? Make a woof."

He looked around. Beneath the depthless sky lay an expanse of placid, silver-blue water—a lake, a sea. Children sat at the edge. Some were naked, at least one of them a teenage girl. A bee buzzed past. Further down the strand a colorful merry-go-round was turning.

"Come on, Leon, give me a bark."

"Rrrow-rowff!"

"Good boy." She roughed his hair.

The air was thick and hot. The sand squeaked under his heels. His penis burned in its bandage.

Sarah helped him step up onto a weathered boardwalk and led him to the edge of an expanse of dimpled, bluish water that seemed to reach to the horizon. He waded in to his knees, mingling glances with a few of the other children. A matron in a floppy straw hat sat in a chair nearby, watching a group of four or five smaller boys. They were in up to their waists, swirling the water with their hands. Tranquilized, all of them.

"Hello," Leon said to a dark-haired girl who'd been shyly watching him. She wore gold hoops in her ears. Her crimson smock clung to her rump. "Where do you live?" he whispered. She lowered her eyes and turned away. "What's your name?"

"Come along, Leon." Sarah led him across the beach and into a dense garden of tropical plants, palms, citrus, and broad-leaf trees. He could hear a brook. Plantings of bamboo, bougainvillea, and philodendron defined nooks, each with a few lounge chairs, a painted table, and lanterns on poles.

They came to a raised terrace of sand-swept tiles. In the middle, under an awning of palm fronds, was a long, polished steel counter—a bar with swivel chairs. No one was there. On the far side of the terrace, behind trellised roses, red and pink, was a wall faced in gray marble.

"Now where do you suppose they're at?" Sarah said. She clipped Leon's leash through the arm of a chair. "Back in two shakes."

A shirtless boy wearing a necklace of shells and loose cotton trousers approached him out of the garden. He was carrying a large basket. Tangerines and kumquats, crusty breads and sweet rolls, rounds of cheese, grapes, cherries, dates, and olives. He jiggled his basket. "Cinnamon loaf?"

"No, thank you." He felt half-dizzy with hunger, but he didn't dare. "Who are you?"

He only smiled.

"It's all right. Really, you can talk to me."

The boy looked away. "I'm a cherub."

"What's your name? How long have you been in this place?"

"Those are the wrong questions." The boy raised his basket. "Red grapes?"

"Hey." Leon squatted down to him. "My name's Leon. That man with the ponytail, Yuri—he kidnapped me. How did you get here?"

The boy didn't answer.

"I won't get you in trouble, I promise."

"Here in the grove we've left trouble far behind."

Leon straightened. "Right. I forgot."

The boy drifted off.

Yuri and Sarah came through an arch in the wall, the two of them on either side of the Secretary of the Dominion, Clyde Trumble, a heavy-bellied man wearing a white linen jacket with a gold crest on the pocket. Pink complexion, thin silver hair swept behind the ears.

Leon slouched, tracing an arc in the sand with his toe, back and forth, back and forth.

"Leon Krauss," the Secretary said in a high voice. "I am in need of your honest help. The pagan girl you found at the Augie Bazaar. Her name is Polly. We really must find her. The future security of our Christian homeland depends on it, and that is no exaggeration. I promise you I do not want to hurt her in any way at all, but I'm sure you understand . . . " He trailed off. "Is he even hearing me?"

"He hears you," Sarah said.

"He looks comatose. And he could use a bath. He's eaten the sweet? You're sure?"

"This one has a stubborn metabolism, your Excellency," Yuri said. "Maybe a swim would help."

"He can't take a *swim*," Sarah said. "He's just been trimmed." She bent over Leon and took him by the chin. Her breath was terrible.

"All right, then," the Secretary said, annoyed. "Go get him a supplement. I want him relaxed and voluble. You have thirty minutes."

"Of course, your Excellency. I'll take care of it, don't worry."

Yuri gave Sarah a hard look before turning to follow the Secretary.

"OK. We're going to take a stroll down to the medical station," the nurse said. "They'll have just the thing to perk you up. Come along, pup dog."

She led Leon back into the leafy grove. He kept two steps behind her. On the other side of the garden, the calliope struck up a new tune.

He felt a tug in his chest.

Look up.

Balthazar. His X-shaped shadow gliding just above the palm fronds.

Hello.

How did you get in here?

Kill her.

What?

Kill her.

Kill the nurse?

She keeps you.

You want me to kill *her?*

Yes. Now.

How?

Look. Look at me. Three steps . . . One. Two. Three.

Through a bright opening in the tree canopy, something came spinning toward his head. He arched his back. With his hands at waist level he caught it. The cane knife in its riveted sheath. He tucked it under his left arm, heart hammering.

Why? Why?

You will free yourself.

But they'll shoot me*!*

Trick them. They will send you out!

He understood. He had to act like a maniac. By being one.

If you cannot do it, we will leave you.

"OK, I will! I'll do it!"

Sarah stopped and swung around. "What did you just say?"

"I wasn't speaking to you."

"Dear Jesus! You *have* been faking it! Why, you stinking little *shit*!" She yanked hard on the leash.

He fell to his knees, drew the knife, and came up with it flat and level. He slashed the woman in the throat. One hard swing and the carbon steel sliced right through to her spine, where it stuck. He tugged it free, releasing a rooster tail of blood.

The nurse staggered, goggle-eyed, climbing the air. Leon pulled the leash from her grip before she could drag him down with it.

Her blond head slewed sideways. She buckled and slumped into the foot-high ferns, shuddering.

Leon's legs and feet were covered in blood.

She lay there quivering. He retched and vomited.

He could hear singing and laughter. There was no one near.

Sparrows pecked at the ground in a grotto where a stream trickled past. He wiped the blade against his hip and sheathed it.

"Balthazar?"

The bird was overhead. *Go to them.*

Now?

Give them the knife. Be calm.

Out in the glare again, he joined a group of children watching the carousel.

A chaperone spotted him. "Whoa! Dear God, what's *happened* here?" She hurried to him, her wide-brimmed hat flying off. "Dear God in heaven, child, are you *hurt*?"

He didn't answer.

"What's *wrong*? Did someone . . ."

The children chattered to one another, excited.

Leon offered the long cane knife to the chaperone with both hands. "I have killed the nurse. It had to be done."

Her eyes shifted in horror from his face to the blade and back. "Set that at your feet there, right there in the sand," she demanded, backing away.

He did.

"*Sanctuary violation.* Maxine? *Extreme violation.* Quad six." She paused. "Restraints and—" She paused again. "Oh, dear God, it doesn't *matter*. Whoever's on call! *Now*, Maxine!"

Two officers in blue Security jumpsuits came running toward them on either side of the merry-go-round, now idle.

They threw a net over him, huffing. He smelled their coffee and sweat. The chaperone shooed the others toward the water.

☾

He lay on his back, strapped to a reclining chair, looking up into a high ceiling. He couldn't lift his head.

He coughed. His throat was dry.

"Pastor? He's coming around." The Secretary's high voice.

Footsteps. A bald man with white stubble on his upper lip and chin leaned over him. "State your full name and your age."

"Leon Wilfred Krauss. Sixteen." His tongue felt like a lump of chalk.

The bald man straightened. He wore black robes and a filagreed crucifix, the suffering figure of Jesus tacked on. Behind him were rows of empty chairs banked like stadium seats and a stone statue of a blindfolded angel on a pedestal, a set of golden scales hanging from her outstretched hand.

"Are you with us in Christ, Leon Krauss?"

"*Water.*"

"Tea?"

He nodded. Anything.

The pastor uncapped a bottle and tipped it to his lips. Sweet and cool. "Speak to me from the heart, son. Are you redeemed forever through your faith in Jesus Christ, our Savior, the Son of God?"

He said nothing.

The pastor slapped him across the face and shouted, "*Be gone, evil one!*"

Leon's eyes filled.

"You *shall not remain* in this boy's precious form. *Depart* from him! I command you in the name of Almighty *God, Ruler of the Universe*!"

"Enough of that, Reverend Seymour!" the Secretary piped. "Just get me a name."

The pastor leaned over him again, the big crucifix swinging. "Who put that knife into your hands?"

"A bird."

"Leon—my son. *Who?* Who gave it to you?"

"Balthazar."

"Who's that?"

"A bird. A familiar."

"Dear God," the pastor said. "Let us pray."

"Hold on, Reverend!" the Secretary said. "The *witch* gave it to you? Is that what you're telling us?"

"Let us *pray*," the pastor insisted. He closed his eyes and raised both hands in the air, fingers spread. "Banish his demons, O Lord. Allow this boy to accept the balm of your grace, O Lord, that he may live in the light of truth!" He opened his eyes and clasped his hands under his chin. "Tell us, Leon. We must have the truth. It is your solemn duty before God to *tell* us. *Who gave you the knife?*"

"My father. Before I left the dig."

The pastor straightened. "He's either hexed or his mind is gone. I only pray that God may forgive Yuri Vasilevsky for ushering this demon into our midst. I know I cannot. Vasilevsky must be disciplined. And this murderer must be destroyed."

After a moment the Secretary said, "With Jesus all things are possible, reverend. Isn't that so?"

"Of course."

"Then there is a chance the boy may be saved?"

"A slight chance . . . yes."

"Then send him down! He is not to be harmed. He's our link to the witch. The knife proves it."

"That may be so, sir, but I will *remind* you that, by law, whenever *anyone* commits such a *horrible—*"

"I need no reminders! I've made my decision!"

"Yes, your Excellency. Conditions?"

"Solitude. Basic nourishment. No anodynes or sedatives."

20

AT DUSK Polly climbed out of the cart and cast a circle in the half light. She would cone the cart for the night if Balthazar did not return. She sat on the ground just outside the shed, watching the stars appear, listening to wagon traffic, pigs, roosting pigeons, a choir rehearsing in the distance.

Before long, Balthazar swooped in past her, landing on top of the Nomad's bug-splotched windscreen above the pilot console. She could just make him out.

Come with me.

"Where are we going?"

The tower.

"Then what?"

He comes. We follow.

"You spoke with him?"

He is changed.

"Mentally? Or physically?" But the raven would not make that distinction.

"Wait," he said. Judge for yourself, he meant.

"You're a pain."

Pain is necessary.

"Thanks."

Take all you can use. Walk to the pools.

"What pools?"

*Before the tower. Be quick.*He hopped into the air.

Polly stuffed the pack with supplies and set off past dark stables, warehouses, a rank hog pen, a noisy slaughterhouse, following the trolley tracks up the grade until the great plaza lay before her. Lights sparkled. People were strolling along the central avenue. Between the capitol's twin trapezoidal buildings, the Crozier, a cylinder of lit and unlit windows, stood tall against the blackness. Its distant dome glowed like a moon.

The capitol courtyard's topiary gardens and shallow reflecting pools were golden under arc lights, the air still and heavy. She sat on a stone bench to wait.

Balthazar descended into a nearby dogwood.

He is out.

"*Where?*"

In a wagon. On a road.

"Who's with him?"

Three men.

"What should we do?"

Stop them. Use the gun.

"You want me to *shoot* the men?"

Surprise them. If you can.

"Right." She called the quarters, applied her ointment, and spoke the spell. The charge came on fast. Her heart raced.

Balthazar steered her out over the lower city just above the rooftops until they reached the main highway north toward the mountains, where the depopulated wasteland began.

Look there.

A coach with a four-horse team rolled along a quiet boulevard, its roof brightening and dimming as it passed beneath the street lamps. The two coachmen were hidden by the awning, but she could see their boots on the dash rail.

She veered in. It was a transport coach like the one she'd seen here two days ago. Georgia Department of Corrections.

They were headed toward the prison. "*Para el insano y poseidos.*" For the insane and the possessed.

Polly zoomed on ahead, looking for that steel-grid bridge over the drainage ravine where she'd hidden herself before.

There it was. She came down at the end of the span. Circling not far above, Balthazar watched her. She shrugged off her pack and took out the handgun. "How much time have we got?"

He arrowed away.

De-integration, the spell she'd used on Leon's Tracelet, would do. She cast a circle bank to bank and asked that her craftwork be confined to the portions of the span she would rub with her hands.

Here. And here.

B returned. *They come. Fifty breaths.*

She crouched in the kudzu, handgun on her knee. On the high road the coach's running lights flickered against the dull wash of light from the plaza. She listened to the wheels and the hooves of the team until the rig angled down off the high road toward the crossing.

She waited for the lead pair to reach the opposite side. "*Nu. Feran.*"

The heavy carriage's back wheels plunged through the mushy steel. It slammed down onto its rear axle and springs.

"*Geendian.*" The deck was solid again.

The horses reared in their traces, screaming.

The coach driver swore in bewilderment. He swung

around in his seat to gape at the trapped rear wheels, the hazard lights pulsing in his eyeglasses. The horses blew and stamped.

"*Whoa*, girls, *whoa*!" The teamster was on the bridge deck, trying to grab hold of the lead pair's singletree.

The coach's windowless side door slid open. A man in blue uniform leaned out, backlit against the glow from inside. "What in blazes is going on? Benny! What is this? What's happened here?" He wore the CPA's cross-and-sword on his sleeve.

The coachman inspected the rear of the carriage with a heavy flashlight. He kicked one of the sunken wheels. "Goddamn rot, got to be. Damn lucky none of us got *killed*."

"And that's how we want to keep it," Polly said. She stepped into the road, the revolver in both hands. "Back away, both of you. Now. That way."

Neither one moved. The uniformed man hopped down out of the carriage and crossed his arms. "We have no *money*, you idiot! This is a *prison* coach. Crawl back under your rock!"

KA-BOOM. Polly sent a slug clanging into the steel deck a foot from the man's toes. He yelped and stumbled against the side of the coach. The horses reared and snorted.

"Next one's in your gut, count on it. *Go!*" she shouted. "*Now!*"

"Don't shoot!" the coachman said. "Please!"

The two men edged back toward the traces. The teamster peeked at her around the animals.

She gestured with the gun barrel. "Keep moving!"

Leon appeared in the coach's open door. "Polly!"

"Jump down, Leon. Do you need a hand?"

"No, I can make it." But he had to sit on the doorsill to ease himself down onto the bridge deck.

A black bolt flashed past her.

The coachman shrieked. Balthazar ripped off his eyeglasses. His chromed pistol clattered on the steel.

"Run, Leon! Run toward the city. I'll be along behind you."

He took off. He was drugged, she thought. Drugged or in pain. And he was barefoot.

"Anyone who tries to catch us will be shot," she declared. "Let us be."

"You're making the mistake of your life!" the uniformed man shouted. "That boy's *mad*! He's a murdering psychopath!"

She caught up with Leon. He was just shuffling along. "What's wrong with you?"

He stopped to catch his breath. "Where are we going?"

"What *happened* to you?" He had dried blood on his legs and feet.

"I'm going to need shoes."

"We'll find you some shoes." She took him by the hand. "Leon. Tell me what happened. Are you badly hurt?"

"How far do we have to go?"

"To the falls." Probably 40 miles, she thought. With a lot of settled territory to negotiate in between. Without the cart.

"I'm pretty weak. Do you have anything to eat?"

Polly paused to listen. Distant traffic, nothing else. She found him some of Tina's jerky.

He tore off big bites.

"What did they do to you, Leon?"

"This." He lifted the hem of his shift above his hips.

She winced. "Does it hurt?"

"Not anymore. Not too much."

"Why did they do it?"

"For looks."

"*Looks?*"

"It's *horrible*, Polly. They keep all these little kids up there, like—Like in this amusement park. But it's not for fun. It's for sex. With men."

"Great Mother. Did they . . . do anything to you?"

He shook his head.

"How did you get out?"

"I—I killed someone."

She caught her breath. "Who?"

"A nurse. I cut her head off."

The cane knife. "So that was Balthazar's idea?"

"Yeah. He said I had to trick them."

"That's some trick."

He nodded. After a moment, his face softened, and he said, "You know what? You're looking very comfortable with that old wheelgun all of a sudden."

She threw her arms around his neck. "It's so good to have you back, Leon."

☾

The sky cleared. They pushed to the north, jogging along over the crumbly pavement, then walking, until Leon had to stop.

"I can't," he said.

Balthazar was somewhere behind them, watching for their pursuers. They had a little time, Polly thought.

"You sit here and gather yourself," she said. "I'll go scout up a good place for us to cross the highway. I won't be long." She put on her cap. It seemed prudent to use the Dispersal while the charge still held. "If B comes back before I do, just do whatever he says. Don't worry—I'll find you."

"Wait. Polly. Before you take off, I've been thinking about this. And—" He compressed his lips. "I don't think I should go."

"Go where?"

"To the Regions. With you."

Her heart went cold. "Why not?"

"They arrested Malcolm."

"Who did? How do you know?"

"Justice. Yuri told me."

"For *what?*"

"Because we helped you get away. You belong to the Secretary, and he's dead set on getting you back, whatever it takes."

"I don't *belong* to *anybody!*"

"I *know* that. I didn't say it was *right.*"

"Oh, Leon. If they truly put your father in jail, that's a terrible thing. But I can't help him. You have to understand. Neither can you!"

"It doesn't seem like I can help anybody, does it?"

"You've been helping me."

"No, I haven't. I've been holding you back. You know I have."

She took him by the arms. "I need you, Leon, and I want you to come with me. You sit here and think about it a little longer. I'll be back."

Polly tucked in her chin and rose into the night.

21

THE HIGHWAY PETERED OUT after a few miles, fraying into bumpier roads and pathways that went winding on through sparse farming communities, then into woodsy uplands that reached northeast to the mountains. If they could manage to get this far before sunrise, they'd be a lot harder to find.

She circled back to where she'd left Leon, but before she touched down she realized that he was talking to someone.

She came to ground farther along the roadway, gently set her pack down, and drew the revolver.

Whooh, whooh whooh. Balthazar. Flying off.

B! Wait!"B!"

Leon spun around. "Polly! Balthazar says we better get moving. They have dogs."

Balthazar says. She lowered herself to the pavement, stunned by something she should have grasped days ago. Leon had the gift. That was the reason Balthazar had singled him out at the Augie Bazaar. "Leon, tell me something. Was there ever talk of witches in your family? Like in past generations?"

"Never. Why?"

She looked at him.

He understood. "You're not saying *I'm* a witch. Are you?"

"I think you are, Leon. A blood witch."

His mouth dropped open. "A blood witch. What's a blood witch?"

"Just that—a witch by blood. 'A witch unawares,' it's called. It means you have *qualities*, but no knowledge. No craft."

"So are you saying that being a witch is *genetic*?"

"It's actually not all that unusual. But most blood witches live their whole lives without ever realizing they have the gift."

A small plane buzzed over. Leon looked up. "Better get moving, Polly. They're coming."

"You mean you're coming with me?"

He nodded.

"What about Malcolm?"

"Balthazar says Yuri was lying to me. He wanted to trick me into giving you up."

"Well, well. What else is he telling you?"

"He says we need each other, you and I. He says there's a lot that I can learn from you."

She wasn't sure what to make of this. She could teach him the rudiments of the craft. She liked the idea, in fact. But not now. Not on the run like this. "Leon, I don't know if Balthazar can appreciate—"

"Hush!" He rose. "Feel that?"

She listened. Insects. A helicopter in the distance. "What is it?"

"Wait." He held up a hand.

"Leon—" Now she felt it. A tightness in her chest. The corrupted bear. "Do you see her?"

"She's stopped. She knows we're onto her."

Balthazar! Where was he?

"God," Leon whispered, "the poor animal's all in knots!"

"She-bear!" Polly called out. "Show yourself! I demand it!"

With a chesty rumble, the bear emerged from the jungle growth ten yards from where they stood.

Polly stepped back, leveling the gun. "Stop right there."

She looked thin and disheveled. Her anguish was plain.

"One last chance, bear. Do I try to cast a counter spell? Or do I shoot you?"

Leon looked at her. "Are you sure you can undo the other witch's magick?"

"No, actually, but I can't even try unless she asks me to." She stamped her foot at the bear. "What do you want to do?"

"*Try,*" the bear groaned, arching her neck. She shambled up onto the pavement.

"So be it. But you stay *back* now! Do you hear?"

The bear eased back onto her haunches.

Polly handed the gun to Leon. "If she makes a move for me, shoot her in the head. Don't hesitate."

"Got it."

She knew two nullifying and countering spells, both marked in the book with a silk cord. She had not cast either one except in practice, but they were not difficult as long as you could match them well to whatever magick you wanted to counter. They were seldom needed, but they could be helpful if a release should fail for some reason—your own or another witch's. She lifted the grimoire out of the pack and unfolded its goatskin wrapper. She looked up as the bear edged a little closer to her.

"Stay where you are, hear me?"

The bear sat back. She was feverishly anxious, Polly could feel it.

Polly turned the clasp wheel in its silver socket from

one symbol to another, right to left to right. *Mithras, Crescent, Quincunx, Pillar, Cube.* The book felt warm in her hands. That seemed odd.

Here. *Toberstan.* A note in the margin, her grandmother's, read, "also a remedy for directed spells of malice or torment." So, perfect. She left the grimoire open on the ground and got up to sweep a large circle. She'd have to invite the bear into the circle, of course. Allowing her so close would be chancy, even in a protected—

Watch! Watch! Balthazar.

The triquetra hissed against her skin. She whirled around. *What?*

The bear dropped to all fours and charged.

Polly bolted across the road. "Leon!"

He raised the gun.

The bear stopped, twisted her head to the side, and roared. She stooped down. She clapped the book shut and lumbered off with it, wrapper and all, into the kudzu.

"*Shoot, Leon! Shoot!*"

The bear was gone, her footfall shaking the ground.

"Great *Mother*, Leon! Why didn't you *shoot*?"

"*Because!* All she wanted was the book!"

"Oh, Leon!"

"I'm sorry!"

"Give me the gun. She won't get far on that bad hip."

He released the cylinder and handed it over. "You're going after her?"

"I have to. Don't wait here. Wait for me at the falls. Follow the highway till it ends. Let Balthazar guide you after that."

"I'm really *sorry*, but you said shoot if she came for *you*, not the book."

"I know. It's not your fault. Just follow Balthazar, OK? Do what he tells you to do."

Stay with him, B. Keep him safe.

☾

The bear's thrashing path through the green growth was plain even in the dark. She was moving fast in spite of her injury, trundling her hard-won prize back to wherever she had been commanded to take it.

Polly's charge had faded away in all the turmoil. She could only lope along, pausing now and then to listen in case the bear might try to circle around behind her. Though that seemed unlikely. She had what she was after.

After a time, exhausted, Polly slowed to a walk. The night wore on.

Her chase ended just before sunrise. She could smell the bear before she came upon her, curled up on her side in a bowl of crushed kudzu.

Polly leveled the gun at her head. "Surrender or be killed!"

The bear was already dead.

Polly prodded her thigh with her toe. The stench of singed fur stung her nostrils. With both hands, she grasped a fat, hard forepaw and rolled the bear onto her back. A patch of blood-speckled hide showed where she'd had the big book pressed to her chest. No use kicking through the surrounding vegetation looking for it, though she did.

Only death will stop her. Balthazar understood, right from the beginning. This spellbound familiar was as good as dead the moment Theldred crushed her will. If Polly did not kill her, the book would.

A few miles to the south, towering above all the world, the Crozier's milky crown shone like a lighthouse in the first rays of the sun. She could hear motor traffic. Cows. A rooster.

She bowed her head. "Sister of the Braid, whose name

I don't know, may the Great Mother welcome your spirit. Your trials are over. I will do all I can to avenge the abuse you've suffered and to right the wrong you were forced to do."

She dried her eyes, swept a circle with the backs of her hands, and raised her palms to the quarters, entreating the elements to protect her while she slept. That was the best she could do.

She lay down beside the ripe body of the bear and closed her burning eyes.

FOUR

22

A YEAR EARLIER, Polly and Aran and Tessa and Ophine, the two oldest in their far-flung coven, made the long, somber journey by carriage east through the Region's greening hills, up across the craggy Whites, and on over miry forest roads to Bangor for the last Great Gathering of the Old League. Lil and her familiar, Fainstock, had flown ahead.

Polly's life, the only life she knew, was coming to an end. All the same, at home little had changed. She'd swept the tent platforms, cleaned the bathhouse, and rolled the eight courts, all on her own, as she did every May. In a week's time the kids would begin arriving, mostly by private coach, for Session One, an invasion she dreaded. The last few summers she had kept herself apart from the campers as much as possible, the older ones especially. Rich kids from the cities. They were interested only in one another, anyway. They thought of Polly as a rustic and a soulless pagan. Which she was.

Everywhere else, in the villages and across the countryside, the people were in turmoil. No one knew how harsh the purge would be. Would ReBirthing facilities be set up locally for those who chose to stay? Or would everyone be driven out? Why was it necessary in the first place? A purge of the northeast Regions? From the lake to the sea? Did they need the land? The resources? Hardly. Were the people making trouble? Not at all. Aran told her that the reasons were fundamental—greed, fear, and hatred—but that Polly couldn't comprehend. How did those feelings arise? Why couldn't they be overcome? What about the virtues—kindness, compassion, and love? Why couldn't *they* prevail? Where did Christian morality come in? The great, lasting mystery of human nature, Aran said, was where the balance would fall. Compassion or fear. Kindness or hatred. In each one of us. And as clear as it seemed the answer ought to be, far too often it was not clear at all.

Polly closed her book and looked out at the rainy woods. The carriage jounced slowly along.

"Dad?"

He turned to her, bleary-eyed.

"Yesterday when I asked Mom if she thought the League was finished, she said she felt sure it was. But that's not what you think, because if you did, then we wouldn't be making this trip, would we?"

Seated on the bench opposite, Ophine and Tessa pretended not to listen. Tessa's white curls shone against the leather bench-back. Dour Ophine, her arms crossed, gazed off into the drizzle. Her familiar, a calico, slept in her lap. In the footwell, Ilsa pricked up her small ears, alert to Aran's voice.

"The League is divided, that's clear enough," Aran said. "Whether it will fall apart we won't know until the Council stands to vote. Hearts may be swayed in the emotion of the moment."

"I know, but— If the Council does vote to leave, and if Mom sticks with Vincent, we'll still be staying, won't we? We're not going to pack up all our stuff and run north."

Before he could answer, Ophine straightened her shoulders and said, "If we cannot resolve to make a stand together, whether we run or stay won't matter. It will be just a matter of time before we're all hounded off the face of the earth. When that happens, not only will the League be finished, but the craft will be finished as well."

☾

The spring roads through the mountains were bad in many places. By the time they arrived at the meeting grounds it was after dark. All of the Core Council members but Aran had spoken, and the Gathering would have adjourned for the feast if one of the sentries, a swift-flying nightjar attached to Glynnis the Gray, hadn't informed the Council that Aran's carriage had reached the valley.

The torch-lit hall brimmed with talk. Someone was playing a flute. All the Old League, witches young and aged, frail and hearty, commanding and small-minded, haggish and lovely, shy and vital, were here. A thousand familiars made a colorful but confusing zoo of the grounds. What disturbed Polly the most was the way the Braid, like a web of nerves, pulled at you from every direction. It was overwhelming. Ever since her cusp ritual, the year she turned 12, Polly had never really liked a Great Gathering. Lil assured her that she would learn to enjoy the atmosphere of these assemblies, but it might take some time. She stood far in the back where the fresh breeze passing through the wide-open doors soothed her senses.

The long day in that cramped carriage had not sapped her father. The hall's clamor subsided. Witches found their seats. Polly watched Aran make his easy way down the center aisle, mace loosely in hand, pausing to embrace an old friend or greet a child he hadn't met. Ilsa followed at his heels. On the dais, the 11 high witches of the Council had risen from their chairs. A giant red pentangle swayed above them in the smoky light.

Polly had met the Core Council two years before when

they'd convened at the farm in Upper Duxton for Imbolc. Besides the Council head, Miles Sauveur, she recognized Glynnis, of the Lakeland covens, Nyx, the oldest, of the Ocean Islands, Nyx's onetime partner, Enoch, of the West Woodlands, and red-bearded Vincent, of the Marshland group. Her own mother, still in her silver-blue sky suit, stood next to Vincent.

Aran stepped to the dais. He bowed to the others before taking the rostrum.

Miles struck the great bell three times with the knob of his staff. "Before us comes Lord Aran Lightfoot, First Mage of the Granite Hills! The Core Council is complete!"

Aran waited for quiet.

"Merry meet, one and all. First, let me thank you all for waiting to hear me speak before calling the vote." He surveyed the assembly. "I regret that I have missed the words of my fellow mages on the council, and yet I am sure you have—"

"You're too late, Lord Aran!" someone shouted. A warlock down in front, half-drunk, Polly thought.

Aran turned to him. "I may be too late, that's true. If I am speaking before this grand assembly for the last time, then so be it. But I *will* speak. Will you hear me?"

"You're wasting your breath!" the warlock shouted.

"Quiet!" someone scolded.

There was some encouraging applause.

Miles thumped the floor with his staff. "Lord Aran will be heard!"

Aran looked around. "If you have already resolved in your hearts to leave these lands for the far north, then I'm too late, but before the vote is taken, allow me to offer a brighter, braver vision for the hard times ahead. In league, altogether, we are two thousand strong. We—"

"Lord Aran . . . " Vincent McRoy rose from his high-backed chair.

Her father turned to him.

"Two thousand witches against fifty thousand Home Guard troops. That is no 'brighter vision,' Lord Aran. That's suicide."

"Run to the north and what will you gain?" Aran asked. "A few years. Ten at the most. These deranged fools will not rest until the entire continent is purged! Fear fuels their hate, and that fear will *never* be extinguished."

"Lord Aran. You must agree that a later death is better than an sooner one." Vincent, in his 30s, was the new First Mage of the far-flung Marshland covens and the youngest council member, though his Caledonian bloodline dated to the age of the Picts. He was brash and copper-haired, with a musical lilt to his voice. Watching him, Polly could understand why her mother had fallen for him as she had, never mind how much it saddened her. "If you want the League to survive, come with us to the north. There will be many hardships. We will need you."

"And I will need you *here*! You and Lil! And Nyx and Miles and Glynnis the Gray! And Enoch and Erda, Mina and Letitia, Devin and Ariadne!" He turned to the hall. "And Sybil and Keely, Willis and Fioon, Willow-wand, Rowena, Moss, Patrick, Cysley, Elspet and Violet, Serepta and Zeb, and all of your covenmates. As well as all the familiars who rightly respect you. Stay! Stay with me. All of us, *all* of us together, hundreds strong, can cast such a pall of threat over the Regions that no settler will bear it for long. These Christians are moved by their *fears*! We know this! And it is their fears, as long as we can keep them stoked, that will drive them out. *This great thing can be achieved*, I promise you. But it will take every one of us. All of us. *All! Standing and fighting together.*"

Aran's passion was reflected in many of the faces Polly could see. She felt it, too. The hall was quiet. Avian familiars stirred in the rafters. Watching the witches' glances, for just a moment she let herself think Aran was going to win them over. How wonderful that would be!

Down in front a young witch with gold cords entwined in his long hair rose to speak. "Lord Aran! I am Corwin of the Ocean Islands. What you say makes hard sense. Our ancestors are buried here. We have taken our nourishment from this soil, built our homes from the wood of these forests. Our blood and bone belong to these lands. And yet . . . the forces of the government—"

"*Enough!*" Nyx. Her raspy voice. "Enough of this wheedling tripe. We have heard Lord Aran. We all know how we feel. I call the council vote!"

Lil rose and pushed her mace overhead, her silver arm catching the light. "I will second. The Surety of Nine is not in doubt, and so there's no cause to prolong these proceedings. Miles?"

The Core Council of 12 consisted of three committed couples, three unattached men, and three unattached women. As co-leaders of the Granite Hills covens, Lil and Aran had been council members since before Polly was born. By tradition, nine Council members voting in agreement were necessary to secure the following of the Old League, 172 covens altogether.

Aran moved to his tall oak chair. The bell rang out twice.

Miles addressed the council. "With the consent of the hall, the vote is called. The resolution reads: 'In view of the grave threats to the peace, community, and livelihood of its members posed by the adoption into law of the Faith and Redemption Amendment, the Old League resolves to depart these regions for refuge in the far north by summer's end.' All in favor will stand. Those opposed will sit or stay seated."

Aran sat. So did Glynnis the Gray and fierce Mina of the broken covens to the south. The other council members stood, holding their maces high.

"With nine votes in its favor, the resolution is adopted. There being no further business, this meeting, the three hundred thirty-eighth Great Gathering of the Old League, stands adjourned."

Cheers and clapping rolled through the hall. Aran leaned down to say something to Ilsa. Lil turned and kissed Vincent through his coppery beard

☾

At home, once camp was in session, the daytime routines seemed almost ordinary. Her father supervised the counselors, managed lessons and ladders, and arranged evening activities for the campers. Polly avoided all of that except for a few times when Aran asked her to drill with one of the better players. When she wasn't studying and practicing, she worked in the garden or helped Harriet, the cook, in the kitchen. She had Lil's goats to look after now, too. The lonely nights were the worst. Not only did she miss Lil terribly, but after lights-out Aran usually left the farm to fly to one distant covenstead or another. Organizing the resistance.

Nearly a hundred witches had broken with the rest of the League on that somber day in May—the Stubborn Few, they called themselves. They had pledged to stay to fight the purge however they could, using a network of threat and physical disruption—spells they would have to cast, hone, and maintain for however long it took to confound the resettlement.

The summer wore on with no word from her mother.

Lil could have sent her familiar with a message any time, of course. But there was no message, which was a message in itself. The morning after the Gathering, on a sunny bluff above the Penobscot, Lil told Polly she didn't know when they might see each other again, but until that day Polly should never doubt her love for her.

"Then how can you leave me?" Polly said.

"Polly, sweetheart, I am honoring your decision to stay with Aran. In the same spirit, I ask you to honor my decision to leave. I have a duty to you as my daughter and only child, but I have a greater duty to the future of the League and the survival of the craft."

"But if *you* stayed, Vincent would stay. And if *he* stayed the others would, too."

She took Polly's face in her hands and kissed her. "Let's not argue. Here, I have something to give you." It was the triquetra, a thick disk of amber framed in gold on a fine gold chain. Polly had never seen anything more beautiful.

Lil opened the double clasp and fastened it around Polly's neck. "This talisman is charged for your quickness, endurance, and alertness to danger. Always keep it with you."

By September, after the last of the campers had packed their footlockers and headed back to the Dominions for the last time, as the hardwood hills turned orange and gold, Polly's anger and trepidation deepened. In the village, nearly all the houses and shops were empty. The mills, lumberyards, and stables were quiet. The ungrazed pastures were lush, the apple trees and berry patches heavy with fruit. All day caravans of refugees rolled north and east along the highways, raising dust. Polly kept herself busy. But why was she canning tomatoes and making cider when, come January, they would only have to flee to the mountains? Still, what *should* she be doing?

Although Aran said little about how the resistance was shaping up, it was not going well, she gathered. The witches had built shelters in the mountains and put up stores of food, water, and other necessities, but the struggle ahead looked increasingly difficult and uncertain. What's more, everyone was sad, and the sadness corroded their hopes. As the autumn days grew short, the Stubborn Few had grown fewer. Even Aran's close friend Milo, who had farmed the flat lands near the old northerly border with his mother, Bertine, had deserted the cause. For his ailing mother's sake. Aran understood, though Polly could not. It was so wrenching to watch her father's confidence ebb as so many of the once-committed fighters lost heart, made their excuses, and melted away. As, in the end, even Polly herself would do.

But here was the main thing. It wasn't just for her safety that Aran sent her into hiding in Orlando. He had another reason. "A mission," he called it.

"What mission?"

"I want you to take the grimoire. For safe-keeping."

"I can't do that. You'll need it, won't you?"

"We'll have Glynnis's. Besides, our challenge will be more practical than magickal, I'm sure." He meant whether so small a band of witches could weave a web of dire hindrance over so much territory—from the lake to the mountains—and then maintain it indefinitely.

"What if— What if it's too much for you, and you have to leave?"

"If worst comes to worst, I'll leave a pilot taper for you. How's that?"

Polly had never seen one, but she knew what a pilot taper was. It was a large candle—a candle charged to guide its possessor to a certain, specific place. "Shouldn't I take that with me, too?"

He shook his head. He had no plan yet for leaving. "I'll leave it for you down in the ice chest. Don't worry, I won't forget." The ice chest was a thick-walled, slate-lined cabinet down in the basement where they kept family documents to protect them from fire.

"All right . . . " She drew a ragged breath, then crumpled against him in tears.

Here, then, was the source of Polly's deep misery as she sat in the kudzu beside the corpse of the corrupted bear. The grimoire was gone, the grimoire her father had entrusted to her keeping, the grimoire she had been carrying home to him because now, somehow, he needed it. As a maiden witch, a rising Adept, a sworn defender of the craft, Polly had been given one grave and critical responsibility. And she had failed.

She had failed.

23

IN THE FIRST LIGHT of day, from the pine hedgerow he'd been following since the highway ended, Leon spotted a row of domed hayricks out in a misty, cutover field. It looked perfect, but the stubble under his bare feet was almost too painful to negotiate, and burrowing part way in under the prickly hay was worse.

He dozed only a short while before he realized that the ripening hayrick was generating its own awful heat. His head ached. Still, with his face pushed out into the air, he managed to sleep off and on, covered in sweat, until Balthazar woke him.

Come out.

He crawled free, lips cracked and swollen, eyes raw. He was half sick.Beyond a stand of trees at the far edge of the field, a few flat-roofed buildings stood against low, distant hills. Nothing else.

The raven came around the hayrick nudging a bruised peach over the ground with his beak.

"Where did you get this?" He sucked the thick juice out of each mouthful before swallowing the pulp, then rubbed the peach pit over the rash on his arms and shoulders. "Do you know where Polly is?"

The raven cocked his head, hopped into the air, and flapped off toward the hedgerow. *Follow.*

They moved north. Leon glimpsed Balthazar now and then through openings in the tree canopy, the strength of their connection fading and swelling and fading again. After a time, they came to a hog pen behind a sturdy plank-and-wire fence. The wallow held dozens of rooting animals, pink and gray and white and black. Many small, tarpaper-covered A-frames provided shelter from the sun and rain. A metal trough set on cinderblocks along the ground channeled a stream of brown water down the middle of the pen.

Follow.

The raven coasted like a gull a foot above the mire. The hogs paid no attention.

Leon vaulted over the top rail. The stench made his eyes water. A few pigs grunted at him, wondering if he'd brought anything to eat. He didn't doubt they'd be happy to eat him if he wasn't careful.

Balthazar perched on a gate post on the far side. *Choose one.*

Leon looked around. *You mean these huts?*

Give me your robe.

"I can't! I have nothing else!"

Choose one. Give me your robe.

He peered into one of the shelters. The dirt was dry. He crawled in, pulled the shift over his head, and tossed it out into the sunlight. Balthazar flew off with it.

Clay and manure coated his legs like plaster. Flies nuzzled his eyes and ears. The shelter was open at both ends, but the breeze passing through brought no relief from the heat and the insects.At one point he heard a wagon's rhythmically creaking wheels and men talking in the distance.

Later on, a police helicopter passed low overhead, following the hedgerow, then a second one, and then horses' hooves and baying hounds. They passed by just 20 or 30 yards off, following the twisting trail among the trees. The agitated pigs snorted and squealed.

A mockingbird in the hedgerow sang the same phrases over and over. The hours passed. He dozed and woke, dozed and woke.

Balthazar returned after the hogs had gathered at the far end of the pen to eat whatever a farmhand had come to shovel into their fan-shaped feed trays. He didn't light but dropped the bundle he'd been carrying with his feet. A pair of blue jeans, stiff from someone's clothesline. A minute later he was back with a black ankle-top sneaker. And then with its mate. In the second shoe Leon found a small jar of Wei-Fang Shandong roasted red peppers.

He laughed. *Where did these come from?*

Eat. The preening raven glinted rose and blue in the sun.

"You used my shirt to trick those bloodhounds."

Eat.

Did you eat?

"Eat," Balthazar said.

The peppers were spicy, delicious.

☾

The raven led him down crumbling byways and alleys bounded by rubbish and debris. Along the way he found a railroad spike for a club, a burlap carryall with some rotten onions inside, a large wool CPA flag, and a length of electrical cord he put to use as a belt. Dogs barked at him, but no one he passed in the road gave him more than a glance. At one point he exchanged wary nods with a group of tough-looking boys hanging out behind a diner. Later, after the lights thinned out, he saw no more people.

At dawn Balthazar guided him into a field of ripening strawberries in long, neat rows. *Eat only a little.*

But they were too good. He stuffed them into his mouth by the juicy handful, then loaded his carryall.

The sky grayed. In a fine drizzle he followed the raven to the mossy banks of a brook just beneath a steep, forested hillside. He bathed there and drank. And puked up the strawberries.

All that day he traveled through the wooded hills, slowed by brambles and blowdowns and a number of water-filled quarries. Once, Balthazar brought him a piece of barbecued chicken warm from the grill. He sipped some of the water he'd saved in the red pepper jar and napped on a patch of mossy ground with the blue, white, and gold CPA flag for a blanket.

☾

Skirting the towns and settled vales, he followed woodsy paths and logging lanes toward the bluish-gray mountains that he could glimpse now and then from open heights of land. By late in the evening, stumbling up a stony defile, he realized that the steady noise in his ears wasn't the wind but the rush of water. The falls!

"Balthazar? Is Polly here?"

But the raven had gone.

Before dark he found a small, needle-carpeted clearing in a stand of pine and hemlock. He sat and rested, trying to ignore his hunger and bone-deep pains, lulled by the tumult of the falls. He drank the rest of his water. The raven did not come back.

In the last light he scraped together a cushion of pine needles and managed to nod off for an hour or two at a time. His dreams were wrenching. In one dream he still had the cart, but there was something wrong with it—he couldn't get it out of shutdown. In another one he was at the dig, but nobody else was there. The bunkers were empty, the gardens covered in sand, and out beyond the dunes the surf had receded a mile or more.

24

THROUGH MOST OF THE NEXT DAY Polly stayed put beside the dead bear, waiting for Balthazar to come for her. She had no urge to set off on her own, nor any clear idea of where to set off to. So why move? At last, at dusk, he angled in, swooped up, and landed on the bear's dusty, fly-blown leg. He jabbed at the oblong patch of singed hide at her middle.

"It was the book all along," Polly said.

Cunning.

"I should have shot her back in the green belt. You were right."

The book is frozen.

"I know. I'm not even sure I could open it now. That stupid witch destroyed her familiar for *nothing*."

But Balthazar did not agree. Theldred had managed to acquire just what she'd been after.

"How is Leon?"

He waits. At the falls.

"That's wonderful, Balthazar. Thank you."

He is discouraged.

"He isn't to blame for losing the book. That's completely my fault."

The raven hopped to the ground. *Fly?*

"I'm ready."

☾

The flashing, dancing falls were lovely in the starlight. Everything else looked forlorn and abandoned. All this used to be park land, Malcolm had told them, a place where people came for a break from city life. Nature trails, cabins, tours and exhibits, activities for children. A lodge with two restaurants, a gift shop, and a theater. Spectacular mountain views all around. And the noisy splendor of the falls. All that was gone, except for a big swimming pool filled with trash, and the views, and the falls.

Polly banked in at the far end of a lot overgrown with brush and came to ground near a shanty someone had built long ago, from scrap. The stovepipe chimney had fallen, and the door was cockeyed, hanging from a single leather hinge. She sat on a splitting block next to a heap of punky firewood, peeled off her hat and goggles, and shook out her hair.She hadn't bathed since Candy's. How long ago was that?

From her sewing box she took a few leaves of the parchment she used for wrapping dried herbs, and with the flashlight clamped under her arm, she copied the six basic spells she had committed to memory just to make sure she wouldn't forget them. After that she lay back and watched the stars.

☾

Awake.

"Balthazar."She sat up, muzzy-headed.

Come. Now.

"What's wrong?"

Men.

"Where? Here?"

Not yet. Soon.

"Where's Leon?"

Come. Follow.

"All right. Give me a minute." She drank some water. "I smell rain."

It comes.

"We can't fly off now and leave Leon behind. You know that."

Teach him.

Polly searched for the raven in the dim light but couldn't pick him out. "Teach him to *fly*? Is that what you mean?"

He can learn.

"You mean teach a blood witch the trickiest transformational spell there is? So the three of us can take to the sky? *That's* your plan?"

Or hide.

"Hide? Hide where?"

Underground.

"Forget it. How much time do we have?"

Quarter sun. Less.

Under three hours. "Are there a lot of them?"

On the roads and in the sky.

She packed her flying gear and placed the revolver on top where she could get to it quickly. *I'm ready.*

Follow.

He glided above a littered roadway toward the rumpled canopy of the forest.

She found Leon asleep, slumped against the root of a great pine tree with the country's flag, of all things, draped over his shoulders. He flung an arm at her when she shook him.

"Leon! We have to move! They're coming!" She gave him a water bottle.

"Did you get it back? The book?"

"No, I didn't. It's a terrible loss, but there's nothing to do now except keep moving. Come on, get up."

He pushed to his feet, wincing. "If we have to run, I'll tell you right now I won't last long."

"Running's not going to do it. Balthazar wants me to teach you how to use the Dispersal."

He gaped at her. "You mean to fly? Do you think I can?"

"I really don't know, but Balthazar thinks so." She took him by the shoulders. "Listen. Dispersal— Is very dangerous."

"You told me."

"Even skilled witches don't fly very much."

"What makes it so dangerous?"

"It takes a lot of concentration and practice to focus the charge on your Dispersal. And if you start to panic, it's over."

"But then can't you just land?"

"Yeah. Like a sack of rocks."

He was nodding, but she knew he didn't understand.

"OK, I need you to promise you'll pay close attention to me and do whatever I say. Promise?"

"I promise."

With a pine bough she swept a quick circle on the root-laced floor of the forest. While she worked, he asked her what to expect when the charge took hold. How did it feel to leave the ground?

"It's hard to describe," she said. "At first you feel almost numb. Then you feel sort of fiery feeling at your center. But watery at the same time—loose. And extra alert. You'll see."

She called the quarters. "Spirit forces, render the place herein a place apart, the locus of our lifting energy and dispersal. Let nothing untoward intrude."

"Step in close, Leon."

She drew him by the hand into her circle.

She opened the tin of ointment. "A little's all you need."

Polly took her own and closed the tin.

"Spread it in a smooth line from . . . from your balls slowly up your belly to the hollow at your throat."

They turned back to back.

"That's *wild*," he said.

"No idle words. I'm going to speak eleven phrases one at a time. You have to pronounce each phrase exactly as I do. Don't stumble. Got it?"

He nodded.

A helicopter, just to the west of them. Then another.

As Polly pronounced the spell, she listened, phrase by phrase, to the firm echo of her voice in his.

The spell took hold. Leon rose right beside her, wide-eyed.

She let go of his hand.

"*Slow, now.* Slow, slow, slow. We're going to hang still just under the treetops till we can see what's what. Do you understand me?" Branches slapped at their boundaries. Leon had his eyes squeezed shut.

They were in the clear. He was speeding up.

"Leon! *Wait!*"

They rose like a pair of balloons.

Balthazar knifed in beneath them. *Go back. Go back.*

Polly grabbed the lip of Leon's tote bag and pulled on it. "*Stop!*" He turned to her, surprised.

"*Leon!* We have to go *down. Now!*"

"Why?"

"Do what I tell you, damn it!"

"OK!"

With the strap of his carryall, she swung him around.

Out on the winding highway half a mile off, she caught

sight of the cream-colored government Atomic and two horsemen cantering along behind it.

They touched down in the cover of the pines. Leon fell to his knees in the pine duff. He was giddy. "That was *incredible.*"

"It's no good, Leon."

"What's no good?"

"You need *practice.*"

"I know! But I was *doing* it! I was really *doing* it!"

"You can't *float* up there like a kite on a string! Do you think you're invisible?"

"What do you mean? We were *climbing*. Pretty soon we would have been little dots."

"Not soon enough. Besides, you can't out-fly a helicopter."

"But— First you didn't think I could do it, but I *can* do it, and now you're saying I can't? I'm *new* at it, that's all."

"*Hush!* Hold on!"

Balthazar: *They come! Condense! Condense!*

Then what?

Hide!

"Leon. Pay attention. We'll have to try something else."

"What does he mean, *condense*?"

"It's our best chance." She took his hand.

"You hear that?" he said.

Hounds. Also a helicopter, high and to the south. "Come *on*, Leon!"

She retraced her circle.

"What are we going to do?"

"We're going to contract."

"Contract what?"

"Ourselves. We're going to shrink."

"Jesus. How much?"

"A lot."

"Well, how much are we shooting for?"

"About two or three inches.Enough so we can hide where they'll never think to look."

"I'd rather fly."

"This is safer. It won't kill us if it goes bad. There's a release, too—in case we have to bail out." Polly wasn't sure she could remember the release, but there was no better way out of this, not now, B was right.

She looked into the sky. "Spirit forces, I ask that the elements attend me once again and forgive me my haste."

She took a small, hexagonal vial of a brown powder from her sewing box and peeled off the paraffin that sealed the stopper.

"Let me tap a little of this into your palm. It's bitter. Suck it into your mouth and swallow it fast. Then speak the seven phrases just as I speak them, one at a time. When the spell kicks in, focus on the boundary between yourself and forces pressing in on it. OK? It's not all that different from Dispersal, only it's a lot more disorienting."

"OK. Anything else?"

"Yes. *Stick with me.* When your head clears, your eyesight and your reflexes will seem extra sharp. Sounds will be louder, smells will be stronger, and everything'll seem just *rougher*. And you'll be very aware of other creatures—beetles, caterpillars, flies. Keep your distance from *all* of them. Especially the red ants. Got it?"

He nodded.

"One last thing. This spell turns you from a predatory animal into a prey animal. You don't want to be sitting out in the open anywhere, if you can help it."

A helicopter came swinging in close, thrashing the pine boughs and blotting out the baying of the dogs.

Polly held a pine cone in front of her. "We favor this size and no smaller!"

She squeezed Leon's two hands in hers. "Repeat what I say as I say it, Leon, and nothing more. Got it?"

"Yes. Go."

She spoke the spell.

Blod ymbbindeth,
hunig on hyf:
gadreth swa thohe;
thohe thicceth,
nearu swa hnecca,
hnigath swa hunig,
hefig on hyf.

She held her breath as the air around her compressed her limbs and torso. She made herself into a ball. The chopper was churning the air, but it couldn't descend through the trees.

25

HER VISION CLEARED. Leon was kneeling beside her, covering his face with his hands. Swirling dirt and pine needles bit her skin.

"Leon!"

"I'm OK, but, God, I can barely *see*!"

"Stand up and come with me. Hurry!"

Polly pulled him along through the buffeting storm one way and another, until she spied what looked like a hollow in the woods floor.

"Come on!"

The ground was shaking under them.

It was a shallow cavern formed by an arching pine root in the duff. Just protection enough from the downdraft. "First you, Leon—crawl in."

She followed.

"This is insane!" Leon said.

Horses' hooves the size of boulders crashed into the clearing, kicking up clods of earth and moldering pine bark. The noisy chopper veered away.

Hounds bellowed. The horses surged against the tree trunks.

With an ear-splitting "ARRR-OOOO!" the root hollow went dark.

They pressed themselves to the back of the cavern. The dog's wet, pungent breath gusted into their faces.

"Beau! Back, boy, *back*! Beau!"

One of the men grasped the hound's collar with a gloved hand.

Security officers, two of them, in riding boots and blue vid helmets. Three or four dogs.

"Craziest damn thing!"

The horses blew and whinnied.

"Think maybe they circled around?"

"How could they?"

"Hell if I know. I had 'em both, clear as day."

"Where's Lucas? *Lucas?*"

"He's gone. He looped back to the lot."

"They were right *here*, goddamn it. I *saw* 'em. Where'd they go?"

"Girl's a witch, ain't she? What do you expect?"

"*Yuri!* Tell Lucas to fly his ass back down here. Shit, is he on? Yuri! What the hell's wrong with him?"

"He's not even on."

"He's on. *Yuri!* Send Lucas back around, will you? Goddamn dogs are useless. We need *visuals*." He paused. "Are you *listening*?"

"ARRR-OOOO!"

The hound was back, shoving his nose halfway into the cavern.

"Beau! *Beau!* Idiot dog!"

The handler yanked on his collar. The dog hacked, pelting them with spit.

One of the horses neighed. The riders reared around and pounded off toward the roadway.

"That was horrible," Leon said. "What do we do now?"

"Nothing. They'll be back."

"How did they find us in the first place?"

She had no idea. "Some of these drones can detect breathing, believe it or not." Then, too, she'd left their marked-up roadmap in the travel cart—with the falls circled in pencil.

A natural wind stirred the debris around the fissured columns of the pines. A throng of midges tumbled by like starlings. A minute or two passed. They heard the chopper returning.

"Polly. Look."

A fox had ambled into the clearing, nose to the ground. Polly caught the canine's musk as he lifted his nose to test the air.

"He smells the horses," Leon whispered. "Look at the claws on that monster."

"Stay focused, Leon. If we lose our grip on this, we're dead."

"I'm trying."

Balthazar. Help.

As the chopper closed in, the fox bounded off, his brush straight out behind him.

"Hey, look!" Leon cried. "Balthazar's back!"

He came in fast, careering among the tree trunks, towing a long vine with his beak. The trailing end was hitched to a basket. Without touching down, he dropped it in the pine duff. It tipped onto its side.

Get in.

They scampered toward it, Leon clutching his flag-cloak to his chest.

It was an oriole's nest—a deep cup of grasses lined with willow cotton.

They dove in headfirst.

Balthazar circled back, skimming the ground, wings cocked. He snatched up his end of the vine and took off with great, beating strokes, straining under the chopper's wash.

They clung to the lip of the nest.

In seconds they were in the clear, the forest spilling away on all sides, a hundred shades of green and bronze. To the right, the milky sinews of the falls, and beyond that a stark mountain, the first in a chain reaching north and east. Behind them, the blue Security helicopter hovering over the pine stand, and that black-domed Atomic idle in the roadway.

Balthazar beat higher through sheafs of cloud. Leon lowered himself to the bottom of the nest.

"Whatever you do, stay awake, Leon, all right? I'm serious. We have to keep ourselves mindful of the boundary, both of us."

They were far above the gray tops of the mountains. B banked easily with the currents, scarcely moving, it seemed.

On they sailed.

At last Polly began to calm down. As she did, the glum truth returned to her: *the book was gone*. She was a failure.

With that, her focus went slack all at once, like a snapped fishing line. Wait. *No. No! Hold, hold.*

Leon looked up at her. "What's happening?"

"I need to recharge the spell! Let's— *Focus*, Leon."

"I'm feeling weird. It's like I have the shivers—"

"*Focus! Don't talk!*"

Polly's skin was tingling. "Balthazar! The spell's getting squirrelly."

He knew. *Do not enlarge.*

"I'm trying!" *Hold. Hold.*

Leon's head and torso began to blur before her eyes.

"Oh, *God*," he cried. "*Help me!*"

"Leon! Leon, please!" She clapped her hands. "*Condense, contract*! *Blod ymbbindeth, hunig on hyf: gadreth swa thohe. Thohe thicceth—*"

She saw his contours sharpen. His eyes went wide and blue.

She had it back. She raised her arms. "*Thank you*, spirit forces!"

No. He was getting *smaller*.

"*Leon!* Hold! Wait! *Stop! Please!*"

But she could only stand and watch as Leon dwindled to the size of a flea on the floor of the nest.

"Oh, Great Mother! What have I *done*? Leon!" She dropped to her knees. "Leon! Speak! Tell me you're all right!"

She couldn't hear his tiny voice.

"B! Find a place to put down, will you?"

The raven canted himself toward the crooked spine of the mountains. She pressed her mind to keep the spell in focus with her eyes fixed on Leon, not to lose track of him.

Balthazar set the gondola on a stony plateau near a pool of bright, inky water. It tipped over. When she fell, she lost sight of him. The nest was spongy, at least, and forgiving. There he was, sprawled on his back.

She held out her hand. "Climb up here. Can you?"

He got up and placed a foot on her pinkie's jagged nail, boosting himself to the tip of her finger. He raised his arms. He was saying something.

"What?"

"Don't shout!"

"I'm sorry."

"You have to *help* me!"

"I *will*, Leon!"

He covered his head with his arms. "Don't *shout*!"

His voice was so small. "Sorry! I'm *sorry*." She extended her hand from the nest so that he could hop down to the rock. She crawled out after him.

In her despair over Leon, she'd forgotten that she was

very small, too. The thick, leathery growth on the rock all around them wasn't some stunted shrub, she realized—it was lichen.

She had overdone it. She'd let Leon get away from her, and then she'd panicked. Just the same, shrinking him even more had probably saved both their lives. Anyway, the fix for this should be a simple release. Or maybe a counter. It was fixable, she was sure of that. If she had her grimoire to consult, it would not be a problem at all. But she didn't.

"There's water here," she told him.

He couldn't see it.

She leaned down. "Off to your right there's a pool—rainwater, maybe. I wouldn't drink from it, but you can bathe in it. If you want. I think I'm going to."

She watched as he made his way awkwardly over the uneven surface. It was hard for him. She could have lifted him to the edge of the pool.

He scooped up water and rinsed his face and neck. He took off his funny sneakers and jeans and waded into the water.

"Are you hungry?" she asked.

"Where are we?"

"Near the top of some mountain. Carolina, maybe.

"I feel like I'm going crazy."

"You'll be all right, Leon. I'll get you out of this."

"So *do* it then! Cancel the spell like you said before!" His flag-cloak was gone.

Polly walked off a few steps. *B! What do you think?*

The raven was perched not far away in a bony spruce. He opened his wings and closed them. *He suffers.*

"What should I *do*? Should I try the release?" A release would cancel the spell's original purpose. But she wasn't sure whether it would have the desired effect on this doubled spell. And the first rule of spell-casting was if you're not sure what your magick will accomplish, you *do not work the magick.*

Maybe.

"OK. I'm going to try it, B—on both of us at the same time. Any risk in that?"

Maybe.

"What else can I do?"

Stay as you are.

"No. No, I don't want to do that."

The raven dropped from his perch and flapped away, hugging the ground.

"Leon. Repeat what I say. It's four words only. Say nothing else."

"I got it."

Polly addressed the elements. "I ask that we and our belongings be returned to their original form. At my spoken command. I ask for no other change."

She pronounced the release.

Hyf unbind.
Lyf unbind.

26

"Wa-HOO!" His voice rang in his bones. Every bit of him was trembling and swelling. He felt half-delirious with relief.

His vision sharpened again. The body of water beside him was just a pond. The maze of frilly lichens was knee-high.

He spun around. Polly's pant leg looked like the trunk of an oak tree. Her flossy, yellow head loomed against the sky.

"Polly!"

"Oh, no!"

"Shit! It didn't *work*!"

"No, no. It *did* work, Leon. Just . . . just not all the way. I'm back to normal, but you're back to the size we were *before*. Chipmunk size."

"Obviously! So say it again! Say the release!" He couldn't stand this, not one more minute.

"Hang on! Let me *think*!"

He watched Polly pull her sewing box out of her pack, open it, and close it again. She sat cross-legged with her face in her hands.

He couldn't wait. "Say it! Come *on*."

"I *can't*, Leon. I don't know which way it will work!"

"What do you mean, 'which way'?"

"I mean the release *could* shrink you back to your teeny-tiny size."

"Oh, God. But if *that* happened, you could just release it again, right?"

"I don't *know*," she cried. "I'm not *sure*."

"So what do we do?"

"Let's— Let's give it a while. Magick can be sluggish sometimes. It truly can."

"But what if it doesn't let go?"

"It'll be *OK*, Leon. I'll carry you with me. You'll be fine."

"Are you saying I might have to *stay* like this?"

"No! Not forever. It can be fixed. I'm just not sure how to fix it." She got down and pressed her hands flat on the stone on either side of him. The flesh whitened under her chafed skin. "I'll take *care* of you, Leon, I promise. If anything ever happened to you, I'd probably kill myself."

Bright tears splashed at his feet, one, then two more.

His heart went soft. What could he do? All right. He could handle this. He could. If he had to, then he would. He *would,* that's all.

☾

At daybreak they descended through cold, gray reefs of cloud. Raw roads, unkempt farm fields, and thick woods lay below. The chain of mountains was gone.

They coasted over a patch of what had once been settled territory, a town—grids of streets and buildings—but there was no smoke, no noise, no motion. A little later they came to ground on a gullied slope at the lip of a desolate plateau.

Polly removed her hat and shook her hair loose. Without speaking, she helped him out of the pack. She was drained and pale. She coughed. She got out a water bottle and drank. Tawny weeds swayed around her legs.

Balthazar landed with a hop. He folded and refolded his wings.

"This isn't the Exclusion Zone, is it?" Leon asked.

"No, it's coal country. Or it was. Long ago."

"How come we left the mountains?"

"These are the mountains, I think. What's left of them."

"It's like a desert."

"I know. No one lives here anymore. All the water's polluted. But it's safe."

No place is safe.

Polly glanced at Balthazar. "It's safe enough for a few hours." She groaned. "I'm getting sick, Leon. I have a fever."

"Can you cast a healing spell?"

"Yes, and I will. But right now I need some rest. And food."

What do you want? B asked.

"Fruit, if you can find any."

He coasted away toward the shadowy hollows below them.

"How much farther do we have to go?"

Polly rubbed her eyes. "That depends on whether we try to cross the zone or go around it."

All at once Balthazar was back, beating hard. *Drones.*

"Drones!" Leon shouted.

Polly looked to the south, then at the raven. "What should we do?"

Follow.

"By air?"

"Aye!"

Now he could hear their humming.

"I can't, B!" Polly said. "I'm too frazzled to hold the charge."

Run, then. Run.

"Come on, Leon!"She held the pouch pocket open.

He scrambled in.

27

POLLY WATCHED BALTHAZAR drift down the gullied slope of the mountain toward a forest of spindly conifers. Three large Guardian drones spanned all the sky she could see to the south.

She maneuvered among the trees, moving painstakingly through half-dead spruce and fir, clambering over roots and blowdowns and washouts, until she reached a ravine and a brook the color of mustard. She stopped to catch her breath.

Balthazar looped around to wait.

"You OK, Leon?"

"I'm all right. How about you?"

She felt light-headed and weak. Eyes burning, she watched through the branches as one of the slow, blind drones passed directly overhead, the blue-and-yellow CSA shield distinct on its gray fuselage.

"They've got us, Balthazar."

Not yet. Use the time.

"How?"

Hide.

"Where?"

Condense.

"I'm sorry, but I'm not going to condense again unless I absolutely have to. What else can I do?"

Find others.

"What others? Where?"

In the valley.

Other people, he meant. A community where they might blend in. Or ask for help. "Can you find someone?"

Follow.

Polly loped through the woods for a good while, then slowed to a walk when she came to a banked highway. It was lined with empty southbound cars and trucks, abandoned where they'd run out of fuel. They'd all been looted. The whole countryside was deserted—weedy fields, mixed woods, stark ruins.

Central Pennsylvania had emptied out after the devastation to the east, although some communities of farmers and gleaners hung on here and there, despite the dangers. She walked past what had been a manufacturing district. One- and two-story buildings stood gaping. The glitter of broken glass was everywhere. As she approached a settlement where a number of the structures seemed lived in—she could see smoke—Balthazar guided her around it through a large field, skirting a great, flat plaza of empty shops, to a littered highway that wound up among forested hills.

She plodded on.

Late in the afternoon, the raven led her away from the paved surface to a traveled lane that, after a time, became a set of wagon ruts with grass in the middle. The lane ended at last in a hilltop clearing occupied by two buildings with corrugated siding and solar panels, a wind turbine, a simple dwelling with a covered porch and curtained windows, and a domed structure, like a squat silo. There were chickens, red and speckled, and a good-sized kitchen garden. In the shade of an oak tree stood a pretty cabriolet with spoke wheels.

Balthazar must have sensed some kind of sympathy

here—simple good-heartedness, probably, but maybe, she hoped, traces of the Braid. Some solitaries still lived on in the desolate corners of the Dominions—although, like Mrs. Hacker, most of them could not be trusted. It didn't matter who lived here, really. All she wanted was a chance to rest awhile and eat whatever a kindly person might have to spare, enough to recover herself, give her enough energy to work up her healing spell, then the Dispersal. After sundown, with any luck, she could take to the sky.

She squared her shoulders and walked toward the house. "Hello!" she called out.

The screen door squeaked on its spring. An elderly, unshaven man came out onto the porch cradling a bolt-action rifle. "Who's that there?"

"A young woman in need of help."

"What kind of help? What's your trouble?"

"I'm sick and hungry."

After a pause, he said, "This look like a hospital?"

She should not have said she was sick. "I have a head cold, that's all. I would be grateful for a little food—just an egg and some bread, if you have any to spare."

"How did you get up here?" He peered past her down the lane. "You by yourself or is there more of you?"

"I have come a long way on foot. If you can't help me, I'll keep going."

The man stepped into the sunlight, shifting the rifle to the crook of his left arm. "Come closer now. These are old eyes."

She did.

"Jesus, you look like vagabond trash. Where you trying to get to, anyway?"

"To Vermont."

"*Vermont?* What the hell for? Ain't nobody up there but the military."

"I grew up there. That's my home."

He squinted. "But you got out. What you want to go back for?"

"I told you, it's my home. My family's there."

"Christian family?"

She shook her head.

"But you been saved. Surely you been saved."

She didn't respond.

He jabbed the gun at her. "I know what you are. You're a refugee. Goddamn heathen got run out of the Regions and no place to go!"

"I'm not a refugee. All I—"

"Pop!" A shirtless young man came out onto the porch, buttoning his trousers. "It's OK, Pop. I'll deal with this."

"Thank you, sir," Polly said. "I'm a free person on a long journey. I'm no danger to anyone who is no danger to me."

"She's a heathen refugee, Nicholas, and you can bet your ass there's more of 'em close by, sure as she's standing there."

"Christian charity. That's all I ask. A bite of food and a place to rest."

The young man ran his fingers through his hair. "Pop, as far as we're concerned, she's a traveler. Whether she knows the Lord or not makes no difference at this particular moment. I'm going to fetch her a towel and some soap, and then I'm going to show her to the daybed in the observatory. And you're going to fix her a plate of whatever we have left over. OK, Pop?" He turned to Polly. "Do you drink hot tea?"

"Tea would be wonderful."

The old man glared at her. "As God is my witness, you're making a big mistake."

Nicholas sighed. "Wait here, young lady, all right?"

The two men went inside, Pop still grumbling.

"Good job with those guys," Leon said.

"I don't think they're bad people," she said, "but it has to be scary, living out here on the edge."

She looked for Balthazar. There, perched on a stob halfway up a broken spruce. He flexed his wings, acknowledging her. *Take care.*

Nicholas led her up a gravel path to the rust-splotched steel door that opened into the small silo. He explained that the observatory, built long ago by a society of amateur astronomers down in Harrisburg, had been closed to the public for decades.

In the center of the space, among a few straight-back chairs, stood a fat, dirt-mottled tube on a complicated-looking mount.

"Does it still work?" she asked.

"You bet! Seventeen-inch classic Cassegrain. It's old, but it's plenty good enough for what I do."

"You study the stars?"

"When the seeing's good. Mostly I scan for incoming near-earth objects."

"Oh." She had read about this. "You're like a watchdog, right? You watch for asteroids that could smash into the earth."

"Asteroid Warning Network, that's exactly right. There's people think I'm nuts, I don't mind telling you. But it was an asteroid that killed off the dinosaurs—sixty-five million years ago. They don't teach that in science books, but it's a historic fact, and I'll say that to anybody."

"Have you ever seen one?"

"Asteroid? Sure. Two or three a month. They don't have to be all that big to cause a whole lot of damage."

"And what do you do when you spot one?"

"Call Security. Give 'em the coordinates."

"Then what?"

"Up to them, thank God. All I do is bark."

"I think you have a very nice job."

He laughed. "I wish it was! They don't pay me a dime—just the lodging. And my dear wife does not approve."

"Why not?"

"When our Creator decides this world has come to an end, that will be his business, not ours."

"That's too bad. Is Pop your father?"

"The wife's. Margery. She stays in town during the week. Shuffles paper for the Guard."

He showed her into a grubby washroom off a small office attached to the silo observatory, then left to see what Pop had found for her to eat. "There's some bean salad," he said. "I know that."

Polly turned the thumb latch. Leon climbed out into her hand. She set him on the back of the toilet tank while she washed her face and hands.

"How long are we staying here?"

Polly looked out a little window. "It'll be dark in an hour or so. I only hope we have that long."

"Haven't heard the drones in a while."

"That just means the choppers'll be showing up before long."

"Balthazar will warn us when they get close, won't he?"

The observatory door creaked open and banged shut.

"Are you all right in there?" Nicholas called into the washroom.

"Thank you, yes. My name is Polly."

"Polly. Well, Polly, Pop's fixed you a nice sandwich. And a mug of tea. I'm sorry we don't have any honey."

"This is just wonderful of you, Nicholas. Both of you."

"It's nothing. If you need anything else, you'll find Pop down in the garden."

"You're leaving?"

"I'm going to go back to sleep."

"Oh. Sorry!"

The outer door slammed shut.

The tea was weak but still hot enough for her to steep some of her own herbs. Cold chicken on thin-sliced dark bread, vinegary green beans with dill and scallions on the side. She cut some meat for Leon. He sat on the daybed, where he could dive under a blanket if he had to.

"Cool building," he said. "There's a professor in my dad's department that has a set-up like this down in Talla—Dr. Folcarelli."

"Ever get a chance to look through his telescope?"

"Yeah, once. We saw the moons of Jupiter and a bunch of different galaxies."

Polly left to take her plate and mug back to the house, hoping to ask Pop if he could spare a loaf of bread for her journey. After that, she meant to work up her healing spell—*Halian faeste.*

The sun had dropped behind a low, orange cloud.

Pop wasn't in the garden. It reminded her achingly of her own garden at home—the neat wide beds of leaf lettuce, chard, feathery carrots, radishes, and beets, the hills of young squash, the blossoming pea vines on a trellis of bare branches, the walkways edged with marigolds.

Someone was talking inside the house.

At the foot of the porch steps she heard one clear word—"Vermont." That was enough. Pop was on a vid hook-up. She could see the panel's reflection in the glass of the open inner door.

". . . hard to tell. Blond. Yes. No, by herself. They *did*? When? Oh, dear Jesus, that's worse than— Yes. No, but that's what I told him. I know! That's what I *told* him. I know. He's asleep."

The other voice belonged to a woman, but she couldn't make out what the woman was saying. Not that she had to.

"*What?* Oh, dear *God*! Yes. Well, they must have. That's just *horrible*. Oh, I won't! You bet. OK, hon, bye. Oh, I will, don't worry about that. Yep. Bye."

She set the plate and mug on the bottom step and ran back to the observatory.

Leon was asleep on the daybed. She gazed at him for a second, then brushed her thumb against his head.

He sat up, yawning.

"We have to fly, Leon. Right now."

"Now?"

"There's a bounty on our heads. We're evil people, Leon."

"How do you know?"

The observatory door swung open.

"Hush, now." She grabbed the revolver and tucked it under a blanket next to Leon. "Hide." She sat with her hand resting on the gun's checkered grip.

Footsteps, than a sharp knock on the inner door. "Polly?" Nicholas.

"I'm here. Come in."

The door opened. Nicholas entered, then Pop, rifle at the ready. Nicholas pressed a wall switch. An LED array in the ceiling began to glow. He cleared his throat. "Polly, I have bad news for you."

"What is it?"

"We know who you are."

"You *think* you know who I am, but if you will kindly allow me to explain myself—"

"Oh, no, I'm afraid we're quite well informed. Pop and I are going to have to hold you here until Security arrives. I only wish you—"

"Who do you think I am?"

"You're the renegade witch, the little monster they've been hunting for down south for weeks."

"'Thou shall not suffer a witch to live,'" the old man said.

Nicholas laid a hand on his arm. "Pop. They said *alive*, Pop."

Polly drew the gun from beneath the blanket and leveled it at Pop's chest.

He reeled back.

Nicholas raised his hands. "Don't shoot! Dear God, please! Oh, please don't!"

"Pop," Polly said. "You set your rifle on the floor. Nice and easy. Do it now. *Do* it!"

Slack-jawed, Pop squatted and dropped the long gun onto the concrete.

"Thank you. Now, both of you back out of this room. Side by side. Back out into the yard. Move." Polly rose to her feet. "*Move!*"

Pop shrank back, glancing behind him. Nicholas had his eyes fixed on Polly. She walked them out past the telescope and stopped there.

"For what it's worth, I am not evil. I am not possessed. The truth is I am a high witch from birth, and I'm free to think for myself and make my own way in the world."

Nicholas pressed his hands together. "Lord Jesus, help us."

"Get out of here!"

Pop sidled through the doorway. Nicholas backed out into the dusk and slammed the door into its steel frame.

"Nice job!" Leon said. "Now what?" He was standing on the couch.

Polly entered the bathroom to get the dry mop she'd seen standing in a corner. With that she swept a quick circle between the desk and the wall.

"You're not going to condense again, I hope."

"No. We're flying."

"We are?"

"Climb in." She patted the pack.

We must leave this place.

Balthazar! "Where are you?"

Above. He was on the roof.

Polly applied her flying ointment.

They come. In the air and on the road.

Polly pronounced the spell as she repacked the backpack, keeping the revolver clamped under one arm.

"You OK in there, Leon?"

"I'm fine. Do you hear that?"

Choppers. "Yeah."

She dashed out into the observatory. The space was dim, lit only by the glow from the room behind her and the orange brightness seeping in at the doorsill. They could not go out there.

"What's wrong?" Leon said. He clambered up through her hair and onto her shoulder.

"The dooryard's lit up like a train station."

"OK, let's look around," he said.

"What are we looking for?"

"*There*, see? Right there!"

It was some mechanical contraption bolted to the floor—a set of iron gear wheels and an L-shaped crank with a wooden handle. "What is it?"

"It's for the roof!" he said. "The dome overhead rolls off on a track! Just turn that handle."

She gripped the shaft like an oar and pulled. The gears clinked. She felt a chain snap taut. She pulled harder, grunting. The roof began to slide with a scraping sound. She heaved at the crank.

"That's enough, that's enough! Hold still while I climb down."

Leon shinnied down to the pack.

"Hang on now!"

"I'm good!" he yelled.

She swung off the pack, shoved the gun inside, and fitted her goggles into place.

Above the big telescope and the cinderblock wall, a crescent-shaped opening gave onto the indigo sky. She could not see the helicopters, but they were loud now. Beams of light raked the yard.

With a push from the balls of her feet, she rose and zipped out into the darkness.

28

OUT OVER THE BROW OF THE HILL, peering back between her fluttering pantlegs, she could see two blinking Security choppers, the lower one dropping into the observatory compound, the other pouring white light into the yard.

She hurtled through tattered clouds in a daze, concentrating on the sparse lights along the shores of the big river below for direction. Her eyes felt like hot sand. Her lungs were rattly with phlegm.

In less than an hour, she felt the charge begin to stutter in her bones. Her fatigue, her fever, her despair . . . all blunted her focus.

Balthazar sensed her faltering. *Look! Look ahead! Steady on!*

Great Mother. "Balthazar! Help!"

Say the spell! Say it!

She tried but couldn't. The uprushing air tore away her words. *Help me.*

The ground came at her like a platter of sparks.

Thwump. Balthazar rammed his narrow back into her chest, the knob of his head at her throat. He spread his wings, almost as long as Polly's two arms, to buffer the fall, and steered with his supple tail between her legs.

The charge was gone. Down she fell. If her life ended here, no one would ever know. That was not a bad thing.

Feet to the fore!

The raven drew in his wings and ducked away.

The rising river looked like mottled velvet. She tilted back, pointed her toes, and smashed into the water. The pack thrust her head forward as she plunged into the hard cold.

Blackness.

She kicked and flailed until her face broke into the air.

Gasping, treading water. Coughing, spitting.

Slowly her head cleared. Her ribs and neck ached, but nothing seemed broken. She laid her head back, staring into the yellow fog of her lenses, paddling with numb hands and feet—

Leon! Oh, Mother! "Leon! *Leon!* Are you all right?"

Nothing. Her ears were full of water.

She had to get to shore. Where *was* she? She pried up the goggles.

The river danced all around, the near bank bobbing in and out of view at a distance she couldn't gauge in the darkness.

"*Leon!*"

She managed to wrestle the water-logged pack off her back. With her arms free, she set off toward land, scissor-kicking and backstroking with one arm, the heavy pack balanced on her hip. If Leon was dead, she would kill herself.

But she would not drown. She stroked with one arm. Her right shoulder—the one she'd strained that last day at St. Mike's—was bad. With the muscular current, the pack, and the drag of her clothes, it was almost impossible to make progress. She drew with her good arm and kicked.

Drew and kicked.

Drew and kicked.

At last her arm nudged the mud, and her eyes sprang open. The melon wash of a new day filled the sky.

She crawled out onto a bank of mossy rocks. She coughed and coughed.

With wooden fingers she reached into the front pocket of the pack for Leon and gently lifted him out.

His face felt chilled against her cheek. "Oh, Leon . . . Please don't be dead."

She placed him on his back across her thigh and tried to breathe air through his mouth into his airway. But he was too little. *He was too little!*

She clenched her fists. "Spirit forces! Don't *do* this to us! *Do you hear me?*"

Polly shouted the frozen spell's release:

Hyf unbind!
Lyf unbind!

And with that his little body began to vibrate against her leg. She held her breath. *Oh, please!*

She laid him on a flat rock. The sleeve of atmosphere surrounding him went fuzzy. He swelled in small bursts.

In a minute he was again his normal size, but limp as a rag doll.

Polly pinched his nostrils shut and breathed three times into his mouth, forcing in the air. Three more.

He gagged and choked, spitting up water.

"Leon!" She jumped to her feet. "You're back!"

"*Where are we?*"

"Oh— Leon—"

He tried to sit up but fell back, trembling. "What happened?"

Polly was in tears.

"What's the matter? Are you hurt?"

Polly blew her nose and pushed the wet hair out of her face. "No, I'm happy. I'm thanking the stars. Actually, I'm freezing, but—"

"*Hey!* I'm not a chipmunk anymore!"

"Isn't it wonderful? How do you feel?"

He patted his chest and stomach. "Not too bad! Great! Where the hell are we?"

"I don't know. The sun'll be out soon. Let's find some place where we can rest out of the wind."

He was rubbing his arms. "You know, magick is amazing, and I love doing it, but that shrinking spell is a loser."

"You're only a beginner, Leon. What amazes me is that you can do any transformative magick at all."

"I know. Without you I couldn't. Not a chance."

At the top of the bank, beyond a raised railroad bed, stretched a broad expanse of crumbling asphalt, brush, and trees with a large, blocky ruin at the far end. In the other direction the tracks curved with the river into deep green woods. Out across the rough water a row of derelict warehouses and many sagging barges lined the far shore. She couldn't see a boat anywhere.

Balthazar came flapping up the railroad corridor, low to the ground. He veered off toward the ruin. *Follow.*

They climbed on weary legs over the tracks and crossed the empty lot toward what had once been a shopping mall. Broken glass and weather-beaten trash. Pigeons gurgling. The recyclers and scavengers had left next to nothing. Even the door frames and floor tiles were gone.

Balthazar settled himself on top of the facade above the entrance plaza. High on the pebble-textured wall was the shadow of a word, *JCPenney.* The sign was long gone.

Inside, glittery shafts of sunlight emphasized the darkness. In the big oval basin on the plaza there was a bouquet of pipes at one end and the remains of a succession of campfires at the other.

They sat on the stone rim of the fountain and emptied the pack. The contents of Polly's sewing box were unharmed. Leon wiped down the revolver and dumped the bricks of ammo so the cartridges could dry.

"I've been wondering about Theldred," he said.

"Wondering what?"

"I don't get why she would want your book in the first place. If she's a high witch, like you, wouldn't she have her own book?"

"No. No, the old grimoires have been lost or destroyed. Most of them, anyway. Some whole covens today have only one to share—and those tend to be rudimentary. There's no grimoire like *The Craeft*. My grandmother once had the twenty-four standard spells and releases transcribed in an abridged version. She gave it to my mother as a wedding gift. But most of the book has never been copied."

"So it's quite valuable."

"It's priceless," Polly said, miserable all over again. When she sobbed, her clogged lungs crackled.

29

AFTER A MEAL OF SOGGY BREAD, Leon tried to get some sleep with his head on Polly's thigh, but the chill wind across his wet clothing kept waking him. Clouds covered the sun.

He sat up. The birds and locusts seemed loud. Out beyond the railroad embankment the tumbling river turned from olive to gold with the gusts.

He jumped to his feet when he felt a rumble in the ground. A train, from the south.

"Polly!"

She jerked and cried out.

"Duck down!"

He pushed the pack out of sight behind the low fountain wall. They squatted there, watching the freight clatter past—a black steam locomotive and a string of red and orange boxcars, each with the silhouette of a buffalo and big white letters. "BRC" and "Buffalo Rail Carrier." Rolling north.

Polly's eyes were closed, the lids twitching. She moaned.

He touched her brow with the back of his hand. She was burning up. "What can I do to help you?"

"I need—" She coughed. "I need—"

"What?"

He waited. She didn't say anything more.

Come away. Now.

He couldn't find the raven in the glare. *Where to?*

Follow.

"Polly isn't well. Not at all." But of course he knew that. Balthazar was impossible to argue with. "Hang on a minute." He still needed to plug the cartridges back into their foam bricks.

Come now.

"Why? Helicopters?"

Hurry.

Balthazar swooped in front of him and angled off to the east. *Follow.*

Leon smoothed Polly's hair. Her face was hot. He opened one of their water bottles and sprinkled a little on her forehead. "Balthazar has some kind of a plan. I'll be back soon. You rest, OK?"

"Mint and warm honey," she said.

Follow.

Balthazar led him down a roadbed lined by scruffy woods and brambles. He paused to listen for aircraft but heard only birds, insects, and the wind in the trees.

He walked on.

The road was untraveled, covered with broken branches and leaf litter. He came to a place where the graded surface and the stone bed underneath had been washed away by floodwater. A footpath crossed the deep wash-out, cutting back and forth through a wide gully filled with sumac, alder, thistle, and ferns.

After that, the route leveled off, broadened, and passed among ruins Leon glimpsed through the trees on both sides. Gutted vehicles. Glass. Rubble. Chain-link fence decked with scraps of insulation like pink fish caught in a weir. Cockeyed power poles. Wires, cables, corrugated pipe. Side streets came and went. A small herd of reddish deer lifted their heads in his direction but didn't run away.

He topped a rise that overlooked a vast bog—dark green cedar brakes and tea-colored water broken by reeds, lilies, bulrushes, and cattails. A pair of long-legged herons glided away as he reached the shoreline. The roadway disappeared beneath the water. In the distance, ducks bobbed on the rippling surface. Dragonflies stitched the air.

Wait here.

He watched the raven slip out of sight beyond a small stand of leafy trees in the distance. A kingfisher made a ratchety call.

He sat on a guard rail, waving at deer flies and wishing he'd brought along one of the water bottles. What help could there be in this swamp? Eggs? Some healing herb?

Soon Balthazar returned with something dangling from his beak. He dropped it at Leon's feet. A wristwatch with a plastic band. It was running. 1:08.

"Where did you get this?"

Go. Bring her here.

"What for?"

Help. Soon.

He imagined the raven might have hunted up another witch in hiding, the same way he'd come upon Leon at the bazaar. He draped the wristwatch over the guard rail, but Balthazar told him to keep it.

He stuffed it in his pocket. "I'll hurry."

☾

He found Polly slumped against the fountain wall. She had spilled both water bottles. He coaxed her to her feet. She wasn't seeing him.

"Can you walk?"

"Nyx has one, too."

"Here now, I'll carry the pack. You take my arm."

Her knees buckled. "Sorry. You go ahead. I'll wait."

He knelt beside her. "Polly. We can't stay here."

"But it's OK. I can hear the water. Just wake me when he comes back."

"Polly, listen to me. We really have to go. Come on, you can do it." He took her under the arms and steadied her until she found her balance. "Hold on to me, Polly."

Their progress was halting. By the time they reached the edge of the bog, a misty rain was falling.

He looked around. "Balthazar?"

"I'm going to lie down," Polly said.

He helped her to the ground. He took a rag from the pack and dipped it in the water to cool her face and neck. She shivered. "Tell her I can't. I'll have to forfeit."

A goose honked overhead, a loon warbled, and then, somewhere out on the water, he heard a man's low voice.

A boat was moving through the mist—a punt, with two men in it, one standing and poling, the other seated in the stern with a long gun across his knees.

Leon raised his arms and waved. The punt turned broadside to the shore and held there. The men wore beards and sleek capes.

"Which one of you's the witch?"

"She is." He nodded toward Polly. "She's very sick."

"You have that watch?"

He pulled it from his pocket. 3:48.

"Count her heartbeats for thirty seconds and double that figure."

He placed his fingertips on her wrist. "Ninety-eight," he called out.

"That's bad. Where have you been the last week or two?"

"In the mountains—in the woods."

"And before that?"

"Carolina. Georgia. New Florida."

"Does she have spots? Green phlegm?"

"No. It's a bad fever, but she hasn't slept in two days, and we're out of food, so . . . "

"How about you?"

"Me? I'm all right."

"And you've been with her since Georgia?"

"Since before that, actually."

The man with the pole nosed the punt's square prow into the grassy bank.

His partner slung the rifle over his back and stepped out. He looked like a caveman, his mane merging with his curly beard.

He leaned over Polly to examine her, then straightened. "If you can get her into the boat, we'll take her to see Daphne."

"Who's Daphne?"

"Closest thing we got to a doctor."

☾

The refugee band were evacuees from Philadelphia, theater people and musicians mostly, who had joined a freethinkers' commune in rural Ohio after the devastation 16 years earlier. They had been struggling ever since, subsistence farming, giving music and acting lessons, staging plays and concerts, making candles and holiday wreaths, until last summer, when the immanent crackdown sanctioned by the FRA convinced them to set up a survivalist camp in a place where maybe they could ride out the upheaval. Last fall the ten of them moved southeast to a bunker they'd constructed on a half-acre island surrounded by a marsh where, as a boy, Randall used to trap and fish.

The ten were Randall and Mojo, the two men in the punt; Jinx and Quinn, their twelve-year-old twin daughters; Audrey and Frank, an older black couple; tall, slender

Daphne, whose husband had been a pediatrician; her son, Eric, a violinist, and Jenny and Flo, another same-sex couple, actors in their 50s.

They'd managed to pass the winter in four, dingy, timber-frame rooms built into the side of the island's south-facing limestone escarpment, which also contained their stores of propane, medical supplies, ammunition, tools, batteries, solar chargers, a library, and a selection of seeds, along with lots of dried fruit, flour, tea, beans, sugar, and brown rice. They had rigged up a gravity-fed water system and sun pipes to guide a little light into the interior. They'd stocked a small pond with brown trout, too, but otters took every one of them in less than a week. The winter was hard. Although the bunker proved warm enough, it was dank and infested with rodents and spiders. Long stretches of rainy weather made hunting next to impossible, the onions, squash, and carrots froze in the root cellar, no one imagined the twins would start menstruating, and neither of their radios would pick up a signal.

"But we weren't *too* miserable," Daphne said with a laugh. "We stayed upbeat. Did yoga, read books, sang songs, played plenty of games—you know. Food's been . . . well, *plentiful*, let's say that. And, from the start, anybody that wanted to bug out could bug out, no questions asked."

"Where would you bug out *to*?" Leon asked.

"The zone is all there is," said Mojo from across the room.

"But then you'd die."

Mojo shrugged. "Better than getting shipped off to some work camp in the desert."

"Live free, die free," Daphne said. "We're committed, Leon."

After bathing Polly outside in a wooden tub, Jenny

brewed two teas for her, peppermint for her cough and catnip for her fever. Daphne made a tincture of fresh sage for her throat.

Polly lay on a cushion of ticking filled with duck down, her wet hair combed out, in one of Jenny's nightshirts. An herbal compress covered her eyes and forehead. Her skin seemed clear and smooth—cheeks, neck, shoulders. How could that be? Leon himself was all scabs and scratches.

Daphne knelt next to her. "Just gargle this stuff and spit into the basin." She set the tray on the floor.

Polly pulled off her compress and, in a hoarse voice, announced that she was going to cast a healing spell. She asked Leon to sweep a circle for her.

Swaying a little on her feet, she extended her upturned palms and faced the quarters, speaking under her breath. She intoned five phrases while Audrey and the twins watched in fascination, silhouetted against the soft light in a room beyond them.

"I'll sleep now," she said. "But first, which one of you did Balthazar approach?"

"The raven?" Daphne asked. "That was me! I'm in the garden de-bugging the potatoes, and I look up, and there's this big, black bird skimming the water, coming right *at* me like a drone, and I'm thinking, holy moly, he doesn't even *see* me. But then he hits the brakes and lands maybe six feet down the row. I go, 'Aren't *you* the friendly one?' and son of a gun if he doesn't *answer* me. Like, 'Help us.' I couldn't believe it."

"He's a familiar. He can tell when someone has the gift," Leon said.

"Well, I guess so!"

"Do you practice the craft?" Polly asked.

"*Me?* Hah! I'm totally clueless. But you know how sometimes, as a kid, you would go around thinking you're *different* from everyone else on the entire planet? That was me, brother—I *knew* I was special. My mother always said that my Grampa Percy was a witch. But nobody knew for sure."

"She was probably right," Polly said.

"Where *is* that raven, anyway?" Daphne asked. "Out in the rain?"

"He likes the rain," Leon said. He was about to add *he's a wild animal*, but that seemed wrong.

☾

Polly's fever broke in the night, and by noon the next day she was clear-eyed, calm, and beautiful again. Later, when Leon had time alone with her, he asked if some day she would teach him her healing spell. Also how to fend off harm—just a few of the basic spells. She said she'd be glad to. She would teach him everything she knew. It was almost too much to believe.

Balthazar returned while everyone was out fishing and foraging for supper. Leon felt the tug just after Polly did, but it took him a minute to spot the raven, a dot perched in a lightning-blasted hemlock far up on the bluff. He hesitated to come closer, Polly said, because a pair of bald eagles was nesting not far away. Leon waited while she climbed up through the scree to the heights above the escarpment to consult with him.

"The choppers went and followed the river toward the Adirondacks," she said when she came back down. "But drones are still scanning the valley."

"Scanning for what?"

"Can't be just visuals or else they wouldn't bother. Balthazar thinks they replaced your chip down in Atlanta."

Of course. Why hadn't he thought of this? "Guess you'd better fry it like you did the first one. Sooner the better."

They walked down to the end of the garden. Leon slipped off the overalls and flannel shirt Eric had given him. He probed and squeezed in the likely places—buttocks, forearms, calves, belly, earlobes, scalp—but couldn't find anything unusual. He dressed again.

Balthazar grawked, gliding down to the hoop of a cold frame on the edge of the garden. He perched and stretched his wings, looking around nervously. *I can find it.* He cocked his head.

Polly nodded. "Let him try."

Leon stretched out on his back. Balthazar hopped onto his chest, feet sharp and hard. He smelled like fish. He poked at Leon's forehead, then walked down his sternum and across his pelvis to his knee. *Turn over.* He hopped off.

Leon rolled onto his belly.

The raven jumped onto his rear end and stood still for a few seconds. He jabbed at Leon's overalls with his hind toe. *Here.*

Leon reached around and touched the spot—the scar he'd acquired on the back of his leg where he'd been gouged once by a broken sofa spring. "Good job."

B perched again on the cold frame.

"I have an idea," Leon said, sitting up. "Let's cut out the chip and have Balthazar take it and drop it in the river. Right? They'll think I drowned."

"Hm. Balthazar should love that," Polly said after a moment. "OK, let's have a look."

He lowered his overalls. "Here." He touched the small lump of tissue a few inches above the back of his knee.

Polly leaned down to it. "I think I can see an incision. Wait—I'll be right back."

She ran to the bunker and returned with her backpack and a few things she'd borrowed from Daphne—a scalpel, some gauze and tape, and a bottle of hydrogen peroxide.

She had him adjust himself so that the sunlight fell on the scar. "I'm going to numb the skin a bit. It's cloves and juniper."

He nodded.

"Keep still. If it's too painful, say so and I'll stop."

He felt the bite of the knife, then pressure.

"All right?"

"Yep."

"I'm going to open it."

That hurt. He gritted his teeth.

"There! I *got* it, Leon!"

She daubed the spot and taped a bandage in place.

"Take a look at this thing," she said.

It was a glossy green capsule the size of a grapefruit seed—not a wafer, like all the chips he'd seen before. More like a little piece of hard candy.

Polly taped the capsule to a small stone. "Balthazar, old boy! Kindly drop this item in the Susquehanna for us, will you?"

He swooped down.

"*Wait,*" Polly whispered. "Stop!"

"What is it?"

"Something's wrong."

Leon felt it, too. A stab of fear—not his own.

Balthazar hopped to the stone and eyed it. *I am marked.*

"What's he mean?"

Polly shaded her eyes and looked off into the summer-blue sky. "All right. Never mind, we can do this later. You go. Be safe. Leave now and come back after dark."

But instead Balthazar clutched the stone in the toes of one foot and launched himself, swooping from the bluff out over the shimmering expanse of the marsh.

He didn't get far before a dark shape came rocketing toward him out of the glare.

Polly grabbed her pack, pulled out the gun case, and flipped it open.

Balthazar drew in his wings and rolled to his right. The raptor ripped past him, turning. Balthazar tumbled and dived for cover in the wind-tossed bulrushes. But he carried no speed.

The eagle screamed and wheeled around, wings back, talons outspread. He struck sideways. Black feathers spun away.

Polly had the big revolver raised, but the two birds were grappling with each other and tumbling as they fell.

The eagle drove Balthazar into the water with a splash. Wings cocked and beating, he held the flailing raven under the surface.

"Nooo!" Polly screamed. "NO!"

BLAM! The blast rolled over the marsh. *BLAM! BLAM!*

The great bald eagle gave a scratchy cry and rose, trailing cords of water. His head gleamed like pearl. Balthazar was gone.

BLAM! BLAM! BLAM!

Someone shouted, "*Stop!* Stop *shooting*! What the hell are you *doing*?"

"*Balthazar!*" Polly called out. "Where is he? Do you see him? *Balthazar!*" She held the revolver in both hands, its smoking barrel up against her collarbone.

Leon watched the spot. Water lilies and cattails broke the bright plane, but if the raven was floating among them, he couldn't make him out.

Randall came jogging up the path with a shotgun. "Put down that weapon!" he demanded. He was out of breath. "Are you *crazy*? What are you shooting at?"

"That eagle!" Leon said, pointing. "He just attacked Balthazar."

"That's Rex!" Randall shouted. He was furious. "Jesus

Christ! Rex and Lady Jane have three unfledged chicks over on the crag."

"Balthazar's no danger to them!"

""The hell he isn't! Ravens *eat* eaglets."

"Not Balthazar!" But he knew it must be true.

Polly plunked the .357 on top of its case and rummaged in the pack for her bird glasses. She scanned the water, finally lowering the binoculars. "I have to go to him. Now."

Someone else was running up the path.

Audrey, wide-eyed. "Everything all right?"

"The girl here just tried to shoot Rex."

"*What? Why?*"

Polly regathered her things. She slung her pack over her left shoulder and pushed past Audrey, stone-faced. Leon followed without trying to explain.

In silence he poled her out to the place where the two birds had hit the water. There they found him, a dark clump suspended beneath the water lilies.

Polly lifted him into the boat. His eyes were closed, his stout, ebony beak parted, his wings dangling like empty sleeves. Polly pressed him to her chest and wept.

FIVE

30

SHE TOLD HERSELF this was how every braided relationship always ended. In death. Balthazar had lived a full life, longer and richer than most of his kind, and he'd fathered many broods. Nor did she doubt that, in the eagle's place, he would have attacked the intruder. Nothing helped. Balthazar was gone from the world. She was shattered.

Another night here was impossible, not under such sorrow and tension. They had to move on. At supper, Polly told their friends that they would be leaving the camp as soon as it was dark.

The men nodded, grim and approving.

"Will you fly?" one of the twins wanted to know.

Polly looked into her eyes and shook her head.

"Well, if you do, can we watch?"

"We won't be flying," Leon told the girl. "But when we're ready to leave, I hope you'll come out and say goodbye to us."

Leon was a very kind person. Far kinder than she was.

After Audrey had provisioned them with water, some bread, and a little dried venison, Randall and the twins escorted them to the inlet. He helped them into a dented aluminum canoe. The twins waved as Randall paddled them out into a channel.

The canoe slipped through pooling sheets of mist toward the east edge of the bog. Polly carried Balthazar in her lap, sewn into a muslin shroud. Farther to the east, Randall told them, lay miles of rolling scrubland, woods, and ruins, mostly uninhabited. The dirty winds and bad water this close to ground zero had driven all but a few people to the west and south.

"Sounds like a wilderness," Leon said.

"Too bad it's not," Randall said. "It's a frontier. There's no law out here, and the people you run into like it that way."

"Scavs?"

"Some. Exiles and criminals, mostly."

"Any wolves?" Polly asked.

He shrugged. "Probably."

In the northern forest there were wolves. Plenty of them. Polly knew more than one witch who had a wolf as a familiar. She might like a wolf herself, she thought, if she could find one. Though maybe not. She was used to the advantages of a winged companion. Her mother had had three familiars, all winged, and her father three as well. Their lives were short, that's all. The trouble was, after you'd had a partner in the Braid for any length of time, it was so diminishing to be alone while you waited to cross paths with another. How long would that be, she wondered. After her mother's last familiar died, Lil had been alone in the craft for almost five years.

☾

The crescent moon was down by the time the canoe nosed into an eroded bank under a thicket of alders. Randall steadied it for them as they stepped out into the cold water.

"Head north along the bank. After a while, you'll come to a wire fence. Keep the fence on your right until you get to an old railroad cut—it's actually more of a cart path these days. Follow that to the northeast. The cart path intersects a bunch of roads. Any one of those will eventually take you to Highway 81, just so you know."

"No highways," Polly said.

"That's what I mean. The 81's the only north-south thoroughfare between here and the zone, so it'll be busy. I assume you'll want to avoid that."

"Thanks. Thanks for your generous help, Randall—all of you."

The big man shook his shaggy head. "If I were you two, I'd fly. Unless that was all bullshit."

"Flying is a lot harder than most people think," Leon told him.

Randall snorted. "I don't doubt that."

☾

The woods were thick with vines, brambles, fallen trees, and rubble. When they reached the railroad cut, they stopped to eat. The mosquitoes were terrible. They put on bug repellent and slept back to back in a stand of ferns above the right-of-way.

In her dream Polly had arrived back at the farm. It was summer. Balthazar had made it back before her. He'd rejoined his family and reverted to normal, so that he behaved like the other ravens—shy, nervous, selfish, unfriendly. Polly was hurt but relieved. Her relief lingered now, as she lay looking up into the brightening sky.

She stood and stretched. The ties and rails were gone from the cut below, and the ballast was host to mullein and burdock. Wheel tracks and hoof prints showed that the way was still traveled.

Peeling their last orange, she began to hear through the birds' dawn chorus the rhythmic sounds of an approaching wagon.

A boy sang out, "Rahhh-bert! *Don't!*" Children squabbling. A creaky wheel hub, the jingle of fittings.

A woman spoke in a scolding voice.

Polly pushed the ferns aside. It was a harvest schooner

drawn by a pair of mismatched horses, the kind that once was common out on the plains where it was flat and windy, back before the water ran out for good. This one had fiberglass topsides and twin cowl vents. Its mast was missing. Polly hadn't seen one like it since she was a little girl. Three brown kids with yellow hair rode on the back deck, their bare feet swinging. From this angle she couldn't see the front bench. Migrant family, she thought, heading north to pick grapes or apples in the Mohawk Valley.

They walked on, keeping to the top of the embankment and off the cart path as much as possible so they would not be overtaken by surprise. They crossed a few roads, none of them much used by the looks. Later they hid in the brush as a hunter plodded past on foot, heading south with a gutted deer over his pack mule.

They made good time and saw no one else until just before evening when Leon stopped still to peer ahead along the cart path. "Hey," he said, nodding, "isn't that the migrants' rig?"

Yes, the high plains harvest schooner, pitched off to the far side of the railroad cut. No horses, no people, not a sound.

"Think they lost a wheel or something?"

"Doesn't look like it."

The ballast had been gouged up by many feet. Plastic crates and a small cast-iron cookstove lay on the side of the path.

"Let me have the gun, Polly."

The wagon's aft hatch had been bashed in and the cargo bins broken. Strewn over the ground were a few books and pieces of clothing—a straw hat, a white brassiere. A split sack of grain. A toy sword. A hairbrush.

A rising breeze rustled the treetops. A veery was calling.

On the other side of the wagon, they found two bloody

corpses in the milkweed, covered in flies. Both men. Hacked to death.

Polly turned away. "Who did this? Scavs?"

Leon shook his head. "Slavers."

"They just *slaughtered* these two."

"Waylaid them at the bend here. Not hard to tell which way they went—couldn't have been more than an hour or so ago."

"We can't do anything for them, Leon."

"You don't know that."

"Even if you still had your carbine, we'd have to be crazy to chase down a gang of slavers."

"Not if we could fly in—after they were all asleep."

"Well, we can't fly in."

"If we had Balthazar, we could."

"If Balthazar were here," she told him, stung, "in deference to us, he would refrain from eating the eyes and tongues of the dead, and that's about it." B would care nothing about the kidnapped children. Familiars understood violence and affection and fear and misfortune, but not moral abstractions like mercy or pity or vengeance. Many witches had a hard time keeping that in mind.

After a while he said, "I wish I had a familiar."

She gave him a look. "There are more witches without familiars than there are witches who have them, you know." Somehow the notion that Leon might find one for himself hadn't occurred to her. Keen as he was, though, she saw no reason why he shouldn't.

"Do you think you'll get another one?" he asked.

"Sure, some day. A familiar isn't something you go out and look for. Making a connection is usually a matter of chance."

"So what do you do? You just . . . discover each other?"

"Sort of. A few witches know how to hone a familiar in the wild, but that's a rare thing."

"So then. Getting a familiar is like falling in love."

"I guess it is," she said. Her cheeks tingled.

Leon set the gun on the ground, took her by the hands, and drew her to him. His mouth tasted sharp and warm, like berries in the sun.

☾

They found no shovel in the ransacked wagon. Leon dragged a musty sail from a cargo locker to use as a shroud. They weighed the corners down with stones and deadwood.

At dusk they reached a slough where beavers had flooded the rail bed. The water extended for some distance, it seemed. Here, the traveled route skirted the beaver bog on a mossy corduroy causeway. Difficult walking, especially in the dark. There was woodsmoke on the wind. They heard distant voices.

"You think that's them?" Leon asked.

"I don't know, and I don't want to find out."

In the other direction it was all snags, stumps, pitcher plants, and muck.

"What do we do now?" Leon asked.

"Turn around. Find a better route."

He groaned. "Polly. How are you feeling?"

"Sad. Tired. Sore—my back, my feet . . . Why?"

"We can't keep on like this." He made a fist. "We have to *fly*, Polly, it's the only way. You *know* I'm right."

She looked into his face in the half-light. "We can't. Without Balthazar, it's just too chancy."

"He would want us to try. You know he would. One night! One night straight across the zone and we'll *be* there."

"Come on, Leon. One night? You haven't held the charge for *five minutes*."

"I know that, but I did the shrinking one. Anyway, if I can't make it, I can't make it, but if we keep on like this, neither one of us is going to make it. That's the truth, Polly."

She sat on her pack. "Oh, Great Mother."All she wanted to do was sleep for a while and then keep walking. Sleep and walk, sleep and walk, on and on.

"We can do it, Polly. We'll stay close to the ground. If I have to land, I'll just land. After that I'll take my chances."

"If I lost you, too, Leon, I don't think I could stand it."

"You won't lose me. Whatever happens, I'll find you again."

She knew he was right. If it turned out that her magick wasn't strong enough to get her home, then so be it, but she could not allow her fears to trump her abilities.

"All right," she said. "We'll try. But this time you have to stay with me and do *everything* I say."

"Got it."

"I hope so."

She cast a circle in the roadside lilies and called the quarters. Leon stood beside her, tense and focused. They each took a dab of ointment. Looking into each other's eyes, they charged themselves.

First Polly spoke the phrases, then Leon, one by one, the seven and then the four:

Swa sunne slaecceth
bone to waeter
swa swegel uncnotteth
ond ich lyftlich.

They rose together, holding hands. And grinning, in spite of everything.

31

BECAUSE HE WAS KEEPING his unprotected face aimed toward the ground, Leon had to hold on to Polly's pant leg with one hand so he wouldn't lose her. Moisture streamed into his ears and flew from his chin. The wonder and sheer joy of it all seemed to help him hold the Dispersal's focus in his mind. Incredible, he was *doing* it. Flying. How he wished he could tell Tina about all this.

Wood fires dotted the piebald landscape. He could pick out steadier, artificial lights here and there, too, but after they crossed a wide north-south highway—the 81, flickering with traffic—there were no lights in any direction, none at all.

Leon knew his wavy-haired mother only from photographs—running after Tina into the waves, sitting on a stool at her loom, laughing with friends at a table in a sunny restaurant. She'd been vaporized. "Didn't feel a thing," Malcolm had said more than once. Leon did not believe it, but it didn't matter. The devastation was too big to comprehend, too big to even think about.

"You're doing great!" Polly said. "Soon as you feel tired or a little tingly, be sure and tell me. *Don't wait*, OK?"

"I will. You know what, Polly? My mother's down there."

"Aha. So she is. Blow her a kiss!"

He did.

They flew on to the northeast, climbing a little. The air grew colder. At one point he realized that Polly was singing to herself. They passed through thickening clouds. Once, far above them, he caught the rare sight of a plane blinking its way to wherever.

☾

The intensity of the effort was thrilling and tiring at the same time, and that, he decided, was the trick to keeping a sure hold—you used the thrill to offset the stress. After a while, in the depthless blackness, his focus began to waver. Having to keep his burning eyes closed only made it worse. The first time he nodded off, just for a moment, he recovered. The sky out ahead was beginning to brighten, he realized. That was encouraging. They'd be putting down soon—an hour, no more. When his twitching bones woke him a second time, he knew he'd lost it.

"Polly!" Oh, God. "I have to go down!" The terrain below was a tangle of roads and ruins divided by a wide, silver river filled shore to shore with barges and container ships. It looked like a logjam.

"It's OK, Leon. Glide. Just glide and stay with me!"

"I *can't*! I can't keep my . . . my . . . " Terror took his breath.

"It's *OK*! Ride my back! Do it!" She tucked her shoulder and slipped beneath him, shoving her backpack into his collarbone and her butt against his belly.

They plunged together toward the cityscape.

Leon hung on, lips taut, flesh tingling. The rippling hems of his overalls stung his ankles.

Polly whacked him on the hip. "OK! When I say *heave,* push out your chest and draw in your knees. When I say *stick it,* open your arms and spread your legs front to back. We're going to hit the deck on the run. Got it?"

"Got it!" They were dropping toward a bridge—a highway overpass.

"Heave!" Polly's head banged him in the chin.

He thrust out his chest. They swooped up . . .

"Stick it!"

They hit the ground at a rough gallup. Leon skidded in the grit and fell, sprawling onto his chest and stomach.

He couldn't breathe.

"Are you hurt?" She was on her knees beside him.

"Yeah. A little." He had blood in his mouth.

"Let me have a look."

Scraped knees and hands, bruised ribs, bitten tongue. Was that all? Seemed to be. He was lucky.

Polly got out a roll of gauze and some disinfectant.

"I fell asleep. Just for a second."

"That's all it takes. After that, if you start to panic, it's very hard to get it back. You did well, though, Leon, just the same."

He shuddered, looking around. The rich chorus of insects emphasized the larger silence. "Where are we?"

A cockeyed sign below the overpass read, "Barrow St. Exit 14S ½ MILE" There were gas cars down on the highway, doors open, hoods up. Some with their windows smashed. Inside a fenced equipment yard stood two rows of diesel tractor-trailer cabs, painted blue, each with a golden crossed-keys emblem on the door. Redbrick apartment buildings with awnings, iron fire escapes, and air conditioners in the windows. Light poles. Wires. Debris. Streets drifted across with trash and dust. In the distance, a field of fuel storage tanks in many colors. They looked like pieces on a game board.

"Well, we're a long way from ground zero," Polly said. "That's a good thing."

"How long do you think we can stay here before we get too contaminated?"

"I have no idea, but at least we're up off the ground. We'll just rest here for a little while and then take off."

"No, Polly. I can't do it. Not soon. Maybe not ever."

"So we'll have to walk."

"Through this?"

"Why not? If we keep to the asphalt and stay out the buildings, we'll be fine."

"We'll get sick, Polly. And before that we'll run out of water. And food."

"Well, if we can't fly, walking's all there is."

"No. *You* can fly. Just a few more hours. Right?"

"Don't make me leave you here, Leon."

"Come on. I'll be along later."

She shook her head.

"Really," he said. "I mean it. Write out the spell and leave me some ointment. I've got the ritual down, pretty much."

"You've never cast a spell all by yourself."

"So what?"

Her eyes brimmed. She looked away. "We don't have to decide yet. How about some jerky?"

They wiped their hands and faces with a damp cloth, ate a little, and slept for a time in the sun, using the pack for a pillow. When the wind rose later, Polly cut lengths of gauze for them to use as masks. Out over the empty avenues and the ragged green lots between the quiet buildings, all that moved were the sliding shadows of clouds. The numb buzz of locusts was the only sound.

☾

Chin thrust out, arms at her sides, Polly rose. Leon could feel the charge, too, but he couldn't make himself trust it. He wasn't ready.

Polly arced around and returned, her goggles reflecting the low sun. She held herself at an angle a few feet above him.

"No go?"

"It's too soon. I'm too— I'll just panic and lose it." In all this ruination it would be impossible to find a good place to crash-land if he had to, even with light enough to look for one. He couldn't chance it.

Polly touched down and pulled off her hat and goggles.

"Don't, Polly. You don't want to stay here."

"Leon, I *told* you—"

"*Listen!* You can't let me keep you from making it home. For God's sake, I've already cost you your book *and* your familiar."

She didn't argue.

"Don't worry," he said. "I'm not going to give up now. I'll get there." Or die trying. "Upper Duxton. Ethan Allen Tennis Camp."

"There's no camp anymore. I don't even know if there's still a farmhouse." She eased out of the heavy pack. "All right. Find the village cemetery. Whatever else they do, they won't mess with the cemetery. It's right by the river. Go to the back and walk along the fence until you come to a pink granite obelisk that says 'Lightfoot' on the base. I'll leave a message for you there if I can, under the pedestal."

She gave him the last of their bread and dried venison, a water bottle, the flashlight, and Tina's survival kit. From her sewing box she took a scrap of parchment with the flying spell written on it. She put a big dab of ointment into the paper and folded it at the edges.

“This may come in handy, too.” She gave him the handgun case and a fistful of cartridges. “You need anything else?”

“Just your belief in me.”

“You’ve always had that, Leon. Right from the beginning.”

He dried his eyes with his sleeve. “I’ll find you again. But I can’t take to the air until I know I’m ready.”

“That’s the right thing,” she said. “You can’t fake it.”

He took her by the wrist and pulled her to him. “Polly. You know this, but I have to say the words. I love you.”

She paused and then she kissed him. “I love you, too, Leon,” she whispered.

He wanted to say more, but nothing came.

Polly worked her goggles into place. She gave him a last look, her chin trembling, and that was it. She spun on her heel and hopped into the purple sky.

He watched her till she was gone. They’d probably never see each other again, he understood that. But this was for the best. He sighed.

He took one of the plastic water carriers from Tina’s kit to use as a tote for his provisions, slipped the revolver butt-first into his overalls’ chest pocket, and set off in no certain direction as night fell around him.

32

IT WAS STILL DARK by the time Polly crossed out of the zone, a transition marked by the spangled shore of what she thought must be Lake George. She was 30 minutes from the Regions, maybe another hour from the village. No chance she'd make it before full daylight, but she could do what she'd come to do on foot if she had to. Return Balthazar and retrieve the taper. As long as the ice chest was still there. And the farm.

No hurry then, but, close as she was, she couldn't help pushing hard toward the mountains and the eastern highlands beyond. The Granite Hills. Home. She swept over the shimmering, southern reaches of Champlain in the half-light, speeding up as she neared the Regions. Great Mother, she was *back*.

Unhhh! A piercing blow to the gut.

She doubled up in agony. An arrow? What, a *meteor*?

She tumbled, wailing and struggling to unclench herself, squeezing her triquetra in her left hand. Down she fell, balled up. Down and down. Helpless.

In an instant, seconds before she would have crashed to her bloody death in the dark woods, the crippling pain vanished, and she managed to unbend enough to angle off through a seam in the trees.

She came down in a bowl of sand and stones—an old gravel quarry on the bank of a small river—and collapsed to her hands and knees, sick with shock.

What *was* that? She hadn't been shot. And the Dispersal hadn't failed—the charge was strong. Something else. A purposeful interference. From the outside. In the air.

Counter-magick.

An *Encumbrance*. That was all it could be. A boundary shield. But why would any witch cast an Encumbrance over the Regions? It made no sense. The Guard wouldn't be affected by it. A spell like this would only stifle the *resistance*, because if the witches couldn't take to the sky—

That was the reason.

Theldred.

Theldred had intercepted *The Craeft* not for herself, but to keep it out of Aran's hands. He had not imagined the resistance might have to deal with a traitor's counter-magick. But *why*? Why the treachery? Why would any witch want to help the invaders?

The road up out of the quarry was steep and rough. Hopping a gully, Polly found that she could still leave the ground—as long as she kept herself beneath the treetops, anyway, heeding the electric pressure of the shield not far above her. It felt awful.

She followed stream beds and tree-covered lanes, coasting low and slow. Trash littered the roadsides. It looked as if all the homesteads, shops, grain mills, and barns had been looted. Many had been burned. The biting stench of carrion came to her again and again. Roads empty, pastures lush, winter-worn corn fields gone to weeds and wild turkeys. For mile after mile, she saw no sign of the re-settlement anywhere. So why all this travesty?

Following the river, it wasn't until she reached the outskirts of Upper Duxton that Polly detected any sign of human presence—the smell of bacon. She set down beneath the black willows on the bank, a few feet above the water. On Central Street, Abe Rosen's slaughterhouse and the tin-sided livery barn were standing but vacant. The hydro station, the redbrick Cooperative Trust Bank, the stone library, the Passumpsic Valley Community School building, and the North Baptist Church seemed the same—although the 14 Victorian houses that ringed the common appeared to be occupied. A few had hydros and electrics parked in front of them. Most of the village green—along with the granite horse troughs, the gazebo, and many of the oak trees—was gone. In its place were a concrete helipad, a hangar, and banks of dully gleaming solar panels. In the center stood a tall flagpole surrounded by a beds of petunias and begonias.

She caught the murmur of a radio. A child's high-pitched voice. The faint splashing of water in a bathtub.

She flew on. Between the cemetery and the river, in the field behind the town hall, where the village held the harvest fair every fall, stood a row of small, blue-and-yellow government helicopters. Also two camouflaged, double-rotor cargo ships, a corrugated quonset hut with satellite antennas, ranks of diesel-powered military vehicles—trucks and troop carriers—and four huge fuel tanks on concrete piers.

She followed the East Branch up into the hollow, gliding just beneath the overarching cedars through clouds of midges and mist. The old steel bridge at Pease Crossing lay the river, the work of the resistance, she suspected. A little further on, Kitcherer's sawmill was a charred heap.

To her relief, the two farmsteads before her parents' farm—the Batchelders' and the Duncans'—were still standing, sheds, barns, and wooden silos. But they were empty.

Not the Lightfoot place. She caught the smell of wood-smoke before she could see the house. Up on the plateau, she could see an orange wind sock atop a pole—they had turned the eight tennis courts into a landing pad. As she got closer, from the fold in the lower pasture she spotted that pale-yellow government Atomic, parked in the lane under the maples.

So. Yuri was waiting for her. She wasn't surprised.

She veered off into the uncut hay and skimmed the north mowing to the stone wall at the edge of the sugarbush. Here, no one would be able to see her from the house.

She sat on the wall to rest while the sun rose above the ridge behind her. New light poured down the opposite hilltops and turned the ripe hay all to gold. Bobolinks darted after insects. The beauty hurt her heart.

She raised the binoculars. On the far side of the brook the tent platforms were bare. Someone had put in a kitchen garden, and the lawn had been scythed. Four horses grazed in the high pasture. The tulip bed beside the house had been buried under a neat stack of stovewood.

Balthazar's family roosted each year in the last sugar maple across the lane from the farmhouse. Beyond that, the cedar hedge on the far side screened the lane from the first-floor windows. Upstairs, someone had drawn her mother's blue curtains across the twin dormers.

She stretched out on her stomach and shoved off, slipping through the dewy hay like a beaver on a pond. Pollen smeared her lenses.

As she approached the fissured trunk of the last maple on the road bank, the ravens left, flapping away over the hayfield, three of them, grawking in consternation. They didn't know who she was.

Behind the house the screen door slammed. A woman appeared, walking toward the gardens. *Harriet*. Harriet Cole, the summer camp cook for as long as Polly could remember. Only there was no camp.

Polly placed Balthazar's body between two root humps at the base of the tree and cut the shroud's stitching with her knife so the others could see him. Then she shoved her pack out of sight in the ferns and darted across the road.

Harriet was on her knees plucking chives. Polly whistled a low note.

She twisted around. "*Polly!*"

"Harriet! What are you doing here?"

"Dear God, you scared me half to death—" She glanced toward the house. "What are *you* doing here?"

Polly knelt beside her. "My father sent for me, so I came back."

"But he's *gone*, Polly. He's *long* gone."

"Where did he go?"

"Who knows? *Everybody's* gone!"

"You're not gone."

"Well, because I'm *saved*. I'm a bondservant now."

"That's *terrible*. Who for?"

"Authority. That's all there is around here anymore, is Authority. Duxton's the administration center for the whole western region."

"And all the witches are gone."

"Must be. We ain't had a terrorist incident since before Easter."

"Then the Resistance is finished."

"They never stood a chance, Polly."

"What happened?"

"They got drove out."

"They put up a fight, didn't they?"

"Oh, they did great at first. New Year's Day, just like they said they would, the Guard come across the lake on barges. Turned out the terrorists put a curse on 'em so in the middle of the lake they all went to mush, like they was made out of cardboard. You know that water was awful cold, too. A lot of 'em drowned. Hundreds. After that, the Guard just come straight up from Albany in troop trucks, and the terrorists—there never was too many of 'em, I don't think—they got overwhelmed."

Polly nodded. Theldred's Encumbrance had made sure of that. "Then what happened?"

"Oh, Lord, it was horrible. Out of control." She closed her eyes. "We had Christian soldiers comin' through here—eighteen, nineteen years old—drunk and wild, blowing away heifers for laughs, busting into homes, stealing anything wasn't nailed down and burning the rest. Killing and looting, that's all it was. For weeks."

"Killing?"

She nodded. "Plenty of people didn't leave when they said to, you know. Too old, no place to go, no passport, no cash. What were we s'posed to do? Nobody expected the Guard to come stormin' through all crazy like they done. Some of 'em, Polly, if they caught you, they just stood you up against a wall and *shot* you. Just like that. Pow-pow-pow-pow. And then they'd rob the jewelry off your dead body."

"I'm so sorry, Harriet."

"Took four, five weeks for Security to show up. By then that first wave was all over. But *then* what happened, Easter Sunday, Authority puts out this list. The 'Enemies of God and Country' list. Which, every night at the end of the Bulletin, they scroll down this list, and every night it gets shorter. Authority was everywhere. Plus they had informers. In the village it was Karen Piscopo, Lorraine Walsh, Jerrold Upshaw, and all them from North Baptist. They told the soldiers who to look for and where to find 'em. And when they found 'em, like I say, they shot 'em. Except if it was a witch. The witches they burned alive, Polly, I hate to tell you. Down on the common."

She clenched her teeth. "Who did they burn?" She had to know.

Harriet shook her head. "I never went. I couldn't."

"They didn't burn Aran, did they?"

"No. The head of the terrorists? Oh, Lord, no. They woulda been dancing in the streets if they put him to the torch."

"Is that who's using the house now? Authority?"

She nodded. "They made it into a guest house for people that come up from the Dominions to meet with the governor. I'm the housekeeper."

"What governor?"

"Regional governor—Donleavy. Him and his wife live down to the village."

"So who's in the house?"

"Right now it's this Executive Branch agent. He's up here checking out the real estate opportunities."

"Is his name Yuri?"

This startled her. "How'd you know that?"

"He's not looking for property, Harriet. He's looking for me."

"But he's up from Richmond! What would he want with you?"

Polly took her by the shoulders. "Harriet, I need your help. I believe my father left something for me in the basement—in the old icebox. It's a candle. Will you get it for me?"

"There's an icebox in the basement?"

"Opposite the wood furnace. It says 'King' on the door."

She patted her knee. "Let me go see. You slip in the henhouse and just wait, OK?"

The layers started fussing when Polly unlatched the door. "Hush! Hush, now. I'm not who you think I am." She fended off the rooster with her foot.

The ravens' agitated knocking and screeching down across from the house told her they'd found Balthazar. She wondered whether there could be another familiar in Balthazar's family. That happened sometimes. Not that she would ever get a chance to find out.

A helicopter. Through the clouded plexiglass window in the door she watched one of those blue-and-yellow CPA choppers land on the plateau in a skirt of pink dust. A Security officer jumped out and helped someone else step to the ground. A tall man in black. He strode down the slope, crossed the lawn, and passed behind the far side of the grape arbor, heading for the kitchen door.

A moment later Harriet came down the porch steps with a basket and a bowl of scraps for the chickens.

The layers rushed out, raising motes and dander. Harriet slipped in and closed the door. "I got you some breakfast!" A dish of chive-flecked scrambled eggs and a scone.

"You're wonderful, Harriet. Did you find the icebox?"

"Yep. It was in there, the candle, in a sock. But when I come up the stairs, the governor was right there lookin' for his coffee, so I stuck it in the cutlery drawer."

"Good. So, the tall man who just arrived, is that Governor Donleavy?"

She nodded. "Drops in for breakfast when there's guests. Soon as I get 'em set up, I'll be back with your candle. Anything else you need?"

"It would be great if you could pack some food for me. I have a lot of traveling ahead. And if my flying leathers are still in my bedroom closet, I could use those, too."

"Might take a little while. What I could maybe do is I could bring it all out into the yard in my wash basket, like it was laundry."

"That's perfect. You'll find my backpack in the ferns

under the last maple across the lane. Just stuff it all in there, if you can."

"I'll try."

"Don't forget the candle."

"I won't. Is it *magickal*?"

"It better be."

She ducked out.

A second later, hearing her voice, Polly peered through the plexiglass. The governor's Security detail from the little chopper was quizzing her.

"Nobody! Just a town girl. A beggar."

Polly stepped back.

The door flew open and banged against the outside wall. The Security officer stepped into the doorframe, helmet closed, riot gun pointed at Polly's chest. The strip above his visor lit up the whole henhouse.

He lowered the gun. "'Town girl'? I'm not reading *town girl*. I'm getting nothing here."

"I don't know about that. She's just hungry, is all."

The officer stepped inside. "What's your name?"

"Polly Lightfoot."

He raised his visor. "You related to *Aran* Lightfoot, the warlock?"

"Aran Lightfoot is my father, and this is our home."

"Well, praise Jesus. How'd *you* get left behind, Polly Lightfoot? You sick or what?"

She said nothing.

"Could be you're a spy, I don't know. Governor's gonna be glad to meet you, I know that much. Turn around."

She did.

"Hands behind your back." He cinched a strap around her wrists.

"Excellent. Lead the way, Harriet." He stepped outside and dropped his visor. "Now you, witch. Nice and slow."

33

LEON TRUDGED ON. The dark, humid night glimmered with fireflies by the thousands. What a spectacle.

He was miserable. Dirty, starving, alone. Alone forever. Good thing Polly had given him the revolver. Now, if it came to that, at least he could blow his brains out. The bad part was knowing she would have stayed with him if he'd asked. Why hadn't he?

So she would make it. She *would* make it, he was sure. Polly didn't need her familiar. She was the most capable and determined person he'd ever met. He was the one who needed a familiar. Like a horse. Or a pterodactyl. He laughed to himself.

He hewed to the north as much as he could. Some big machine had cleared the road long ago, so the walking wasn't difficult. He saw many tracks in the dust—deer, coyote, rabbit, fox. No sign of human life—no smoke, no sound. A few of the buildings had been boarded up, though most had not. Wire and cable snaked along the roadsides and drooped from cockeyed poles. Gas cars, vans, and trucks in all shapes and colors were all over the place, most of them intact, some even with belongings inside. Plenty of commercial goods, too, probably. In the south, all you ever saw were stripped shells. Fuel stations occupied almost every corner, too—big, blocky pumps with canopies overhead—Gulf, Sunoco, BP. Why did they need so many?

Late in the night he found a nook between two cars that some desperate person had enclosed with scrap metal and plastic, not recently. He inspected it with his flashlight, then went in.

Much later he crawled out into a still, overcast morning, groggy and stiff. He drank a little water and bit off some jerky. The muggy air was dense with the smell of honeysuckle, the buzz of insects, the liquid chorus of the birds. He retied the gauze over his mouth, gazing down the road. Was that north? With no sun to judge by, he'd have to check the compass.

Hell. Tina's survival kit was gone. He'd forgotten to put it back in his pocket yesterday after taking the plastic bag out of it. The compass, the water purification tablets, the waxed matches, the fishing line and hooks—it was all back at that overpass, a place he couldn't find again if he wanted to.

He rubbed his face. Stupid. Now he didn't know which way to go. All he could he do was wait till the sky cleared. The road passed through a deep thicket of locust trees, sumac, grape, and blooming honeysuckle. He sat for a while, then rose to stretch. He picked a few of the small white and yellow blossoms and pulled off his mask to taste the nectar. Just as he touched the end of one to his tongue, he felt a nugget of warmth form between his lungs. He swallowed hard. Was he getting sick? Already? No. No, it was something else, something outside of him—like another self. His and not his.

I will help.

He held his breath, glancing around. "Who is that?" He

stared at the makeshift shelter between the cars. *Where are you?*

Here.

A whirring sound. A small blur in the air, like a smudge on a mirror. The whirring stopped. A ruby-throated hummingbird. Perched on a locust twig a few feet overhead. His gorget looked almost black.

"Is *that* you? The hummer?"

Yes.

"What are you doing out here?"

We are feeding.

"Who's with you?" Another witch?

Family.

Other hummers. "Did Polly send you?"

I found you.

"What do you mean? You . . . *felt* me?"

Yes. Do you fly?

"Well, I can, but not very well. Are you a familiar?"

The bird trilled.

"Do you know what a familiar is?"

I knew one. Long ago.

"You knew a familiar?"

Yes.

"Another bird?"

No.

"Have you ever been a familiar yourself?"

Not with your kind.

What did that mean? "OK. First you need to know I'm a beginner at all this—magick and everything—but as long as you don't expect too much of me, would you consider being my familiar?"

I am now.

Leon laughed. "I guess you are! Fantastic!" He had a familiar! But the bird was so small! Tiny! How was this going to work? "My name is Leon—Leon Krauss. What's yours?"

Nothing.

"Do you have a name?"

No.

"Familiars are supposed to have names, I think. Do you want to me to give you a name?"

You can.

Leon's favorite storybook years ago featured a bull named Burt and a rooster named Razzmatazz. "How about if I call you Razz? Does that sound all right to you?"

Yes.

Another hummer swooped down between them and buzzed back and forth several times before settling on a high branch. A pale-breasted female. She trilled at Razz. He approached her, chittering, then dived and vanished into the thicket, the female right behind him.

Leon packed his things, rolled the bag closed, and waited, chewing venison. Only yesterday he'd been wishing for a familiar, and now he actually had one. Maybe his wishing had something to do with it. Polly would be amazed. What would she say?

Minutes passed. The cloud cover began to thin, and the disk of the sun brightened beyond the tops of the trees. The little bird didn't come back. The longer he waited, the more he had to wonder whether their strange meeting had really happened. Had he actually been talking to a hummingbird? Maybe he was going crazy.

But in another moment the bird returned, zoomed once around his head, and halted inches in front of his nose. Leon felt his wings' vibration on his lips and eyelids. The bird looked at him through one black eye and then the other.

You journey to a certain place.

"That was the plan, but I'm stranded here. I was trying to get to the northern forest. On the other side of all this."

You must fly.

"Right. Only the last time I tried that I almost killed myself."

Flying is the way.

"For you it is."

For you too.

"Not if it kills me."

Try.

"If I try and I still can't do it, will you stay with me?"

Until you die.

He gave a laugh. "That's good to know. I think." But the hummer was right, he had to try. Even if it killed him. He was a witch, wasn't he?

Try! Razz zipped up a foot and then back to eye level, whirring.

"Give me a little time to get ready. I've never done this by myself."

Razz darted up and back and lit on the same locust twig he'd perched on before.

Leon decided against sweeping a ritual circle—not to stir up any dust. Instead he defined a circle with the toe of his sneaker, stepped into it, and bowed to the quarters. He asked for the spirit forces' help just as he'd watched Polly do it. He unfolded her paper and took a little ointment.

"If this works, I think I should stay close to the ground. In case it goes bad. What do you think?"

One danger or another.

There would be dangers no matter what he did. True enough.

Now. Now.

"Right. Here goes."

He applied the ointment in one smooth stroke and

spoke the spell's eleven phrases, the seven and the four. In seconds, the icy flame of the charge spread up and through him and into his limbs.

Razz felt it. He darted from his twig with a buzzy call.

Leon tucked his bundled belongings under one arm and launched himself. The focus was like an incandescent wire at his center. "Fly on, Razz. Stay low, OK?"

The hummer zipped ahead through a tunnel of vine-shrouded locust trees. Leon lost him immediately. This was no good. He couldn't fly through this clutter, not without a helmet and goggles. He wiped the cobwebs from his face.

Razz was back, whirring at his shoulder. *Up high?*

"Right!" Leon cried. "High!"

Razz vanished in the filagree of branches. Leon followed, shielding his eyes with one arm.

☾

Up and up and up. The higher he climbed, somehow the less taxing the mind-work seemed to be. That he hadn't expected, but it made sense. A kind of serenity came with the altitude. He kept his chin tucked in to his collarbone. Whenever he opened his eyes he could look only straight down, but his grip on the Dispersal felt sure.

Was this his familiar's doing? He thought so—partly, at least. Razz reappeared every minute or two to check on him, then zipped ahead again, blazing their course. His agility was phenomenal. All Leon could do was bumble along like a log in a river. But as long as he held this calm focus, he was sure landscape would keep flowing beneath him the way it was now, like a quilt endlessly unfurling.

34

POLLY CLIMBED THE STEPS to the side porch with the hulking officer on her heels. Harriet held the screen door. "Sorry, Pol," she whispered.

Polly patted her doughy arm. In the corner of the kitchen, where the maple trestle table and four chairs used to be, stood a made-up cot, a washstand, and a sheet-metal wardrobe. Harriet's.

A platter of her buttery scones sat on the soapstone counter.

The two men out in the sunroom halted their conversation at the sound of Polly's footsteps in the uncarpeted hallway, then pushed up out of their seats at her appearance. A rush of blood rose to her scalp when she saw their places set with her great-great-grandmother's Irish porcelain. And Lil's old collection of Inuit ivory animals—seals, bears, fish, foxes—was missing from the credenza.

The tall governor eyed her, smiling faintly. The stocky man beside him in the silk blouse and gray ponytail was Yuri. He knew who she was, too, she was sure, though he gave no sign.

"MacKenzie?" the governor said.

The officer had removed his vid helmet. He stepped up beside Polly. "Pardon the interruption, Governor. The cook said you hadn't started." He shoved her forward. "I found this girl hiding in the chicken coop. She says her name is Polly Lightfoot."

The governor's eyes narrowed. "And is that your name?"

"Yes, it is. What's yours, please?"

The governor made a small bow. "Excuse me. James Donleavy, Regional Governor, Western Sector. My guest this weekend is Yuri Vasilevski, chief aide to His Excellency, Clyde Trumble, Executive Secretary of the Second Dominion."

"Thank you, Governor," Yuri said. "I have been looking forward to this moment for quite some time. This girl is the runaway bondservant I've been pursuing for weeks."

"I'm sorry, Mr. Vasilevski," the governor said, "but if this girl is who she says she is, she's no runaway." He turned to Polly. "Your father is Aran Lightfoot, the terrorist leader? Is that correct?"

"My father is not a terrorist. *You're* the terrorist. You've driven my people from their homes."

"*Hah!* Your *people* have no home on this earth! Indeed, every breath you take defiles the Lord's creation."

She shook her head. "Witches defile *nothing*."

"Governor," Yuri said. "Secretary Trumble has made a considerable investment in this slave girl. As you know. He *will not rest* until she is in his possession."

Donleavy turned to him. "As *you* know, Mr. Vasilevsky, my task since the day I landed out here has been to purge the heathens and eliminate the terrorists."

"And you have succeeded."

"Not quite! But now, praise Jesus, the last of the witches is in my grasp. The spawn of Lightfoot himself. When I have disposed of *her*, by the grace of God, the peace and purity of the Regions will be ensured."

"Please, governor. In view of the debt you owe the Secretary for your impressive success, surely you can show a greater regard for his interests."

"For a *witch*?"

"This girl belongs in servitude to Secretary Trumble, Governor. That's the truth. It's not for you to *dispose* of her."

"Is that so?" Reddening, Donleavy slammed the table with his open hand. The cups clattered in their saucers. He unclipped an instrument from his belt and spoke into it. "As the Regional Authority's chief governing officer in the Western Sector, and by the light of the Lord God's revealed truth, I deem the witch before me to be the last witch left alive in the Outlying Regions. As such, she shall be consumed in righteous fire tonight on the village square. So I decree."

"That's a decree you will regret, Governor," Yuri said.

The governor ignored him. "MacKenzie! Sequester the witch in the woodshed. Don't leave her alone. Watch her closely. If she starts muttering, gag her. Do you understand?"

MacKenzie ushered Polly out through the mudroom and into the old workshop. It was bare now—all the hand tools, benches, and cabinets gone. He shackled her ankles and padlocked the shackles to a length of chain attached to a ring in the floor next to a stained mattress and a slop bucket.

Out in the mudroom he settled into her mother's bentwood parlor rocker, leaving the sliding door open between the mudroom and the shop so he could keep an eye on her. He propped his shotgun against the wall.

If she could get a scrap of time to herself, just three or four minutes, she could work up a de-integration spell. She sat erect, watching for the opportunity through half-closed eyes. But the morning passed, and the officer did not once leave his chair.

☾

The shop door scraped across the floor. She could not remember anyone closing it. She blinked in the light from the mudroom. Yuri. With a tray in his hands. Wearing a pistol in a flap holster. The Security officer wasn't in sight. Oh, Mother, she'd missed her chance!

"Harriet's fixed you a bite of supper. Smells delicious. Can you eat?"

"Untie my hands. Please."

He set the tray on the floor and cut the plastic ribbon around her wrists. She folded her swollen hands into her belly.

A fried brook trout and a mound of steamed, buttered spinach. "Thank you." She could hardly grasp her fork.

Yuri crouched beside her. "Polly. I want to help you. But if I'm going to get you out of this, you'll have to listen to me."

"I'm listening."

"Do whatever they ask you to do. Do *not* try to escape. They'll kill you if you do. Don't worry—you will be rescued. I promise you. I have it arranged."

"Who's going to rescue me? How?"

"It's better if you don't know."

"Well, if you want to rescue me just to make me a slave, forget it."

"No witch can be a slave. You know that."

"So then why did you buy me?"

"I'll be honest with you. For the grimoire."

"*My* grimoire?"

"It *was* yours. As I understand it, that's the reason it can't be opened."

"It can't be opened because it was *stolen*. By a traitor named Theldred."

He shook his head. "Never mind all that. The important thing is this predicament we're in. *You* don't want your life to end in agony. And *I* don't want to watch your execution. Are we together on this?"

Polly nodded.

"Fine. Do nothing. You will be rescued."

Footsteps. Yuri straightened.

The governor and two officers crowded the mudroom behind him. One wore a shotgun, body armor, and a bandolier.

"Last supper?" Donleavy said.

Yuri said nothing.

"I'll be going on down now in the chopper," the governor said. "Thompson and Puente will deliver the witch in the hydro. You're more than welcome to join the festivities, Mr. Vasilevsky. This will be an unforgettable occasion."

"I wouldn't miss it," Yuri said. He gave Polly a nod and left.

"No rough stuff, Jasper," Donleavy said. "And no drugs. We want her conscious and aware."

He and MacKenzie crossed the porch and headed out toward the landing pad.

The husky guard with the shotgun kicked Polly in the hip. "On your feet."

She scrambled up. "There's no need to hurt me."

It wasn't a bandolier he had across his chest but a leather belt and a length of chain. He fastened it around Polly's waist, then freed her feet from the shackles. "Start walking. Down the steps and to the left." He pointed out across the lawn to the overland coach idling behind Yuri's government Atomic. "Move it."

35

As THE DAY FADED behind them, Razz led Leon out over the wide body of water dividing the Third Dominion from the Regions to the east. Lake Champlain, the last stretch. The lavender peaks ahead on the eastern horizon held the last of the light.

The hummingbird veered in close to his ear. *Down, down, down.*

"What's the matter?"

Follow.

Why?

A killing wall. The bird disappeared.

Hold up, Razz. Slow!

They slanted down toward the wind-streaked surface of the lake. In his scalp and on the skin of his face, he could feel the threat of pain. Or maybe he was feeling Razz feel it. Cold and sharp, like electricity. It brought back the time he'd touched that Atomic.

The hummingbird leveled off a few feet above the choppy water, and from there they arrowed on like a pair of mallards, straight and low, toward the stony shore.

What's going on, Razz?

He had no answer.

They skimmed the rooftops of a harbor town. Streets vacant, nothing moving, no lights, no smoke, out above a roadway between empty farms and fields, then on over dark, fragrant hardwoods.

Razz led him into highway corridor that traced a river valley. That they followed for a short time before his focus began to fray. He landed at a trot on the concrete pavement, wheeling his free arm for balance.

He sat in the road to massage his legs. Misty fields, black trees. The sky was starless. "Is this a safe place?"

No place is safe.

"I guess that simplifies things."

Beware.

"Of what?"

Your kind.

People? Or witches? He could hear crickets, the rush of water, a few nightbirds far off, nothing more. "Seems empty to me." He combed the bugs out of his wet hair with his fingers. "How are you feeling? All right?"

I feel.

"Are you hungry? Anything like that?"

No.

"I'm starved."

He hadn't thought much about how he was going to find Upper Duxton. He knew he couldn't risk asking for directions. He would just have to press on to the northeast, keeping an eye out for road signs.

He took out the flashlight and the revolver and set off.

"I'm searching for a certain village," he said.

And another witch.

"Another witch, you're right."

With yellow hair.

"That's Polly. Do you know her?"

You carry her. And the black bird.

That was true. "What else do I carry?"

Waves. Sand. Blood.

"I killed two people," he said after a moment.

Living is killing.

That was true, too, he thought.

Fly?

"I need to find something to eat, Razz. I'm too weak."

He walked on, listening to the river. It was a big one. In the morning, if he still had those fishhooks, he might catch a nice fish. But he didn't have any fishhooks. The night air was sweet and cool.

He followed a ramp off the high road. After a time, he came to a lonely intersection bounded by fields that surrounded a flat-roofed brick building with two rows of dark windows. It looked like a factory.

"Razz, will you go see if anybody's in there?"

The bird returned a minute later. *Not your kind.*

Leon switched on the flashlight. A row of cast-aluminum letters spanned a high wall:

Bassford Town School

☾

The front doors had been smashed in. Crumbs of glass twinkled on the vestibule floor. He smelled dust and mold. He could hear water dripping in the walls. The desks were gone from the classrooms, and so were the interior doors, the gas-light fixtures, the stair rails and sheet metal, though not the porcelain fixtures or the chalkboards. Sheets of paper lay all over the place. Inside glass display cases lining the foyer, under a sagging "*Go Bobcats!!!*" banner, was a display of plaques and athletic trophies. In one classroom a few of the cubbies still had mittens and jackets in them.

The kitchen and cafeteria had been picked clean. In the carpeted library withered plants in glazed pots sat in a row on the windowsill. The bookshelves hadn't been touched.

His flashlight drew junebugs and little white moths that kept fluttering into his face, but after a few minutes in the reference section he found what he needed: *Vermont: A Natural Geography and Road Atlas.*

Further down the road he came to a farm with a carriage barn across the way. The house had been gutted. In back, in an overgrown garden, he found some young asparagus and rhubarb and several rows of last year's parsnips. He ate, studying the atlas. Razz busied himself in the primroses.

☾

The Lamoille. That was the river. Just trace its course upstream to where the Black River joined it and traverse the range of hills to the east. After that, heading north up the next valley, eventually he would come to the long covered bridge just to the south of Upper Duxton village.

He swept his circle on the floor of the barn, cast the spell, and set off again through the damp air, cruising just above the placid watercourse. He dodged tree limbs and slipped beneath unlit bridges.

Later, he began to notice a strange, reddish cast to the cloud deck overhead, and soon after that he came upon it, the covered bridge. And beyond that a helipad in a square where lights burned in most of the windows.God, they had occupied Polly's village! Why?

He set down in a playground next to the village cemetery, both tucked into an oxbow. The grass was wet and long. A dog barked out by the road. Somewhere not far away a piano was playing a snappy version of a hymn he remembered from his childhood, "Joy, Joy, Joy." He jogged across the ball field and scissored over a low stone wall into the cemetery, where the overcast night seemed even darker under the canopy of maples and looming pines.

He couldn't chance the flashlight, but without it, finding the Lightfoot obelisk might take some time. Drawn by the music, he followed a gravel lane among the headstones until he came to a pair of iron gates chained open. On the other side of a narrow yard, inside a well-lit meeting house with a squat steeple, the pianist was playing another hymn he knew, a sad one, "Abide With Me."

He crouched among the gravestones, watching as the settlers walked across the common toward the meeting house, some alone, some in groups. Many with children. In the lamplight at the building's entry he saw that the men were carrying vid helmets—federal Security officers, almost all of them. The women wore long skirts and head scarves.

The music stopped with a flourish. The hall grew quiet. In one voice they pledged their allegiance to the flag.

"Welcome, everyone!" A man's booming voice. "Bless you all on this, the sixty-third day of the Resettlement. Praise Jesus."

"Praise Jesus," they echoed.

"Before we link to the feed from Richmond, I have wonderful news. It's the word we've been praying for through all our days of trial and tribulation. At the guest house this morning, first officer Harold MacKenzie captured a teenage witch." The crowd murmured. "A witch who happens to be the spawn of *Aran Lightfoot*, the terrorist warlock! A witch who stands *divinely revealed* as the last witch in the Regions! The *last witch*, my brothers and sisters, is *ours*!"

They broke into cheers and applause.

"Thank you, Jesus!" someone yelled.

"Where's she at?" a woman called out.

"*Burn* the thing!" another woman cried.

More clapping. Some stomped their feet.

"*Patience!* Please! Have patience, good people, and

rejoice! By order of the Governor, it pleases me to announce that the last witch's earthly form will be consigned to the pyre tonight on the square, directly following our gathering."

Everyone cheered.

The five-note chime sounded, signaling the start of the Nightly Bulletin. The meeting house windows brightened as the big screen flared.

Where was she? Where were they keeping her?

Beyond the cemetery walls, the houses he could see were mostly dark now, and the helipad's glow seemed hellish in the moist air.

"Razz?"

He was right overhead.

"Can you feel another witch's presence? Anything at all?"

No witch is near.

"Well, she can't be far off. If you spiral out from me here, do you think you could get a bead on her? Would that work?"

Maybe. He was gone.

☾

Leon stood listening to the Bulletin from a rise at the rear of the cemetery, a prospect that offered a view of the village common and the illuminated helipad down through the black shapes of shrubs and monuments. As the last notes of "America the Beautiful" died away, the people began filing out of the meeting house, talking and laughing in their excitement. They stooped to pick up pieces of scrap lumber and deadwood from piles heaped along the sides of the street. For the pyre.

Farther off, from within a steel-sided hangar next to the helipad, pairs of men appeared, rolling big drums one after another toward a raised platform at the center of the green. Ten of them. The men positioned the drums around the platform and the bare flagpole nearby. Others attached ramps on opposite sides of the platform and erected a girder in the middle.

A generator blatted to life inside the hangar, then another, and all at once each great drum loosed a pillar of light into the thick sky.

The glow washed back over the noisy crowd, men to one side, women and children to the other. Officers with riot batons took up positions around the burning place.

A flare whistled up and exploded in a shower of sparks.

A tall man in black bounded up one of the ramps and stood in the platform's yellow footlights, arms raised.

"Bless you, bless you all! What a glorious night it is! A night fit for a burning!"

People clapped and cheered.

"Good Christians, this is a time for celebration. Since the day we first arrived in the Regions, the Lord has tested our determination, our courage, and our faith. All the while, Satan's servants never ceased to hound and torment us. Not for one minute! Until tonight. In the name of Jesus, now is come our time of victory! Tonight we reap our reward for our steadfast courage and unshakeable faith. Our prayers have been answered! The power and glory of Almighty God are tonight confirmed in our final and absolute triumph over the arch-fiend himself!"

The crowd cheered.

Razz? He was back.

She comes. In a coach.

"Where? What coach?"

She is bound.

"Razz, we have to *stop* this. What can we do?"

He had no answer.

On the far side of the common Leon saw an approaching transport with green running lights and, just behind it, that government Atomic. Yuri. Damn. She'd flown right into his trap.

A number of officers with batons and plastic shields kept the crowd back from the burning place, as two others escorted Polly to the platform. Her hands were tied and she was hooded to the shoulders, but it was Polly—he recognized Tina's canvas pants.

The crowd jeered at her and shouted.

Leon checked the cylinder and slipped the revolver into his overalls pocket. If he could not save her life, then he could take it. He could cross the common and push through the crowd until he was close, right up front. And as soon as they set fire to the sticks heaped around her, he could leap up onto that platform and shoot her in the heart.

Then himself.

36

THE TWO SWEATING MEN removed her leather restraints and pushed her back against a cold, iron post, then bound her to it at the ankles and the waist. Her burlap hood and her pounding heart dampened the clamor of the crowd. All she could see were her frayed cuffs and her shoe tops. These people had come here to see her tortured to death. What kind of human being could find pleasure in watching another person's terrible suffering? They were insane. All of them.

Nothing would stop this now. There would be no rescue. "Great Mother," she pleaded aloud, "make it end quickly."

"Kill the witch!"

"*Burn* her! Burn her! Burn her!"

A guard peeled off her hood. She gazed out over a hundred pale, straining, shouting faces. They waved branches and sticks of lumber above their heads.

"Build the pyre!"

A woman ran up and flung a piece of wood at her over the guards' blue helmets. A child did the same. Then another.

A trumpet sounded. The searchlight beams went still.

"Good people!" The governor. Donleavy. He was right behind her.

He stepped around without a glance at her, raising his arms overhead. "Good people!" It was starting to sprinkle. "Good Christians! Make ready! The time of our deliverance has come!"

He waited. Their excited voices grew still.

"Praise God! The spawn of Satan stands ready to receive her fate. Come, all of you! Let us send this witch back to her craven master on wings of *flame*! *Come! Build the pyre!*"

They hurried up a long ramp on her left, jostling one another, men first, then the women and children. They dropped their offerings at her feet, cursing her as they did. Some spat at her. Polly covered her face. "Why do you hate Jesus?" a girl asked in a squeaky voice.

Guards with long-handled forks heaped the accumulating firewood high around her. She shut her eyes and pressed her hot triquetra to her heaving chest. *Help me. Oh, Great Mother, don't let me suffer long.*

"*Polly!*"

Leon?

It couldn't be! But it was. It was *Leon*, his wreath of wild blond hair on the other side of the loose pile of sticks.

Their eyes locked. Leon leaned in until he fell against the heaped-up wood. Before one of the guards could grab him, he pushed himself back, thrusting the big revolver butt-first through the pile. "Kill her!" he yelled. "Kill the witch!"

He let go of the gun. It slipped down into the mesh of sticks. Polly groped for it. She couldn't reach it.

A guard took Leon by the arm and spun him around. "Hold on! You're no *settler*! What in God's name . . . ?"

Leon pulled free and leaped from the platform.

"Grab him! *Catch that boy!*" a man was shouting behind her. Yuri. "*Stop him!*"

But Leon zigzagged through the crowd and disappeared in the night.

Polly twisted in her chains. They gave a bit. Just a little more . . . more . . . *There.*

She drew the gun through the pile to her thigh.

A trumpet sounded.

An official in white robes marched up the ramp carrying a staff topped by a flaming cross. He handed it to the governor. "Deliver us from evil!"

"So I shall!" Donleavy brandished the cross of fire. The crowd cheered.

He turned to Polly. "Raise your cursed hands, witch. Beseech the Lord for any mercy he may deign to show you . . . *for we shall show you none!*"

Polly met his gaze and lifted the revolver.

BLAM. She sent a slug through the small of his throat. *BLAM.* Another to the chest.

He dropped the cross and sank to the platform. People screamed. A guard whacked Polly's arms with the handle of his fork. She dropped the gun.

In the same instant the heavy black mass of cloud above them burst to a blinding white. *Ka-RACKKK!* A flash split the air.

The flagpole exploded. People near it crumpled to the ground. Others yelled and ran.

The searchlights went out all at once.

A sudden, hammering rain blotted out the shouting crowd.

Yuri was right beside her. "*Get her into the car!*" he yelled. "*Be quick! Bind her hands and feet! Move! Now! Now!*"

Two men kicked the pyre apart with their boots. One of them bent to unwind her chains, the deluge dancing like gray fur on his helmet. He cinched strips of plastic around her bruised arms and ankles and dragged her down the ramp to the waiting Atomic.

He shoved her onto a plush seat in the rear compartment. The overhead brightened.

Yuri slid in beside her, out of breath, his pistol in one hand. The door shut, and the overhead dimmed.

Yuri pulled back the hood of his cloak. He was flushed, his eyes wild. "You didn't have to *kill* the man, for Christ's sake!"

"Didn't I?"

"I had it all *arranged.* I *told* you!"

"You had what arranged?"

"The lightning! The torrents of rain! *Everything!*"

"You're in league with her, aren't you? You and Theldred."

He shook his head, disgusted.

"Where are you taking me?"

He was watching the road behind them in a drop-down monitor. The mounted escort came into view far to the rear, their helmets lined in blue. "Why in God's name couldn't you *listen* to me? Christ! *Five seconds*, just five seconds more and we'd all be free and in the clear. Now . . . *hell.* The Secretary himself can't save you now."

The Atomic sped up along the river flats. She could feel the bumpy road. At the new mill bridge they slowed and then turned up into the hollow. The rig braked to a hard stop at the farm, but Yuri waited, seething in silence until the escort caught up with them.

Soon as the side door slid open, Polly's eye went straight to the covered porch, drawn by the thrum of the Braid. Silhouetted in the light from the sitting room window, Theldred sat on the wicker loveseat, arms crossed.

Yuri climbed out. A drenched horseman reached in,

seized her by the arm, and pulled her out onto the muddy road.

The rain had stopped.

"Make it quick," Yuri said. "This girl just killed the governor."

"I saw," Theldred said in a weary voice. "So tragic."

Yuri opened the Atomic's front compartment and drew out an oblong bundle. The grimoire.

Theldred rose from the loveseat. Her coarse, broom-straight hair fell past her shoulders as she leaned down to take the bundle from Yuri's hands. She had articulated pads at the shoulders and knees of her gray flight suit and spiny glide wings that opened when she extended her arms. The large delta-shaped headpiece beside her on the porch floor looked more like a fairing than a helmet. She wore a gold pentacle at her throat. "Come closer now, Polly Lightfoot. Come." She placed the bundle on the porch floor and unfolded the oiled goatskin.

"I can't walk," Polly said.

"Unbind her, Vasilevsky," Theldred said. "She's mine now."

At Yuri's nod, one of the horsemen snipped the restraints. Polly rubbed her chafed skin. Her right wrist was swollen. With the butt of his shotgun a guard prodded her toward the porch steps.

The tall witch had the sole of one boot pressed down on the grimoire's silver clasp wheel. "First, dear maiden, fair warning." She snapped her right arm and sent a blue-white spear of light into the terra cotta planter on the porch rail. *BOOM*—pot shards and clods of smoking soil flew everywhere. The guards cringed, and Yuri let out a yell in spite of himself. Down in the lane the harnessed horses reared and whinnied.

"Plasma channel," Theldred said. "There is no more

excruciating way to die. Apart from being burned at the stake."

"I'm not afraid of you," Polly said. "I'm not afraid of dying, either. I am—"

"Never mind your fears!" she rasped. "Answer me this! Can you *see*? Can you *hear*?" Theldred's mouth was a slot in her pale face. "You owe your *life* to me, you idiot! To *me*!" She kicked the grimoire. "In your gratitude, you will open this book. Do it now. *Now!*"

Polly glanced toward the sky. "The Encumbrance. That's your doing, isn't it?"

"Of course it is. And if you had any sense, you'd be grateful for that, too."

"For what?"

The witch sneered. "For letting them leave with their *lives,* that's what! Without *me*, without *my* merciful intervention, they would all be *dead*! Or were you stupid enough to imagine thirty-nine desperate witches could defeat the righteous forces of God Almighty, Creator of Universe?"

"You broke their magick! Why? Why did you do it?"

"I just *told* you! Because in the end they would have been *roasted*, every last one of them!"

"Get *on* with this business, will you?" Yuri shouted.

"*Speak the release!*" Theldred raised her right arm like a mule driver with a whip. "*Speak it now or die where you stand!*"

"I *can't* speak it. I don't know it. And I wouldn't speak it if I *did* know it. Not for you."

Her long face tightened again. "No? Not for your *father*? Not for your loving *mother*? Not for all the others shivering in their wretched huts up on the tundra? Don't you *care* about them? Don't you want to *see* them again?"

"That book's forbiddance spell is as old as the book itself. For all I know, no one can release it, not even me."

"Oh? Well, we're going find out! Come on! *I'll* give you the words to try! Come! Come up here into my circle." Theldred lifted her boot and stood straddling the thick grimoire.

A siren wailed down toward the village.

"Damn it, that's *enough*!" Yuri yelled. "Cuff the girl. We're leaving!"

But before Yuri could take back the book, Theldred stomped on it. "*Leave* then, little man! Go! The book and the witch stay with me."In the next second she froze, shoulders hunched, listening. She whirled toward the house and stooped over to peer into the living room. She turned on Polly. "*Who is that? Who's with you? Tell me!*"

Polly felt it, too. "I don't know."

"It's that murdering *boy*! Isn't it? *Isn't it?* He's *here*!"

It wasn't Leon. It was a finer presence.

Theldred pointed to the guard. "*You there!* Find that boy and bring him here to me."

Yuri drew his pistol. "That's *enough*! Do you hear me? Security's going to be all over this place in two minutes!"

Theldred pointed at him. "A threat to my life has arisen here, little man, and it must be dealt with here. We cannot *leave*!"

"What threat?"

Take the book. Now.

Polly gasped. A familiar! Where? She looked toward the house. Nothing.

Take the book. Run. I will defend you.

How? Who are *you?*

A big double-rotor chopper was throbbing toward them out of the west.

I am with Leon.

You are? *Is he here?*

Take the book! Now! Now! Now!

Now. Right. One of the helmeted guards was easing open the front door while Theldred looked on. Another guard jogged down across the lawn toward the Atomic.

The huge helicopter descending to the red clay plateau had Yuri's attention.

Polly lunged and grabbed the book from between Theldred's legs. She broke for the lane and the fields beyond.

"*Stop her!*" Theldred bellowed. "*Stop the—*" She shrieked in pain.

Polly ran. A bolt of plasma split the air beside her, *KA-BLAMMM!* Fire engulfed the Atomic.

Yuri was yelling in a high, cracked voice.

Polly scrambled up the roadside bank. The pack was right where she'd left it. She crammed the book inside. Across the lane, Theldred's shrill howls echoed between the house and the cedar hedge. She'd been wounded somehow. Badly. Polly could feel it.

The grass whipped her legs. The little familiar stayed close as she bounded through the overgrown pasture. A bat, she guessed. Bats made excellent familiars—long-lived, sensitive, nimble in the air.

She stopped in the fold to listen and catch her breath . . . Wait! She recognized that sound. "Great Mother, you're a *hummingbird*!"

I am.

"That's fantastic! I've known many familiars in my life but never a hummingbird. *You saved my life!*"

You are brave.

"What did you do to that witch?"

I stabbed her eyes.

"Yow. Is she *blind*?"

She may heal.

"What about Leon? Is he all right?"

He waits for you.

"Where?"

Among the dead.

At the cemetery. Polly could see him leaning back against the granite obelisk in the Lightfoot plot. "Do you have a name?"

The bird had perched somewhere. *Can you fly?*

"I can fly, but I have to get ready first."

Get ready now. Hurry.

Looking back, against the faint glow of the farmhouse, she saw four men lumbering toward her through the tall grass. Up on the plateau behind the house, the big chopper was already lifting off and hooking around back toward the village.

☾

Polly coasted in over the iron fence and landed in the gravel lane just below the obelisk. Leon threw his arms around her without a word. He was chilled, shivering.

Commotion gripped the village—shouting, lights, vehicles.

"Those people were going to *burn you alive*!" he said hoarsely.

"They're insane, Leon."

"That's no excuse!"

"'They know not what they do.' Right?"

"That's no excuse, either."

The generators had started up again. Polly squeezed his arm. "We have to get out of here."

"Where to?"

Far, the hummingbird advised. *Far.*

"Did you find your father?" Leon asked. "And the others?"

She shook her head. "They're gone. They left weeks ago."

She swung off the pack. Inside, under the grimoire, her flying leathers, and two scones in a folded dish towel, she found the pilot taper in a cotton sock. *Thank you, brave Harriet.*

"*Hey!*" Leon said. "You got the *book* back! That's it, isn't it?"

"That's it."

"Fantastic. How did you manage to do that?"

She pressed two fingers to his whiskered chin. "Long story. How did you find the familiar?"

"I didn't. *He* found *me*. He's cool, isn't he?"

"He's cool, all right. And you're very lucky."

She cast a circle and tapped the ground with her toe. The air around them went still, even as the tops of the pines swayed against the stars and the tattered clouds.

She slipped the pearl-gray candle from the sock. It was fat as an ear of corn, with a coppery wick. "My father left this at the farm for me."

"What is it?"

"It's a pilot taper. If we follow its smoke, it will take us to him. I hope."

"By air?"

"Yes. Are you OK with that?"

"I think so. How about you, Razz?"

Always.

"Great," she said. "Everybody ready?"

"I am."

"Still charged?"

He nodded.

Polly set the candle on the shoulder of the pedestal and

touched a match to its wick. A green, unwavering blade of fire reached straight up.

She looked into Leon's eyes.

He took her hand.

She blew out the flame.

☾

A thin feather of smoke ushered them north along a winding highway to a knife-shaped, glacial lake between two granite monadnocks. They followed the shoreline, gliding under dripping birches and willows toward the lake's rain-swollen outlet, then skimmed on down the stony waterway through the hills until they crossed the old border into what had once been the Province of Quebec.

Theldred's Encumbrance abruptly faded. They climbed.

Later they stopped to rest on the brow of a mountain that overlooked the valley of the St. Lawrence. Stars filled the sky.

Polly dug out two of Harriet's scones and a jar of apple butter.

Leon leaned back and raised his arms toward the whirl of the galaxy. "Wonder of wonders!" he said.

"Is it? Look there, Leon."

He straightened. "Where?"

She pointed. "Down there. In the valley." Criss-crossing strands of tiny lights. A small village.

"Street lamps," he said.

"Yes. There's your wonder of wonders."

Leon gave her a look. "What's so wonderful about street lamps?"

"They're a lot rarer than stars, for one thing."

"Hah! All right. But what makes them *wonderful*?"

"We do," she said.

"*We* do?"

"Sure. We created them. Nothing else in the universe can bend energy to its own purposes. Only us."

He thought for a moment. "So then *we're* the wonder. People. Not street lamps."

Polly smiled.

Leon laughed his easy laugh, reached over, and drew her against him. She rested her head in the crook of his shoulder.

ACKNOWLEDGMENTS

THIS FANTASY would be in no one's hands today had it not been for the encouragement, advice, and contributions of many of my good friends and partners in the craft.

In particular, I want to thank poet Adrienne Raphel, who wrote the two elegant magick spells (Dispersal and Contraction) in Middle English; Miranda Dutra, who generously provided me with a description of life at a Florida tennis academy; Dan Cohen and his student, the dairyman Himar Escalente, who rendered the scavs' vulgar language into Spanish; Gary Moore and Dounia Bredes, who offered careful counsel and criticism all along the way; and Howard Morhaim, my tireless literary agent, who helped me to shape Polly's story and to focus my vision for it.

Dede Cummings, my astute editor and publisher at Green Writers Press, has stood enthusiastically behind Polly and her inspiring message from the start. My old friend Howard Mosher, indefatigable guide and champion to all of us who work at writing, has been crucial in making sure this novel would find its readers. And I am most grateful to my wonderful wife, Eileen Boland, for sticking by me at every turn on this long and winding road.

READING GUIDE

Polly and the One and Only World

1. What do you think the author means by "the One and Only World"? How might this phrase refer to Polly's environment and the people she meets?

2. Throughout the novel, the power and knowledge of familiars are significant elements. Why is the human-to-animal connection so important to the plot and themes of the story? Do you find the familiar characters more complex and dynamic than the human characters, or less?

3. What did you know about witchcraft before reading this book? Do the methods and beliefs of witches as they are depicted here resemble what you previously understood about witchcraft?

4. Why is witchcraft so associated with the Outlying Regions (New England)? Does this have to do with the area's history, or is the author using witchcraft to evoke something particular about that part of the country? What does witchcraft represent in relation to the culture of the Dominions?

5. How does fear affect the judgments and actions of the book's characters? Consider not just Polly and Leon, but also the many secondary characters that they meet on their journey.

6. Why does the author choose to leave Theldred's motives and intentions unresolved? Balthazar declares that what Theldred seeks is power. Does Polly agree?

7. Despite Polly's witchcraft, the revolver that she and Leon carry with them appears essential to their progress. Would you consider the gun to be a character in itself? Does it carry any metaphorical meaning?

8. The book of spells that Polly is summoned to deliver to her father embodies so much value and significance that others' desire for it puts Polly and Leon in danger from the start. What does the status of the book suggest about a culture's need and reverence for information?

9. Near the book's end, a familiar tells Leon that "living is killing." In what ways could such an assertion be true?

10. The author includes many specific details of the natural world—plant life, weather, and Polly's awareness of how to forage for food. Are these details purely plot related—that is, in accord with the characters' immediate needs and observations—or do they have a deeper purpose?

11. Why, at the end, after all the hardships of their journey, does Polly feel the need to correct Leon when he calls the stars "wonder of wonders"? Why do you

think the author chose to end the book with the last leg of their journey still ahead of them?

12. How does *Polly and the One and Only World* fit into the post-apocalyptic genre in narrative fiction? Does the gloomy future the novel depicts resemble any place on the planet in the present day?

CPSIA information can be obtained at www.ICGtesting.com
Printed in the USA
LVOW11s2308060115

421559LV00002B/2/P

9 780989 983891